THE HOUSE
THAT
HUSTLE BUILT

THE HOUSE
THAT
HUSTLE BUILT

NISA SANTIAGO

www.melodramapublishing.com

Library of Congress Control Number: 2014943094
ISBN-13: 978-1620780442
ISBN-10: 1620780445
First Edition: February 2015
10 9 8 7 6 5 4 3 2 1

Interior Design: Candace K. Cottrell
Cover Design: Candace K. Cottrell
Model Photo by Marion Designs

BOOKS BY
NISA SANTIAGO

ONE

Roosevelt Field was the second-largest full-price shopping mall in the state of New York, anchoring over two hundred stores, such as Bloomingdale's, Macy's, Nordstrom, and Neiman Marcus. The mall had some of the best merchandise in the metro area, but it also specialized in undercover cops posing as shoppers, so it was a paradise *and* a curse to shoplifters like Pearla.

Retired NYPD officers and a group of security guards provided security at the mall, and they were good. *Very* good. Nassau County Police Department also had a foot post assigned to the mall.

But this didn't intimidate Pearla and her crew. They were determined to pull off another one of their shoplifting schemes.

Pearla strutted through crowded Roosevelt Field mall on a mission in a white Bebe sundress and teal stilettos, her long, sensuous, black hair falling past her shoulders. Her pretty eyes hid behind a pair of dark Chanel sunglasses as she walked around Bloomingdale's taking a mental note of everything she liked.

Pearla, who had been hustling since she was thirteen, had single-handedly put together a crew of skilled, get-money bitches, which catapulted her into notoriety throughout Brooklyn and even Queens. Her tight-knit crew, a ring of boosters in her area, was able to steal anything that wasn't nailed down. In fact, everything Pearla wore was stolen. She had a stable of customers who would purchase the stolen merchandise, not to mention her website, where she advertised and sold things on eBay, and craigslist. She had even set up a PayPal account so that the money could be direct-deposited into her account. Once the funds cleared, she distributed the profits to her crew.

Pearla was known to have a different crew of jostlers who were pickpockets. Since the average person didn't carry around a lot of cash, they came off with the debit and credit cards. The money-makers were merchandise gift cards, which were charged on stolen credit and debit cards from stores like Bloomingdale's, Saks Fifth Avenue, Macy's, Victoria's Secret, Sears, and Target. Pearla was able to sell the gift cards for half price.

Her business was booming, and with her two best friends, Roark and Jamie, by her side, she felt like she couldn't go wrong with anything she did. Now nineteen, she had already made a name for herself throughout her borough as a thoroughbred, a hustler.

Roark, soft-spoken and about her business, was a thin brown-skinned beauty with Native American features. She had light eyes like Pearla and mostly kept her long, silky hair in two braids. She was nineteen as well and had come up through humble beginnings, living in a cramped two-bedroom apartment with sisters and brothers toppling over each other. With her parents steadily out of work she got into shoplifting and scheming with Pearla.

Jamie was stunning. At five feet four, with bronze-colored skin and sleepy eyes that hung low, her hair was a mane of flowing Senegalese twists, and her grace and style matched Pearla's. Some might say she was bougie or standoffish. Even though she was from the hood, she acted like she grew up somewhere in Beverly Hills. She was twenty-one, and her mother was an associate at a law firm that paid handsomely. She was the only child to divorced parents, who showered her more with gifts and cash than love and attention. Jamie stole not out of need but because it was exciting to her. She hung with a bad crew, not wanting to be the odd person out in a rough Brooklyn neighborhood.

✳✳✳

Pearla exited the mall with money and business on her mind. She strutted through the parking lot toward her silver Mercedes-Benz 240. Though it was a used car, it was in mint condition. Pearla was meticulous when it came to her appearance, meaning her wardrobe, her jewelry, and her car, which she had purchased for $22,000 from a hustler she'd known and fucked, saving up cash from her illegal business.

As she got closer to her car, her cell phone rang. She reached into her purse and looked at the caller ID. She immediately answered the call.

"Benny, talk to me. What you got for me?"

"Mami, we got some nice things fo' you. Can you meet wit' us today?"

"Of course. You don't even have to ask me twice. Just say when and where."

"You know the spot—the warehouse on Atlantic, an hour from now."

"I'm there. And hook me up this time, Benny, 'cuz you know I'm good peoples."

"I got you, mami; you ain't gotta worry."

Pearla hung up beaming with joy. Whenever Benny called, it meant a profit for her. Burberry, Gucci, Fendi, Louis Vuitton, and Chloe—he had it.

Benny was her connect in the garment district. The short Puerto Rican thug from the Bronx ran with a tight-knit crew that regularly boosted cars and committed B&Es and robberies from Long Island to New Jersey. They had access to it all, from clothing to high-end appliances.

Pearla was only interested in the clothing because, in her world, it was easier to move. Clothing didn't come with VINs and tracking devices.

When it came to shoes, she made a fortune off them, since shoes were the essential piece to a bad bitch's wardrobe. Everyone wanted to dress and look like Beyoncé, to walk into a room and catch everyone's attention.

She popped the trunk to her Benz, and inside was pricey clothing wrapped in plastic to shield it from dust and damage, and a few boxes of shoes. She had her own clothing store happening inside of her trunk.

She nodded as she went over her merchandise. Tina from the beauty salon on Fulton Avenue had called and placed an order. It was the sixth order in two days from ladies looking to get right for some upcoming event at Platinum, a high-end club in downtown Brooklyn. It seemed some major rap star and his entourage was supposed to show up and take the stage. So every bitch in Brooklyn had to look their best from head to toe to snatch them up a baller or player. They came to Pearla, knowing she had the good stuff for the right price.

Jamie made her way toward the car carrying the large shopping bag. She smiled Pearla's way, indicating that everything went smoothly.

"You got the dress?" Pearla asked.

Jamie threw her hand on her hip and shifted her weight to the right leg with a slightly domineering posture. "Am I a bad bitch?"

"Yes, you are," Pearla answered easily. She peered inside the bag at a few pricey dresses out of the store, even the one she'd just tried on.

"I swear, they need to give out fuckin' awards for shoplifting," Jamie said.

"And y'all would win everything."

"Bitch, you know that's right."

"Where's Roark?"

"You know how it goes—security stopped the bitch, thinking they caught her red-handed, and Roark probably leaving out of there with muthafuckas having egg on their faces, and she should be coming our way in five, four, three, two—"

"Y'all miss me?" Roark hollered from a short distance, hurrying out of the mall with a big shopping bag. She was all smiles, her adrenaline flowing from boosting. She couldn't wait to do it again.

Roark felt like she was around family as Pearla and Jamie greeted her. She simply wanted to please Pearla, who always looked out for her, from cash to clothes.

The trio climbed into the car and hurried away from the shopping mall.

While driving, Pearla hit her girls off with a few hundred dollars, showing her appreciation for all they'd done. Without them, she wouldn't be where she was today.

To Jamie, it was nothing but pocket change, but to Roark, it was cash she truly needed. Roark smiled broadly. Pearla dropped off her girls and headed West toward Benny.

She parked her Benz and walked toward the two-level commercial warehouse a block away from Atlantic Avenue. The area was industrial/urbanized but quiet, with the sun fading and most of the workers going home. It was a risky area, not too far from the projects, and the goons were known to lurk around the place. But Pearla wasn't intimidated. Brooklyn had been her home all of her life.

She knocked on the side door. It didn't take long for Benny to answer. He was grinning from ear to ear when he set his eyes on her.

"I'm glad you came," he said, allowing her inside.

"You think I wasn't?" Pearla replied.

Benny was pale-looking with a slim build, tattoos running up and down his arms. A long, bulky gold chain with a diamond-faced Jesus pendant hung around his neck, and a Puerto Rican bandana was tied around his head.

Pearla walked into the 18,000-square-foot warehouse with the storage and half bath on the first floor and on the second floor more space, an office, and another bath. The place was a ghetto Wal-Mart with electronics, flat-screen TVs, guns, and of course, her favorite—clothing.

"What you got for me, Benny?" she asked.

"You know you always get first pick of anything new we bring in," Benny said, still smiling.

Pearla knew he had a crush on her, and she flirted with him to get what she needed. She followed him to where he stashed the clothing. Inside the room looked like a scene from *The Devil Wears Prada*. Designer clothes were everywhere along with pricey shoes, from Red Bottoms to Manolo Blahnik. It was a dream come true for any woman.

"How much for it all?"

"Because I like you and you stay coming to me, four thousand."

It was an excellent deal. On the streets, she could make close to $15,000 or better. She reached into her stash and peeled off $4,000 like she was paying for something at the grocery store.

"It's always good doing business wit' you, mami."

Pearla smiled. "The pleasure's all mine."

After Benny's men loaded everything into the backseat and the trunk of Pearla's car, she drove straight to Tina's beauty salon on Fulton Street and hustled a bulk of her clothing there. The ladies were practically knocking each other over to purchase an outfit or shoes from Pearla. They all knew her shit was authentic, and she had stuff that was hard to come by.

"Pearla, you're my favorite bitch. I love you," one satisfied customer exclaimed.

"Pearla, when you gonna get me that Dolce and Gabbana dress?" another customer asked.

"Give me until next week," Pearla replied.

"Pearla, how much for these Red Bottoms?"

"Pearla, you got this dress in a size six?"

"Pearla, can I get these shoes for a hundred? 'Cuz you know a bitch gotta get her hair done too."

"Pearla, you gonna be at Platinum this weekend?"

The business and the questions swamped Pearla, but she didn't mind. She gave them great deals and joked and laughed with them.

Hitting three salons in one day, Pearla nearly sold out. She doubled her cash and was ready for more items from Benny or from the mall. Exhausted, she parked her Benz in front of the three-bedroom home in East New York and entered the place.

The minute she walked into the room, she heard her mother, Poochie, exclaimed, "Bitch, where the fuck was you at all day? And where's your fuckin' half of the fuckin' rent, Pearla? You know I don't play that shit! You think you gonna live here for free? Bitch, don't get it twisted!"

Pearla didn't feel like arguing with her mother over bills and money. "Mom, I'm tired," she said lifelessly.

"Bitch, I don't give a fuck if you're tired or not! I want my money!"

Out in the streets, Pearla was that bitch, a hustler and go-getter, knowing all the hustlers, being cool and respected by any nigga that had a name on the street, while driving a Benz and making money. But, at home, her mother made her feel low, and her space was limited to just the bedroom.

She also resented the fact that she had to split all the bills down the middle but could only fully occupy her bedroom. To Pearla, money wasn't the issue. It was the principle—the fact that her mother spoke to her like she was her archenemy, and also because she always treated Pearla like she was an adult even when she was a kid. It forced Pearla to grow up quickly and learn how to take care of herself.

Pearla knew that sooner or later she had to become fully independent, which meant she needed to move out and build her own household.

TWO

Cash took a pull from the cigarette burning between his lips as he gazed out the passenger window looking for the right car to steal. The green Accord he drove around in crept through the Cobble Hill area of Brooklyn. Three young black men in the car cruising slowly through an Italian neighborhood stood out easily, so they had to be subtle and quick.

The Accord moved across Smith Street, a commercial street mostly lined with family-run shops, Italian meat markets, barbershops, and trendy restaurants. The young boys were taking a huge risk trying to steal a car in the middle of the night, because police were always patrolling the area. But it was worth it, since Cobble Hill had the cars they were looking for.

Cash had been stealing cars since he was twelve years old, so that's what he loved and knew best. He was able to hot-wire anything within a heartbeat, and he could drive anything—stick shift, motorcycles, even eighteen-wheelers. Before his first arrest, he had stolen close to one hundred cars before he was sentenced to prison for car theft. Honda, Toyota, Acura, and General Motors vehicles were some of his favorite cars to steal. They had good resale value, so the parts were in demand. Tonight, he and his crew were searching for a certain Accord.

Darrell was slouched behind the wheel, navigating the car coolly, and Petey Jay was in the backseat trying to roll up a blunt. They'd all grown up together and been best friends and partners in crime since middle school.

Darrell was the car thief and master mechanic. He could take apart and put together any car effortlessly, and could repair anything. Petey Jay could easily bypass any alarm system, and Cash was the jack-of-all-trades—master car thief, skilled driver, and criminal—but stealing and selling cars was his forte. They learned from each other, and the three of them became the best car thieves in the tri-state area.

They avoided cars parked in front of houses and in driveways because they were too wide open and visible. Dark, secluded locations, such as apartment buildings and complexes, carports, underground parking, and parking garages were more appealing to them because they could have their pick of vehicle in one location, and they could hear if someone was coming.

"Yo, we need to hurry this up," Cash said. "I got this bitch waiting to suck my dick when I show up."

Darrell chuckled. "Nigga, you's wild wit' these bitches. Get ya fuckin' mind off of pussy and focus on makin' this money."

"Nigga, if you knew how good this bitch could suck a dick, you be rushing to get to her crib too." Cash grinned. "I'm tellin' you, *D*, this bitch could suck the skin off my dick with her strong, full lips."

Darrell and Petey Jay laughed.

"Hook us up then, nigga," Petey Jay suggested.

"Nah, nigga, can't do that. I got this bitch for keeps."

"Selfish muthafucka," Petey Jay spat back playfully.

"You still fuckin' wit' Stephanie?" Darrell asked.

"Nigga, who you think I'm gonna go see tonight? That bitch is a freak, yo. She can't get enough of this big fat dick."

Cash was a pretty boy with a low Caesar haircut with waves. With his flawless skin, snow-white teeth, beautiful black eyes, and long lashes, he was a magnet for women. He didn't come from or ever had a stable home, mostly sleeping on friends' couches. Cash never had a legitimate job, and had a string of girlfriends and jump-offs. He couldn't be faithful to any woman even if he wanted to.

"What we lookin' for out here?" Darrell asked, turning the corner onto the next street, approaching an apartment complex.

Cash took another pull from the Newport then exhaled. "A Honda Accord."

"Nigga, we stay stealing Accords. We need to be stealing Beamers or Benz," Petey Jay said. "I would look so fuckin' fly in one of those."

"Well, for the moment, Perez needs an Accord. He needs the parts."

"As long as he payin' the cash, we deliver the cars," Darrell chimed.

Cash fixed his eyes on a silver 2012 Honda Accord with its king-sized cabin. It was parked in a secluded area near the parking garage, sitting there on factory rims, no tints, and looking regular. "Bingo!" he said, pointing to it.

Darrell nodded and drove closer to the car. At 2 a.m., the area was quiet and still. It was a golden opportunity. Darrell stopped the car, and Cash, knowing the routine, quickly jumped out with the slim jim in his hands. He promptly scoped out the car and went into action. He preferred to steal a car without an alarm, but if there was one, he was able to disable it and drive off.

There was no blinking red light inside; the alarm hadn't been activated—a big mistake for the owner of the Accord. In case there was an alarm on the car, Cash didn't want to take any chances setting it off. He positioned himself on his back and quickly maneuvered himself underneath the engine and looked for the alarm horn, which would usually be on the passenger side, nearest to the firewall. He yanked that, and then *poof!* If there was an alarm, then there would be no sound, only fun lights.

He removed himself from under the engine and inserted the slim jim carefully between the passenger door window and the weather stripping.

He moved the tool slowly back and forth until it grabbed the lock rod. The lock flipped over, unlocking the door. No alarm, no lights.

Cash hurriedly jumped inside and began to hot-wire the car. Knowing the make and model of the Accord, he knew what to do. He removed the plastic cover on the steering column and tried to find the wiring joining the connectors, a coil of electrical wires.

Darrell and Petey Jay were waiting in the idling car, keeping cool and keenly watching their surroundings. If anything looked wrong, they were ready to abandon the mission.

Cash worked his magic while remaining out of sight, and within seconds, the Accord came to life. He popped up behind the steering wheel, looked over at his cronies and smiled.

"Who fuckin' wit' me?" he exclaimed jovially.

"Let's get the fuck outta here," Darrell said.

Cash put the car in drive and followed behind his friends. Another stolen car meant more money in their pockets. They were on their way to Perez's chop shop on Liberty Avenue. The crew got two grand or more a car on average, and they stole no less than ten cars a week from all over the city.

Cash turned on the radio and tuned into Hot 97. He nodded to Jay-Z's "Empire State of Mind," as he cruised through Brooklyn, out of Cobble Hill and closer to his stomping grounds. He couldn't wait to get money and see his bitch later on. His dick got hard just thinking about Stephanie sucking his big dick. For good measure, he dialed her to make sure she was still awake, and she answered after the second ring.

"You still up, right?" he asked.

"Yeah, I'm still up. Damn, Cash, what's takin' you so long?" Stephanie whined.

"We 'bout to hit the shop now, and it ain't gonna be but a minute. So keep them lips suckable for me and that pussy nice and tight 'cuz you know I'm ready to stretch you out like a rubber band."

Stephanie chuckled. "You so silly, Cash. But hurry up before I get too tired."

"I'm already there. Play wit' your pussy or somethin' to stay up. A'ight?"

"Bye, Cash."

Cash hurried behind Darrell, but he couldn't drive too fast or too reckless in a stolen car. Even though he outran police a few times in a high-speed chase, he didn't want to wear out his luck. No matter how late it got though, he knew Stephanie would wait up for him. She wanted him just as bad as he wanted her.

With his share from the chop shop in his pockets, and on his way to see his freak bitch Stephanie, Cash was a happy man. It was four in the morning, and he was far from tired. On his mind was some nasty sex, smoking weed, and having a good time. Cash loved the life he lived. He was a young kid who grew up around poverty all his life, so stealing cars was a goldmine in his eyes. Even though it came with risks, he felt like he could do it until the day he died. One day he hoped to maybe run his own chop shop and drive the baddest car in the city. He loved being a playboy. He loved the streets, he loved the hustle, and he loved his crew.

He pulled up to Stephanie's apartment building in another stolen car, checked himself in the mirror, licked his lips, and smiled. He was ready. He climbed out the stolen Buick and hurried into her project building on New Lots Avenue in East New York.

Stephanie lived with her grandmother above a corner bodega in a graffiti-covered, three-story building that had seen better days. It was a violent, crime-ridden area, but Cash wasn't worried because he was a familiar face. He walked into the lobby and through the broken security door. He went up the stairway and knocked on her door. It didn't take long for Stephanie to answer her door—buck-naked.

Cash smiled broadly. He couldn't wait to get the party started.

Stephanie wasn't what most would consider beautiful; she had big eyes and a big nose and looked good from afar, but not too good up close. But her phat ass, luscious curves, and balloon tits could arouse envy from a few bitches that didn't have her wonderful body. She'd been one of Cash's jump-offs for almost two years. Out of all his bitches, he loved fucking her the most. She always had the wettest pussy and gave him the best head.

"Damn, nigga! You took long enough. You lucky a bitch didn't fall asleep on your fuckin' ass and let you suck ya own fuckin' dick," she barked, her hands on her hips.

Cash looked at her shaved pussy. Her dark nipples looked like Hershey kisses pasted on her breasts, and her dark skin glistened like neon. "Damn!" he uttered at the sight of her raw nudeness. "You miss me? I know you did."

Dropping her attitude and smiling at his humor, Stephanie replied, "You a fuckin' trip, nigga." She stepped to the side and allowed him inside.

Stephanie's grandmother was out for the night, probably spending the night at her boyfriend's place, gambling in the casino, or drinking and playing cards with her friends. Stephanie didn't care. It gave Cash and her all the privacy they needed.

The minute Cash was inside the apartment, he unfastened his jeans and dropped them to the floor, along with his boxers, eager to show off his big, black dick that was hardening in front of her eyes. He touched himself as Stephanie approached closer with a strong, sexual gleam in her eyes. Fast cars and fast women—who could ask for anything more?

Stephanie reached down and grabbed a fistful of dick and stroked him gently, causing him to moan. "What you want me to do wit' this?" she asked with a teasing smile, her tone dripping with lust.

"You know what I want. Stop playin' wit' me."

Cash didn't like foreplay. He wanted sex right there and now, starting with a blowjob from her full, wet lips, and then he wanted to fuck her in every hole.

The two tongue-kissed fervently for a moment, and then Stephanie slowly went down on her knees before him, his big, throbbing dick still wrapped in her fist. She leaned closer to his sexual tool, opened her lips, and covered his hard flesh with her mouth.

"Ugh!" Cash groaned, his eyes shut. His knees trembled, and he was in complete bliss. "Oh shit!"

Each stroke of her tongue made him shiver. The perversion she catapulted him into seemed endless. Each time her tongue would wrap completely around the base and slide up to the tip, his mind went haywire, and his body felt like putty.

With her hands wrapped around his dick, she started kissing and sucking on the head. She released his dick from her mouth but not her hand and looked up at him. Her eyes seemed distant, but hungry at the same time.

Cash stared down at her, and she became the most beautiful woman in his eyes. He was about to say, "Don't stop," and it seemed like she read his mind.

She continued, her suction and salivating mouth bringing him closer to ejaculation. He could no longer stand, and pedaled backwards toward the couch and plopped down with his legs spread and Stephanie in between them, lowering her lips around his erection again. She cupped his balls, her nails tickling the back of his scrotum. Her other hand gripped the base of his cock and became like a vise, not allowing anything to get past her fingers as she sucked him harder than he ever remembered her doing. She moaned while giving him head, and the vibrations flowed along his shaft past her fingers and into his balls.

Cash grunted and moaned. He threw his head back against the couch and placed his hand around the back of her moving head, causing her to deep-throat him more. She sucked his dick so good, there was no way for him to keep his flood from rushing forward.

"I'm gonna come!" he cried out.

Just as he was about to reach the point of no return, she suddenly stopped. Cash gazed at her dumbfounded and asked in exasperation, "Yo, what the fuck!"

"Uh-uh, not yet."

Stephanie straddled his dick raw dog and fucked him on the couch. The two of them had an intense fucking session. Cash threw her against the wall and pounded her doggy-style on the floor. Then they went from the floor to the bedroom, from the bedroom to the bathroom; the entire apartment was their realm.

Stephanie had fallen in love with Cash, but he didn't know the meaning of the word *love*. All he knew was sex, cars, and just doing him day by day. He was a young goon with a provincial way of living; anything outside of Brooklyn or Queens was a stretch to him.

Nestled up against Stephanie, Cash was sleeping like a baby. Her big tits and soft skin were comforting like a cushy pillow. Their intense sexual encounter had drained them both. After busting multiple nuts and fucking their brains out like high-paid porn stars, Cash plunged into la-la land and planned to be there for hours. He was never a morning person. For him, seeing the sunrise was like seeing the bottom of the ocean. It was never going to happen, at least intentionally anyway.

Stephanie's apartment was a temporary place to stay, since he didn't have a place of his own. Though it was messy and cluttered with clothes and looked like the living room in *Sanford and Son*, she had food, weed, liquor, and cable TV, which was bliss to him.

Cash's cell phone ringing in the morning made him wish he'd put the damn thing on vibrate or left it in the other room. It was loud, chiming 50 Cent's "I Get Money, Money I Got." He tried to ignore it and go back to sleep. He winced from the sound and spun over, wrapping his arms around a sleeping Stephanie and giving his back to the phone. Whoever it was, they would stop calling.

The cell phone rang again. Whoever was trying to reach him wasn't going away. Agitated, he spun back over and gruffly snatched the phone off the nightstand and looked to see who was calling him. It was a number he hadn't seen before. Reluctantly, he answered the call with an irate tone. "Who the fuck is calling me?"

"Cash, it's me, baby. I need you to come bail me out," he heard her say hastily.

Cash sighed heavily. He didn't respond right away. He was sick and tired of her. It was a perpetual thing with her, getting locked up for prostituting herself and looking for him to bail her out. *When will it ever end?* he thought. Cash closed his eyes and asked, "How much is it this time? And where are you, Momma Jones?"

"I'm being arraigned downtown Brooklyn. They say my bail is fifteen hundred this time," his mother said tensely.

"Fifteen hundred?" Cash repeated loudly, taken aback. "Are you serious?"

He sat erect now, clutching the cell phone tightly to his ear and gritting his teeth. Why were his mother's problems always his problems? Fifteen hundred was nothing to sneeze at, and he didn't have that type of money at the moment. From last night's score, Perez had paid them $2,500 for the stolen Accord, but the money had to be split three ways, leaving him with a little over eight hundred dollars. With the four hundred dollars he already had on him, it still wasn't enough to bail his mother out of jail for prostitution.

Cash sighed once again and wiped the sleep out of his eyes. He looked at the time. It wasn't even 10 a.m. yet. He was upset at being awakened so early in the morning, especially after a late night. He wanted to curse his mother out, but he held his tongue.

"Baby, I don't wanna be in here. Can you come get me out?" his mother pleaded. "I don't belong in a place like this, and you know it. It's goin' to kill me."

"I'm comin', Momma Jones," he replied nonchalantly. "Just chill out."

"I owe you, Cash. I love you. You're my favorite son."

"I'm your only son," he reminded her.

Cash hung up, feeling even more agitated. He wanted to go back to sleep or fuck Stephanie again, but for some reason, he felt obligated to help out his mother, though she was never in his life, and most times, he despised her.

"Stephanie . . . Stephanie," Cash said, nudging his jump-off in her side, trying to awake her.

"What, Cash?" Stephanie exclaimed, obviously annoyed Cash was disturbing her sleep.

"I need five hundred dollars."

"What?"

"My moms got locked up again."

"And why you think I got that kind of cash on me?"

"'Cuz I know you do. You workin', right?"

"So what? That makes me your personal ATM now?"

"You know I'll pay you back. I'm good for it."

Stephanie sighed. "You better."

Cash smiled. He then added, "And I'll pay you back with interest wit' this tonight." He grabbed his flaccid, big dick and played with it in front of her then rapidly moved his hips left to right, making his penis flap side to side against his thighs. It was an impressive trick. Stephanie couldn't help but laugh at his silly and perverted antics.

Cash had Stephanie wrapped around his finger. Whatever he needed from her, he didn't get much resistance. The way she gave up pussy, money, and a place to stay was proof that she loved him.

Stephanie worked at a doctor's office in Sheepshead Bay, and though she was ghetto, rough around the edges, and trashy, she had a good job and was reliable.

Stephanie, laughing at Cash's playfulness, removed herself from the bed and went into her purse to give him the five hundred he needed. She'd recently cashed her paycheck, and her bills weren't due anytime soon. She handed Cash the money, and he snatched it without a single "Thank you," from his lips.

"I owe you," he simply replied.

"Pay me back by eating out this good pussy tonight," Stephanie said with a wayward smile.

Cash chuckled. He wasn't too eager to go down on any bitch and was going to, somehow, some way, talk his way out of giving her oral sex. He would pay her back, but it wouldn't be a priority on his list. She always gave him money when he needed it, and he always promised to pay her back, maybe giving her half or a small percentage of what he owed her when he had it. In his head, giving her some good dick was payment enough.

Cash quickly got dressed. He walked out the building on what was a gorgeous, warm spring day. He wasn't in any rush to bail out his mother for the umpteenth time this year. He jumped into the stolen Buick parked out front and revved the engine. He hated to cough up that kind of money to the city, but he had a good heart and couldn't let his moms rot in jail. However constantly aiding his mother with her legal fees and addiction, he would have to steal over a 100 cars a week to be able to help her out every time she got into trouble.

Cash lingered for a moment behind the wheel. With Stephanie's five hundred, he was up seventeen hundred, minus the fifteen hundred bail money; he would be left with two hundred dollars to his name. Shit was stressful on him. Tonight, he and his crew would simply go back out, cruise a neighborhood, and steal another car to sell to Perez.

THREE

Pearla woke up with the morning sun seeping through her open window. It was another day, another hustle. She had a lot of things to do—orders to fulfill and merchandise to snatch up. She and her crew planned on hitting Roosevelt Field mall again that afternoon. They had run their shoplifting scheme over a dozen times at that mall. Long Island was risky, since mall security and Nassau County police were harsh, and that particular mall had the latest high-tech security in place to deter shoplifters or catch them in the act. But nothing deterred Pearla and her crew.

The minute Pearla climbed out of bed, she heard the loud music playing from the living room from her bedroom, a clear indication that her mother was already up, probably drinking, and certainly had some male company over. It was the only time she played music so early in the morning—when she had dick in the apartment. Pearla's mother loved fucking to blaring R&B music.

Pearla decided to linger in her bedroom for a moment, afraid to walk out and interrupt something. Her mother had no shame in her game, from her constant profanity to her vulgar sexing anywhere in the apartment without caring who saw.

***

One time, Pearla walked in on her mother riding some big-dick nigga on the living room couch in the early afternoon. Pearla was mortified. She stood there like a deer caught in headlights.

Poochie had said to her daughter then, "What? You gonna fuckin' stand there and watch us fuck until we finish? Ain't you got some place to fuckin' be? Let a bitch come in peace."

Pearla had no words. She hurried off and locked herself in her bedroom that afternoon.

Poochie was a trip, though. She was selfish, loud, aggressive, ghetto, mean, whorish, and a judgmental hypocrite. She believed in "Do as I say, and not as I do." It was hard for anyone to believe she was a 38-year-old federal correction officer working in lower Manhattan. She had ten years on the job and loved every bit of it.

Working around violent and unpredictable inmates all day kept her mean and pugnacious. Her mouth was reckless because she always carried a gun, and she would do unruly things that could cost her her job.

Pearla had overheard her mother talking one day to Janet, her best friend. She went into explicit details about how she gave one inmate a hand job as he put his big dick through the slot of the steel prison door and she subtly jerked him off. Both women laughed.

Poochie said then, "Janet, this muthafucka is fuckin' fine though, and he's on twenty-three-hour fuckin' lockdown. Shit, every time I checked on him, he would be working out in his cell butt fuckin' naked. When I fuckin' saw what he was muthafuckin' working with, I was like, 'Gotdamn! Why he gotta be fuckin' locked up?' Bitch, you know I had to touch that big muthafuckin' dick at least one time."

Sometimes Pearla felt like she was the parent and Poochie the child. It was hard to believe that Poochie gave birth to her, because Pearla was more posh, well-spoken most times, and meticulous with her appearance and her room, while Poochie was messy and uncouth.

Pearla's bedroom was her safe haven, a direct contrast to her mother's messy apartment. When she wanted to escape or be alone, she would lock her door and either turn on her radio, write and doodle, or just think. The room was decorated precisely the way she wanted it and was scented with candles and perfume.

Her love for Paris and Parisian antiques showed with her vintage 18th century four-poster bed, crystal lamps, and custom drapes and bedding.

At the foot of her bed was a large retro storage trunk with an array of stuffed Disney animals and Mickey Mouse memorabilia that she kept dear to her heart. They were gifts from her father. She barely knew the man. He lived in Maryland with his wife and kids and always promised to come see Pearla, but he never did, nor did he send money to her. He also never paid Poochie a dime of child support.

Poochie constantly cursed about him and his new wife and kids. "Fuck that muthafuckin' bitch-ass nigga, his fuckin' cunt-ass wife, and his fuckin' bastard kids!" she would always say.

However, Pearla loved the man she barely met. On every birthday, from the time she was six years old, she received a cute, stuffed animal from her father and a birthday card. She knew that one day he would fulfill his promises to come see her.

Pearla slid her feet into her pink slippers, walked to the window, and gazed outside at the beauty of the day and decided to dare it and get ready. She opened her bedroom door, and Mary J. Blige could be heard blaring from the sound system. The hallway was cluttered with her mother's clothes.

Through the music, she heard her mother getting her groove on.

"Ugh! Ooooh! Fuck me! Fuck me!"

Pearla quickly went into the bathroom and locked herself inside. She shook her head, wishing she was somewhere else at the moment. Looking at her reflection in the bathroom mirror, Pearla was still a beauty in the morning without any makeup, her hair wrapped in a blue-and-white scarf. She splashed her face with some water, brushed her teeth, and then shed her bedtime attire to jump into the shower.

As the running water cascaded off her light-skinned flesh, she closed her eyes and thought of a few pleasurable things to get the moment started. It'd been a minute since she'd had sex—maybe too long. She was always about her business and didn't have any time for a boyfriend. Though, there was one boy she did like and have a crush on, but he barely noticed her.

With the temperature of the water set just right, Pearla groaned as she focused on her clit, rubbing it heatedly with her thumb. She then inserted two fingers into her vagina at the same time and moved them slowly in and out. She put the showerhead near her clit and teased it with the water pressure until she came—hard and fast. It was a really good orgasm, one she needed to get her day started. With no boyfriend in her life, her early-morning masturbating escapades were satisfying enough.

She stepped out of the shower and toweled off. Once again, she gazed at her naked reflection in the mirror, where her beautiful face was strong and captivating. She couldn't say the same thing about her body. It was enticing and pleasing to look at, but she couldn't hold a candle to her friends and other bitches with bodies like a video vixens. Her friend Jamie was bad from head to toe, voluptuous and curvy. Even Roark was thicker and more shapely than her. But what Pearla lacked in booty and tits, she made up for in sexiness, style, and wit. She dressed the part and looked the part. One day, with the money and the nerve, she would get a boob job and ass implants to enhance her body image.

Pearla took her time to get dressed. Today, she planned on wearing something simple— jean shorts that flattered her petite figure, a white camisole, and a pair of white Nikes. She wore the right accessories to enhance her look and wore her hair down to her shoulders. She looked like a cute, preppy female ready to hit the town and hang out with her friends.

Before exiting her bedroom, she picked up her cell phone and called Roark. The phone rang a few times before her friend picked up.

"Hey, Pearla," Roark answered. "You ready to make moves?"

"I'm ready," Roark replied, sounding excited. She was always excited when they went out to do a job.

"We definitely gotta keep sharp and swift."

"I know. We hit that mall a million times and never had any problems."

"I just want us to stay sharp and not slip up."

"We won't. We a team, right?"

Pearla smiled. "Yeah, we're a team."

"You talked to Jamie yet?"

"I'm about to call her right after I hang up with you, but I'll be ready to come get you within the hour."

"Okay."

Pearla hung up. She sat on her bed and sighed heavily. For some strange reason, she had butterflies in her stomach about today. She'd never had butterflies in her stomach when they were about to pilfer from any store or mall. She had been doing it for so long that it felt natural to her, like tying her shoes and applying makeup. Her feelings were always concrete. She was smart about the stores or the malls her crew would hit. They would try to rotate their crime wave throughout the city, and their wave of schemes stretched from New Jersey to Long Island. She would never try to hit the same places twice in one month. And she would try to use different girls for different places, to avoid using the same faces. It took skills to steal high-end merchandise from stores with heavy security, but it took smarts and wits to not get caught.

Pearla called Jamie.

"Hey," Jamie answered.

"Jamie, you ready?"

"I was born ready," Jamie responded, moving around her bedroom in her underwear and taking her time to get fresh.

Pearla chuckled. "That you were."

"What we hitting up today?"

"Roosevelt Field mall."

Jamie reminded her, "We just hit them up."

"I know." Pearla was aware of the risk. "But a bitch don't feel like driving to Short Hills mall today, and we can't get the high-end things we need from Kings Plaza."

"You sure you don't want to travel out to Jersey? You know I don't like fuckin' with Long Island like that. Those crackers be heavy out there."

"I know, but there's money out there." Pearla was adamant.

"Well, you know a bitch gotta go where you go, right?"

"Right," Pearla co-signed.

Pearla could hear Jamie having a good time in her bedroom with the music playing. Jamie was a huge Drake fan and always referred to him as "her husband." Her bedroom was decorated with his posters, and his heartthrob image on front covers of several magazines spread out on her table. Jamie always joked that if she ever saw him in person, she was going to kidnap him and have his baby.

"Pearla, I know you're going to the block party this weekend," Jamie said out of the blue.

"What block party?"

"What? You ain't heard? Everybody supposed to be coming through on Saturday, and DJ Mack Red is supposed to be doing the party. You know he deejays at Platinum and shit. Then they supposed to have some big-ass after-party at Platinum later on that night."

Pearla had forgotten. She had been so busy with her hustle, partying became almost nonexistent in her life, but hearing Jamie talk so lively about it and who was coming excited her too.

Jamie asked, "You are going, right?"

"Yeah, I'm gonna go."

"Cool. You know we gotta go out there and represent for real, Pearla. I already know what I'm gonna wear that day, and believe me, niggas ain't gonna be able to take their eyes off me, and bitches gonna be hating us hard. We gotta go lookin' like divas and shit."

Pearla agreed. They never went anywhere half-stepping. From the grocery store to a player-filled party, Pearla, Jamie, and Roark were three eye-catching females not about to get caught slipping wherever they went.

For a short moment, they talked about the upcoming block party then about the club. Then the conversation went on about making money and, briefly, about boys.

Jamie loved the attention she received from the males. Even grown-ass men tried to talk to her and offered to pay any of her bills or take her somewhere nice for a fraction of her time. She and Pearla were in the same boat when it came to attracting the cuties, the hustlers, and the bad boys, but Jamie had a more active sex life.

After her talk with Jamie, Pearla gathered her things and walked out her bedroom. Passing her mother in the living room, she heard Poochie ask, "Bitch, where the fuck you goin' lookin' like that?"

Pearla spun around and looked at her mother with contempt. "I'm going out!"

"Out? Bitch, you ain't got no fuckin' job, and I told ya fuckin' ass about that shoplifting. You think I'm fuckin' stupid, Pearla? I know what the fuck you 'bout to go out there and muthafuckin' do! Ya ass is about to go and steal some fuckin' shit!"

Poochie was nestled on the couch with her new boyfriend, both of them inadequately dressed and looking like two lazy bums. It was obvious they'd just finished fucking. The living room reeked of sex and weed.

Pearla noticed two empty condom wrappers on the coffee table and a half-empty bottle of Hennessy near his legs with two empty plastic party cold cups toppled over on the floor. The man was exactly Poochie's type—a roughneck, brawny, heavily tattooed, black, and bald. In Pearla's eyes, he looked like trouble.

Pearla and the man locked eyes briefly. He smiled her way, but Pearla frowned, tired of the company that came in and out of their apartment. Her mother had no respect for herself or her. Poochie was the epitome of a hood rat. Pearla yearned to gather enough money together and get her own place, somewhere far away from her mother and the ghetto.

"You stupid bitch! I work in the gotdamn muthafuckin' jail, and when you get fuckin' locked up, I ain't gonna be the one to fuckin' bail ya criminal ass the fuck out! You hear me, Pearla? 'Cuz I already told ya fuckin' ass—You need to stop stealin' shit!"

Bitch is funny, Pearl thought to herself. Her mother was always rambling on about her stealing but never turned down any clothing that was her size and sported proudly the stolen clothes or items she brought home. Poochie was the biggest hypocrite. How she was able to keep her federal job as a correction officer was a mystery to Pearla.

"I like them shoes you got on," Pearla replied sarcastically. They were the same shoes Pearla had taken out of a store in Queens a month back, and they were exactly her mother's size.

"You tryin' to be cute?" Poochie retorted.

"No, I just like your shoes," Pearla replied evenly.

"Bitch, you better not be gettin' fuckin' cute wit' me. I don't give a fuck if ya nineteen or not. Bitch, you ain't muthafuckin' grown, and if your fuckin' ass wanna be fuckin' grown, then I will fuckin' come over there and knock the pretty of ya light-skin ass."

"I'm not."

"And don't be out there fuckin' drinkin'!"

Pearla had heard enough. She spun back around toward the door and marched out. Dealing with her mother was like walking barefoot across broken glass—sharp, painful, and plain stupid. She hurried out the building and walked toward her Benz, which was parked a block away.

All the hustlers and bad boys were out today showboating in front of their flashy rides, some gambling, others throwing back liquor and beer, and admiring the lovely creatures roaming about. It was a beautiful afternoon and everyone looked like they wanted to take advantage of the day.

Pearla couldn't walk a block to her car without some nigga trying to talk to her, or some resident asking about an outfit, shoes, or jewelry they wanted her to get, so they would be able to wear it to the block party and club this coming weekend. Everybody wanted something from her. It wasn't a secret in the neighborhood what Pearla did.

She got behind the wheel of her Benz and took a quick breather, checked her image via the mirror in the sun visor, and went on her way to pick up Roark and Jamie.

✳✳✳

It was the middle of the afternoon, and being a weekday, the mall was less crowded. Pearla decided to linger in the food court while Roark and Jamie hit up Bloomingdale's and Nordstrom. Bloomingdale's was sweet. The girls were in and out.

Holding Bloomingdale's shopping bags full of stolen merchandise, Pearla sipped on a milkshake and kept her eye out like a hawk above. She noticed a man seated on the other end of the food court constantly looking her way. He tried to be inconspicuous, but he wasn't doing that good of a job. She had spotted him several minutes earlier—a white boy, young, maybe mid-to-late twenties, dressed regular, in blue jeans and a white T-shirt with short, cropped hair. He had a harmless look about him, but something was off.

He could be a cop.

Then suddenly, Pearla noticed two mall security guards entering the food court area—redneck-looking white boys—toy cops that looked too eager to take their subpar job seriously. Their attention wasn't focused on her yet, but she felt, in a minute it was about to be.

She tried not to look spooked by their presence, but butterflies began to swim around in her stomach. When she caught him looking, white boy averted his attention elsewhere. He sat alone, nibbling on the same French fries for the past half-hour.

It didn't take that long for anyone to eat some fries. Pearla knew better. She played it cool.

He was definitely watching her.

The mall security guards too. They stayed a good distance from her, acting like they were there formally.

Pearla removed her cell phone from her bag and called Jamie. Her instincts told her to abort today's plan. She didn't get this far in the game by being stupid. Somehow, she felt that mall security were on to them. But how? She pushed back her chair and removed herself from the table. Walking away from the food court with the phone pressed to her ear, Pearla heard Jamie's phone ring twice before she picked up.

"Abort! Run away!"

Jamie didn't need to ask any questions. When Pearla said abort, they aborted.

Pearla started to casually walk away from the food court, trying her best not to peer over her shoulders and give herself away. She took a few steps away from the area, and as predicted, mall security started to follow behind her nonchalantly. White boy too—he removed himself from the table, and Pearla found herself with unwanted company coming her way.

She took a deep breath and felt her heart beating a little bit faster. Bit by bit, her easygoing movement started to speed up. She clutched her bag to her chest tightly as she moved toward the exit on the lower level. The mall wasn't crowded. She had plenty of leeway from the top floor to the mall exit on the lower level.

At first there were three, but from her peripheral vision, she noticed another guard approaching from her left, his intense looked aimed at her. Yup, she was marked.

Like a heartbeat, Pearla dropped the bags filled with stolen merchandise and took off running, the men right away giving chase behind her. Pearla sprinted through the mall like a track star, bumping and almost knocking over mall patrons in her way. She headed straight for the escalators ahead of her and went flying down two to three stairs at a time. When she hit the ground, she made a sharp right and went flying by the stores. Security tried to entrap her, but Pearla moved like a fly in the sky, zigzagging through the bottom floor and desperately trying to reach the exit and escape.

"Stop! Stop!" she heard a security guard yell out.

There was no way she was going to comply. She wasn't about to be detained. The chase through the mall caught everyone's attention. People gawked at them like they were watching a scene from a movie. With her arms flaring up and down, Pearla didn't look behind her once. She was too focused on getting away. She could see the exit fifty feet from her, and security was close behind.

With freedom so close, she put a little power into her running and bolted toward the nearest exit like a bullet discharging from a gun. She was young and in shape, and her pursuers weren't. They were already winded—except for the white boy. He was able to keep up, moving like he was a track star.

Who is this muthafucka? Pearla wondered.

Pearla became a blur to the storeowners and mall customers witnessing the craziness unfold right before their eyes.

She rushed through the glass doors like a flood pouring through, nearly shattering one of the doors as she thrust it open, escaping into the parking garage. She had a half a minute window to hide herself somewhere in the garage. She interweaved through the parked cars and hunkered behind a black big-body SUV, her breathing ragged. She kept quiet and looked around her, carefully listening for anyone approaching. She could hear the guards' radios going off as they searched the area for her.

Pearla was scared. Why were they chasing after her?

The guards were heard moving through the parking garage. Their voices and walkie-talkies gave away their positions. With one coming close, she lay down flat on her stomach and shimmied underneath a different car that was low enough to conceal her. She remained quiet and still like a mouse, observing her chasers walk right by her.

"We lost her," she heard one of them say.

"What about her friends?" another one asked.

"No signs of them either," another answered.

What is going on? Pearla asked herself quietly. How did they know about her crew? They were always careful.

She hid for a long moment, hoping the owner of the car she was underneath didn't come back anytime soon. She had scraped her knee and felt dirty and sweaty. It was a low point for her. She hoped Jamie and Roark were able to get away too.

She let a few more minutes go by until she removed herself from underneath the car. She carefully looked around her, and everything appeared to be clear and safe.

Pearla hurriedly went to where she had parked her car and jumped inside. She started the ignition and then got on her phone. She was worried about Roark and Jamie. Jamie's phone rang several times before she picked up.

"Jamie, where are you?"

"Where are you?" Jamie asked, sounding like she was out of breath and running.

"I'm in the car, ready to come get y'all. Roark's with you?"

"Yes. We just barely got away from these muthafuckas."

"Okay, I'm coming to get y'all now. Where are y'all?"

"In the parking lot by the Macy's store, hiding behind some red Chevy."

"I'm on my way."

Pearla wheeled her Benz out of the parking garage and headed their way. She drove inconspicuously around the parking lot looking for her friends, trying not to draw any attention to herself.

She soon spotted Roark and Jamie hastily walking away from the mall. She hurriedly pulled beside them and they jumped inside the car. Roark and Jamie looked somewhat disheveled. No one said a word. Pearla drove farther away from the mall.

Something went wrong, but how and by whom? Today's mission was a complete bust. They had nothing to show for their long journey into Long Island. Going home empty-handed was a disheartening feeling. They never went home empty-handed. Each girl looked puzzled and relieved at the same time.

When they got on the highway, Jamie was the first one to say something. "Rebecca."

"You think it was that bitch?" Pearla asked.

"Yup!" Jamie replied. "I'm for sure."

Rebecca was a young girl that worked in Nordstrom, mostly as a cashier. She was one of the girls that helped Pearla with their shoplifting.

Jamie added, "When I saw that bitch in the store, she was acting funny toward us, and then it happened that you called and told us to abort. The minute after you called, Pearla, security was on us, and Rebecca just stood there looking dumbfounded."

Pearla drove, analyzing the situation.

"We need to fuck that bitch up," Jamie said.

Pearla didn't respond. She continued to drive, thinking not about retribution, but about maybe getting into another line of work. Maybe that's what she needed to do—quit while she was ahead and come up with another profitable hustle. She'd always known it was best to never put all her eggs into one basket.

FOUR

An irate Cash walked out of the downtown Brooklyn Detention Center on Atlantic Avenue with his mother right behind him.

Momma Jones, clad in a short denim skirt, high heels, and a tight red top that left nothing to the imagination, was desperately trying to keep up with him and put herself back together. She tugged at her skirt while trotting down the courthouse stairs.

"Cash, I'm sorry, and I owe you. You are my savior."

Cash wasn't trying to hear anything she had to say to him. Because of her, he was out fifteen hundred dollars. It was too early in the morning to be going through this shit. He hurried toward his car.

"Cash, I'm gonna pay you back."

"It ain't about the money," he spat back.

"Then what's it about?"

Cash stopped walking abruptly and spun around to glare at her. Through his clenched teeth, he said, "You're embarrassing me. That's what the fuck you are—a fuckin' embarrassment, Momma Jones."

"Embarrassment?" Momma Jones uttered, animosity swelling up inside of her. It hurt her to hear her own son speak and think so poorly about her.

"You're forty-two years old, and you still out here dressing like some fuckin' hood rat and suckin' dick for pennies. You think I need this shit?"

Momma Jones glared at her son and threw her hands against her hips. "No matter what you think of me, I'm still ya fuckin' mother."

"Then fuckin' act like it."

It was plain as day to everyone that Momma Jones was a crackhead, sucking dick for twenty dollars and throwing her pussy away for thirty to fifties dollars. For years, she'd been feeding her drug habit via prostituting and stealing. She would rent a room out of a boarding house in some of the slummiest parts of town. She had clientele, because word around town was that she was cheap and gave the best head around.

Cash hated that she sold her ass and sucked dick. Growing up, he'd gotten into plenty of fights around town with young dudes his age bragging about paying his mother to suck their dick and fuck. Cash was no punk or a sucker. He was an affable dude, yes, but when it came to his family, he became a beast and stood up for his mother and father.

Momma Jones's dark skin shined as if she was sweating after a long, hard workout, her blond wig clashing with her skin tone. The hard lines etched into her face and her sunken eyes bore evidence of the hard life she lived, her beauty corroded by years of drug abuse and prostitution.

Cash only dealt with her when he needed to. He couldn't pick his parents, but it was hard to turn his back on them.

"I should have just left you in there."

"And prove what?" Momma Jones shouted.

"Maybe have you detox in there, 'cuz you need to do somethin'."

"Nigga, don't fuckin' tell me how to live my life!"

Cash fired a few crippling and unkind words at his mother and proceeded to walk toward the Buick parked blocks away from the detention center.

It was a beautiful day, and the morning crowd bustled around the area. Cash lit a cigarette and took a few much-needed pulls. Arguing with his mother was the last thing he wanted to do. He wanted to drop her off and get back to business—stealing cars. However, Momma Jones was one to always have the last word. The two bickered at each other.

When Momma Jones saw the gleaming Buick LaCrosse Cash was driving, she hollered, "And who the fuck is you to judge me, Cash? You steal cars for a living. Nigga, you ain't better than me."

Cash simply shook his head, shot his mother an irate stare, and climbed into the car. "You comin' or not?" he asked sharply.

Momma Jones didn't say anything, but her climbing into the passenger seat was her answer.

Cash started up the car and pulled away from the curb.

They rode in silence until Momma Jones asked, "You got another cigarette?"

Cash sighed and gave her two cigarettes from his pack.

"Thanks," she said to him. "I needed one."

After dropping Momma Jones off in Crown Heights, the place where she did her dirty work, Cash needed relief. He wanted to get away somewhere and relax. It was still too early in the morning for him to be cruising about. The sun wasn't even at its peak yet, and his stomach was growling for breakfast. He decided to hit up McDonald's.

Going through the drive-thru, he ordered a sausage, egg and biscuit sandwich, hash browns, and a medium orange juice. He devoured everything within minutes and drove back to East New York. He thought about going back to Stephanie's place, but she was last night's pleasure, and now he owed her five hundred dollars.

His mind floated to a pretty eighteen-year-old he'd met last month named Tyesha. She was five-three and brown-skinned with perfect tits and a booty like a brown bubble.

Slowly cruising down Atlantic Avenue, he picked up his cell phone and dialed Tyesha. After the third ring, she picked up.

"Hey, beautiful," he said charmingly. "What you doin'?"

"Who this? Cash?"

"The one and only."

"I'm sitting here thinking about you," she returned.

Cash smiled. "Oh, word? You thinkin' about me? What you thinkin' about?"

"You care to come over and find out?"

"Beautiful, you read my mind. I was thinkin' about you too. Why you think I called?"

She chuckled like a schoolgirl. "I know why you called."

"Oh, you do, huh?"

"Uh-huh."

"I missed you," he lied to her.

"I missed you too."

"So since we miss each other, I'll be over that way in an hour."

"An hour? Why an hour?"

"'Cuz I gotta stop somewhere first."

"What? You gonna see another bitch?" she asked, a slight attitude and insecurity in her tone.

"No, it's not like that, Tyesha. I just gotta take care of something important, and then I'll be over that way to make it a good morning for you, you know, massage your feet, scratch that itch, and tickle your needs."

Tyesha grinned and chuckled. "I like that."

"I knew you would."

"Cash, you better not take more than an hour to come see me. My parents will be home at three, so don't keep me waiting."

"I won't. Promise."

"Okay."

"And, Tyesha," Cash said, with an afterthought.

"Yeah?"

"Come to the door naked."

She giggled. "Cash, you so stupid."

"I'm sayin' . . . why waste time taking off clothes and shit?"

"A'ight."

Cash hung up. He couldn't wait to get into Tyesha's panties again. Last time, they'd fucked like they were trying to make a baby. Good thing they'd used condoms. The way her pussy would tighten around his dick with his every thrust, it almost felt like a boa squeezing around his manhood. Yeah, Tyesha was one of the unforgettable ones—warm, wet, and tight.

Cash drove the stolen Buick into Brownsville, Brooklyn and parked on Sutter Avenue. He jumped out the car and headed toward a corner bodega across the street from the Seth Low Houses. With the sun still fresh in the sky, the local thugs, hustlers, and residents didn't swamp the area yet. People were at work or still in their apartments, and the streets weren't busy at all, making it easier to find his father.

Cash knew his father was always in the area. If he wasn't lingering in front of the bodega, then he was hanging out in the courtyards of the projects, panhandling for money in front of the local liquor store, or on the streets. His father was homeless, but he was a good man.

Raymond, aka Ray-Ray, was an intravenous drug user. Despite his tattered appearance, he was still an easygoing man with a warm personality. Ray-Ray would dance, crack jokes, and hold the door to the store open for approaching patrons; anything for a buck and some spare change. Everyone knew and loved Ray-Ray, despite him being the neighborhood drunk and drug addict.

Cash walked into the bodega and got two hot cups of coffee. He walked back out of the bodega, sipping on one cup, and headed up the street. He planned to kick it with his pops for a short moment before he got things started with Tyesha.

As expected, he spotted Ray-Ray opening the door for a middle-aged woman going into the liquor store in the early morning. Ray-Ray said something to the woman, putting a smile on her face.

Cash smiled, seeing his father. He walked his way. "You gonna hold the door open for me, too?"

Ray-Ray turned around and grinned heavily, seeing his son approaching. "There go my boy," he said cheerfully. "You know I'll always open any door for you."

"I brought you some coffee." Cash handed his pop the hot cup of coffee and dapped him up.

Ray-Ray happily took it and started sipping on it. "Cash, you always know what I like."

"I see you still got a way wit' the ladies," Cash said.

"You damn sure right, I do. And don't forget where you got the genes from."

"I know, Pop. I didn't forget."

Ray-Ray smiled. He had a weathered look to him with a deep tan and heavy creases on his face—rugged as heck. He lived a hard life outdoors most of his adult life. He survived the cold, the rain, the snow, the heat, and everything else thrown his way. His addiction to heroin had had a crippling effect on his life for over fifteen years now.

Cash always tried to be sympathetic to his father's addiction, knowing he had a serious drug problem like his mother. One was on crack, the other on heroin. He had a dysfunctional family with a capital *D*. His mother and father had contrasting personalities—she was a bitch and a backstabber, and his father was so nice and easygoing, the most lovable guy anyone could ever meet. How the two ever hooked up was a mystery to Cash.

Ray-Ray once broke it down, though, explaining that Momma Jones was once the most beautiful woman in New York City who ran her own escort service in the eighties and early nineties. He became one of her favored customers. He used his charm and humor to melt the panties off Momma Jones, and nine months later, Cash was born. Momma Jones named her son Cash, because that's what she was all about—the money. So Cash became the son of a prostitute/madam who'd gotten pregnant by a frequenting trick. His family's life was a book waiting to be written.

Since he was a young boy, Cash had been a street kid, pretty much raising himself and wishing life would get better when he went days without food, shivering in a cold apartment. It only got better for him when he started stealing cars and making his own money. Cash became more about charm than character, telling the ladies what they wanted to hear to get his way with them. He was no longer hungry or broke. Bitches always took care of him, from money to shelter.

Cash told his father, "I saw Momma Jones this morning."

Ray-Ray smiled, hearing his baby mama's name. "Oh, you did? What she's been up to?"

"I bailed her out for prostitution."

Ray-Ray lightly grinned his son's way. "It never gets old."

"You ain't mad, Pop?"

"Why should I be?"

"Because she's always getting locked up for the same old shit."

"And you keep bailing her out, Cash."

"How could I forgive myself if I didn't?"

"Easy. We all got our demons, Cash, some more than most. Who am I to judge that woman?" Ray-Ray set his cup of coffee on top of a pay phone and lifted his right sleeve to reveal the tracks running up and down his arm. "My life is in these veins," he said.

"It ain't gotta be, Pop."

"Funny thing, Cash—I'm a great swimmer but feel myself sinking every day."

Cash sighed. "You ever think she loved you, Pop?"

"Your mama had a thing for me, and I did love her."

"Why is she like that and you like this? I mean, I can talk to you—you cool, Pop—but I can't ever talk to her. She ain't gonna ever change."

"Cash, if you judge her, then you gonna have to judge me too. We both are doing the same harm to ourselves, dying differently. You know what my father, your grandfather, used to say to me all the time? 'He who conquers a city is not nearly as strong as one who conquers himself.' And you know what? I'm okay with it. I can't conquer this demon, and I don't think I ever will."

"Why you talkin' like that, Pop?"

"I'm just talking, son, that's all. Your mother . . . she loves you . . . we love you."

When Ray-Ray wasn't high or drunk, he was a wise man spilling out wisdom and truth that would have any man thinking and nodding his head. He'd been through it all and had a lot to share, from experience.

"You got a cigarette, son?"

Cash pulled out a fresh pack of Newports from his pocket and handed Ray-Ray four cigarettes.

"I owe you," Ray-Ray said.

"Pop, you don't owe me anything."

"We always owe something to somebody."

Cash continued to chat and spend some time with his father. They talked while lingering outside the liquor store.

The time almost got away from Cash. When he realized how much time had passed, he thought about Tyesha. He said to his father, "You gonna get ya shit together, Pop?"

As always, Ray-Ray replied, "Tomorrow."

It's always tomorrow. Cash promised his father he would come by again sometime that week and hurried back to the car.

He drove Tyesha's way, that pussy heavy on his mind. The day had started off wrong with his mother, but it started to get back on the right track with the conversation with his father and going to see Tyesha.

Before noon came, Cash was knocking on Tyesha's apartment door. She came to the door buck-naked like he'd asked.

He smiled broadly. "Damn!"

"I take it, you like what you see," Tyesha replied with an engaging smile.

"You know it."

Cash stepped into her apartment ready to get the party started. He was completely naked before he walked into the bedroom.

The next three hours were pure bliss for him.

After Tyesha's place, it was back to his old stomping grounds where he linked up with Darrell, Manny, and Petey Jay. The group got high at Petey Jay's place, talked shit, and cracked jokes.

Cash bragged to them about his recent sexual tryst with Tyesha.

"Yo, I was fuckin' that bitch so hard with her bouncing on my lap, I almost put her fuckin' head through the ceiling," he said with the sexual movement, to indicate how he had her positioned on his lap.

"Oh, word, son?"

"Yo, that bitch pussy is mad tight and shit. Yo, but y'all shoulda seen how I had this bitch. Crazy, yo."

Petey Jay took a pull from the burning weed. He laughed and passed the spliff Cash's way.

Cash took it and took two long puffs from it. He was dumb high.

Darrell suggested, "Yo, Cash, you need to start filming these bitches and shit, know what I'm sayin'? I would love to see that shit."

Manny co-signed, "Fo' real, my nigga, I be wanting to see that shit too."

Cash laughed. "Y'all crazy. But, a'ight, I'm gonna start putting these bitches on videos and let y'all see how I get down." He dapped everyone up with the glad hand, and they continued to smoke.

"Cash, you goin' to the block party over Melody's way this weekend?" Manny asked.

Darrell nodded. "Yeah, I heard it's supposed to be off the hook and shit. They got DJ Mack Red comin' through."

"Oh, word?" Cash said.

"Yo, mad bitches gonna be out there Saturday," Manny said. "I'm there."

Cash nodded. "I'm there too."

Manny added, "Yo, and that bitch Jamie and her crew comin' through too."

"Yo, I've been wanting to fuck that bitch," Petey Jay spoke out.

"What 'bout her friend Pearla?" Manny asked.

"Yo, she a fuckin' cutie too, but she ain't fuckin' wit' Jamie though. Jamie got that fuckin' body; you know what I'm talkin' about."

Manny smiled. "Yeah, but Pearla gettin' that money, and she be havin' all these bitches in check."

Cash was listening. It wasn't the first time he'd heard Pearla's name ring out. He was constantly hearing about her, how fly she was, and that she was a born hustler. But he was too high to even think straight at the moment, and he figured in due time, he'd probably fuck all those bitches. One thing was for sure: he was going to be at that block party. It would only be right.

FIVE

DJ Mack Red had the block party in East New York jumping with old-school and present jams blaring from the gigantic speakers. The entire blocked was closed off to vehicular traffic, and residents flooded the street from corner to corner. Kids ran in every direction, playing, riding their bicycles, and yelling. Activities like pony rides, inflatable slides, popcorn machines, dancing, and the smell of barbecue made it the place to be on this sunny Saturday afternoon.

When DJ Mack Red put on "Electric Boogie," everyone immediately got in the mood and danced to the classic song. A flock of people moved to the beat in rhythm, doing the choreographed line dance.

Pearla, Jamie, and Roark arrived at the block party in style. Getting out of Pearla's Mercedes, all three ladies immediately grabbed the attention of every male in the area. They came dressed in sexy shorts and colorful camisoles, wearing their fresh sneakers or flip-flops. Jamie was dressed the sexiest in her micro-mini stretched shorts that highlighted her protruding, plump buttocks, her tits stretching the material of the tight shirt she wore. She absorbed the attention like a sponge, flirting and smiling at the cute boys and sticking with her friends.

The crew needed to take their mind off nearly getting caught in Roosevelt Field mall. Spending Saturday afternoon at a block party was the perfect way to unwind.

"There go DJ Mack Red over there," Jamie pointed out, smiling and gazing at the lean, six-two, 180-pound man wearing a blue Yankees fitted and a wife-beater. He was heavily tattooed and looking like an extra from *Magic Mike*.

The girls quickly mingled in with the block party crowd. Business didn't stop for Pearla, though. She was still getting orders everywhere she turned, with several young girls eager to get their hands on a new designer dress and shoes. Pearla was moving like a politician during election year, and Roark was beside her, smiling and watching, taking in the glory of being her best friend.

Cash, Petey Jay, Manny, and Darrell strolled toward the block party like the young, cocky, handsome playboys they were. They were motivated to get as many numbers possible and leave with some new, pretty bitch the same day. Dressed to the nines in stylish T-shirts, designer jeans, expensive Jordan's on their feet, and jewelry gleaming around their necks and wrists, they were eye-catching to the females swarming everywhere.

"I told you," Manny said, referring to all the good-looking, nicely dressed ladies in attendance.

Cash was the main one turning heads as he moved through the crowd. His strapping physique showed through the fabric he wore, and his waves were spinning like a toy top on his head. Everything he had on was brand-new and fit him perfectly.

The first thing Cash and his friends did was take advantage of all the barbecuing happening around them. The smell of burgers, hot dogs, ribs, and chicken on several grills made their mouths water. Cash sunk his teeth into a juicy cheeseburger, devouring that within minutes, and then he munched down a few hot dogs, some fried fish, and downed two beers.

He was definitely hungry. His friends matched his consumption of food. They walked around with their mouths full, gazing at every beautiful young girl they passed by.

"Damn, I like that!" Petey Jay said, staring at a curvy young woman hanging out with her friends on the other side of the street.

The boys, ready to make moves, were craning their necks in every direction to catch the big booties and cute faces.

Petey Jay was in a daze. "Yo, I like that even more. Shit, they gettin' it in over there."

Cash and the others looked over to see what had Petey's attention as he stuffed a hot dog into his mouth. They saw, and they were hypnotized.

A few girls were twerking in the middle of the street, with thrusting hip movements while they squatted, and a small crowd gathered around them. The fellows were cheering them on, eyes glued to the provocative booty-shaking that had some conservative adults sneering. Jamie was one of the girls twerking, catching all the boys' attention.

Manny hollered, "Oh shit! I like that, I like that."

Cash gazed at her with lust in his eyes, admiring what he saw. Jamie's body was phenomenal, and the outfit she had on made him thirsty to get to know her better. "Yo, shorty is nice," he said to Manny.

"I know, son."

The young kids were taking over the block as afternoon transitioned into evening, and DJ Mack Red played music they could relate and dance to. Future, Lil' Wayne, T-Pain, Drake, The Dream, Nicki Minaj, and many more had the block sounding like it was a club.

Cash and his friends were becoming the life of the party, mingling with the girls and showing off the latest dance steps in front of everyone. Cash especially showed off, moving like he was a backup dancer for Chris Brown. He had rhythm and knew every dance move there was. He was fun to watch. He wanted the attention, and he got it.

The girls giggled and smiled his way, whispering to each other. Pearla couldn't take her eyes off Cash; she'd had her eyes on him for some time, but they barely ran into each other.

"Nigga, stop showing off!" Petey Jay yelled. "You ain't Chris Brown."

Cash smiled, playfully flipped him the bird, and continued dancing. He danced behind a young girl and couldn't keep his hands off her. He touched her hips, and she backed her ass up against him and moved like he moved, on point and in tune.

"That's my nigga right there! That's my nigga!" Petey yelled.

Cash had to be the life of the party. It couldn't be any other way. He loved being seen, and he loved being popular among his peers. It was a great feeling to be wanted by so many beautiful women and respected and admired by his friends.

Cash didn't want the moment to end. He had eight hundred dollars in his pockets for his everyday needs and nice clothing to parade around town in, while munching on free food, and grinding with a few cuties on a Brooklyn street. This was the life. Parked a few blocks away were the two stolen Honda Civics the crew had arrived in, which they planned on delivering to Perez later at his chop shop on Liberty.

Cash laughed and chilled with his friends, while contemplating going over to talk and flirt with Jamie. He was ready for something hot from the oven and new in his life, and the way she'd moved and twerked earlier had him yearning to see what else she could do in private. He had to be patient though, since he wasn't the only guy trying to holler at her.

Petey Jay suddenly tapped him on his shoulders. "Yo, there go Pearla over there."

Cash turned and looked. "And?"

"That's you right there, Cash. She a get money-bitch."

Pearla was alone for the moment, talking to someone on her cell phone. She was beautiful, but she wasn't captivating like Jamie. Cash had always been into girls with banging shapes—nice hips, phat asses with small waists. Weave or no weave, it didn't matter to him. Pearla's body was okay, but it didn't stand out to him like her friend's did. It was her face that stood out. She was pretty—gorgeous in fact—with her long, natural soft hair, light eyes, and pouty pink full lips. Something about her drew niggas' attention, and she looked like a cool girl to hang out with.

Cash wasn't looking for a cool cutie to chill with; he wanted a hot, smoking freak that he could fuck—another trophy piece on his shelf.

"I bet you can't fuck her in a week."

"What? Nigga, I'm Cash—I got bitches lined up to jump on this dick," he said with a cocksure smile. Petey Jay made Cash want to walk over and introduce himself.

"I heard she stingy with the pussy."

"What you tryin' to say? You think I can't fuck that bitch right away?"

"Nah, I don't think you can. She a challenge. She 'bout her paper, and that's all she 'bout."

"Nigga, I bet you a hundred I can get that number today, and another two hundred I can fuck that bitch within a week."

Petey Jay stared at Cash, thinking about the bet. "A'ight, bet."

"Nigga, get ready to pay up like an ATM," said Cash with a grin.

He walked over coolly, his eyes fixated on Pearla from head to toe. She was still on her phone, looking like the conversation was important. He didn't care who she was talking to; he was about to make it about himself in a few seconds.

As he approached, he admired her style and noticed she was a lot more beautiful up close. Her eyes alone were hypnotizing. Her full, glossy lips looked kissable, and her long, black hair definitely wasn't a weave.

The two locked eyes. Pearla looked at him expressionlessly, not believing he was coming her way. He smiled. She didn't smile back but continued talking on her cell phone, trying to ignore him and play it cool.

Cash stood right in front of her and said, "Tell them you'll call back."

"Excuse me?" Pearla replied, looking thrown off by his words.

"I'm sayin', if you're not on the phone wit' me, then it can't be that important."

"You're serious?" She let out a slight chuckle.

"Like cancer."

Pearla stared at him, showing no emotion.

"Cory, I'm gonna have to call you back," she said into the cell phone. She hung up and gave her attention to Cash.

"So, who's Cory? Your boyfriend or somebody?"

"Why is that your business?"

"It's not. I'm just sayin', if you got a man, is he treating you right?"

Pearla chuckled. "Why? Because if he wasn't, then you can treat me better?"

"Oh, I see. You tryin' to clown me."

"No, I'm not, but I've heard it all before."

"Well, I can be brand-new in your life."

"Are you always this cocky?"

"Actually, I'm quite shy."

"If you're shy, then the sky is green," she quipped.

"Then let it be green. Besides, I'm color blind." Cash laughed at his own line.

Pearla chuckled. "You don't even remember me, don't you?"

"Am I supposed to?"

"Wow! Was I that invisible back in the day?"

"Well, you're not invisible to me now." Cash smiled, showing his pretty, pearly white teeth and deep dimples on both sides of his cheek. His dimples and his smile were definitely panty droppers.

"Eighth grade, Mr. Stencil, English class."

Cash racked his memory trying to remember who she was.

"Yeah, how could you remember? You wasn't in school that much anyway, always playing hooky."

"It's obvious that you remember me, though."

"Who can forget you, Cash?"

"I've known a few."

"Yeah, whatever. You can tell me anything."

Cash stared at Pearla, trying hard to remember her from the eighth grade. It was seven or eight years ago. She must have changed drastically.

"You ain't gotta hurt yourself to try and remember me. If you don't remember, then you don't. Like I said, back then, I was invisible."

"Usually, I have a good memory."

"Well, tonight, you just don't."

"So I got an idea. Today, right now, let's start making some memories of our own. Let me take you out tonight."

"What? You asking me out on a date?"

"You turning me down?"

"I didn't say that."

"So, what are you sayin'?"

"I'll think about it," she replied casually.

He slightly laughed. "Oh, you're playin' hard to get."

"No. Who's playing?" She smiled.

Cash matched her smile and replied, "You know what? I like you."

"And I like you too."

The two kicked it, looking like their conversation was golden. They had many eyes watching them, some curious and many hating. They talked for half an hour. Cash was impressed by her intelligence. If she really liked him, she disguised it very well. They exchanged numbers, and he promised to call. She didn't promise him anything.

"So, you gonna call me?" Cash asked before walking away.

"I'll think about it," she teased.

"You gonna call. If you don't, it will be a waste of a half an hour having a wonderful conversation with you."

"And why's that?"

Cash didn't reply. He walked away feeling like he was a step closer to winning his bet with Petey Jay. It was going to take him less than a week to hit that. She didn't have that remarkable of a body, but there was something special about her that impressed him.

✳✳✳

Pearla walked away thinking, *Wow! Did that really just happen?* Everything came unexpectedly, and she liked it. She really did.

She walked Roark and Jamie's way, trying to hide her smile, but she couldn't.

The frown her friends carried on their faces as she approached them made her think something was wrong. They both seemed agitated about something.

The minute she was around them, Jamie said, "I know you ain't tryin' to fuck wit' that nigga."

"Who? Cash?"

"He a dog, Pearla," Roark chimed. "He only cares about himself."

"We were just talking," Pearla said in her defense.

"Please," Jamie said. "That nigga wasn't just talking; he was scheming, looking for another notch on his belt when he fucks you. He a dog, Pearla. A womanizing, nasty ho."

Roark said, "I know, right? Ain't no telling how many bitches he's been wit'."

Whoa! Where did all this come from? Pearla thought. She had heard enough. Her smile turned into a frown. Her own friends hated on her because Cash came over to her and initiated the conversation. "It seems like y'all hating on me."

"What?" they said, dumbfounded by her response.

Jamie asked her, "Why we gotta hate on you, Pearla?"

"Because Cash came my way and hollered at me, and I ain't have to do shit to get his attention. I'm no stupid bitch, y'all, and I ain't no fuckin' ho."

"We weren't calling you no ho," Jamie said.

"Well, don't get it fuckin' twisted. I'm a big girl, and I can handle myself. I know what I want, and Cash is what I want right now."

Jamie and Roark had nothing else to say to her.

The rest of the day, she thought about Cash. If he didn't call first, then she would crack and call him. But she was going to play her hand of cards real cool, because it felt like she was holding a full house.

SIX

Yo, so this bitch calls me in the middle of the night for some dick, right, and I was like, 'Damn, ma! Is it that serious?' And she was like, 'Come over. I wanna see you.' But, yo, why she wanted me to come over while her husband was home?" Cash proclaimed gleefully.

"Get the fuck outta here, nigga!" Darrell said. "Serious?"

"Nigga, I'm so fuckin' serious," Cash said loudly.

"And you went over there?" Manny asked.

Cash grinned. "What you think, nigga?"

Manny said, "Yeah, nigga, you went over there, wit' your crazy ass."

Cash was telling one of his stories about another fascinating sexual rendezvous with another beautiful female. They were all at Petey Jay's two-bedroom apartment drinking liquor, getting high, and watching porn on the flat-screen in the living room. It was guys' night out. Weed smoke filled the living room, everyone's breath was saturated with liquor, and each man had his own interesting story to share with the fellows in the room about sex and the women they'd been with.

Cash had the most attention-grabbing story to tell. He always had an interesting story about some female he'd recently fucked and how they did it, where they did it, and the level of freakiness she was on. He had enough tales in his head to write a book.

"So, what happened, son?" Petey Jay was compelled to ask.

Cash smiled. He took a few pulls from the joint burning in the room and passed it to Manny. "Nigga, I jumped into my whip and hurried over there. I mean, if you seen this bitch that's telling me to come over for a late-night booty call, you would go too in a fuckin' heartbeat."

"Wit' her fuckin' husband home?"

"Yup. Yo, you know me—I love the challenge. But, anyway, I gets over there, right, and I don't knock, 'cuz she don't want to wake up her husband. So I call, tell her I'm outside. She tells me to go around the back, and she lets me inside the back way."

"Literally, right?" Petey Jay uttered.

The room erupted with laughter from his sly remark.

"Yeah, I fucked her in the ass. But anyway," Cash continued, not losing his beat in telling the story, "the minute I walk inside, she's butt naked and all over me, grabbing my dick, tonguing me down, and I'm touching her tits, got my hand between her legs and rubbing her clit, right? She mad wet and shit. But we gotta be quiet; her man's sleeping in the bedroom upstairs. Nigga, I waste no time. I push this bitch on the couch and fuck the shit outta her."

Cash's peoples were listening intently.

"Yo, she was feeling the dick so good, she started moaning, about to get loud and shit. I'm like, 'Shorty, you gotta be quiet, but she can't, 'cuz you know when I fuck a bitch, they can't help but to yelp out. So, as I'm fuckin' her, I gotta put my hand over her mouth to muffle the sound. Man, I ain't gonna front though—that pussy was so good, I almost had to put my hand over my own mouth to keep me from screaming out."

His friends laughed again.

Darrell shook his head. "And you telling me her husband ain't wake up not one time?"

"Nah, nigga. I guess he's a heavy sleeper."

"Yo, that's disrespect right here, fo' real. I would kill a nigga if I caught him fuckin' my bitch in my crib," Darrell stated.

"That's why you gotta know how to creep and be very careful. That shit was fun, though."

"Her husband must be a stupid muthafucka, yo," Petey Jay said.

"Yo, and that nigga's a cop," Cash told them.

"Aaaah, nigga, get the fuck outta here! You lying, nigga!" Darrel exclaimed. "He ain't five-O. Fo' real?"

"Nigga, if I'm lying, I'm dying. I'm telling you, he five-O. His wife showed me pictures of him in uniform and everything. He like a sergeant or something."

Manny said, "Nigga, you fucked a cop's wife in his own home while he was 'sleep? You is either fuckin' stupid or crazy—Which one?"

"Maybe I'm both," Cash said, a grin plastered across his face.

"It couldn't be me, yo," Petey Jay said.

Cash finished telling his spirited tale by saying, "It was some of the best pussy I ever had."

"Yeah, better be worth dying for," Manny told him.

The fellows continued to trade stories. Liquor continued to flow into their systems, and the weed had them so high.

Cash leaned back into the sofa, feeling proud he was the man in the room. He loved being around his crew. Next to pussy, friendship was the best thing to have. He couldn't ask for a better group of friends.

"Yo, what's up wit' you and Pearla?" Petey Jay asked out of the blue.

"Yeah, nigga, I saw you chattin' wit' her for a minute at the block party yesterday," Darrell chimed. "You tryin' to fuck her too?"

"I'm still workin' on that," Cash replied. He looked at Petey Jay.

Petey Jay grinned. "I need me two hundred dollars in my pocket fo' real. Ready to go to the club wit' the cash."

Cash lightheartedly tossed up his middle finger Petey Jay's way and said, "Nigga, it's only been twenty-four hours."

"Time goes by fast, yo."

"Not in my book."

As Cash was about to take a swig from the Grey Goose, his cell phone rang. When he looked at the caller ID, he grinned and nodded his head. *Yeah, that's what's up.* He held up his cell phone to Petey Jay and said, "Yeah, nigga, look who's calling me—I want that in all twenties."

She was five-five, 120 pounds, with a brown face nearly looking angelic as a baby doll in her long curls and ruffled sundress. She stepped out of her building lobby with somewhere important on her mind. It was a beautiful Sunday evening, the perfect day to show off her sexy. There was no need for a jacket, but she carried one anyway, draped over her bare shoulders. It might get cold later on in the evening; better to have and not need, than to need and not have.

The beautiful, petite girl strolled out of her building lobby on the Brooklyn street and walked toward the nearest train station three blocks away, all smiles, looking innocent and eager to travel into the city and enjoy the picturesque day. She was known in the area, well liked, and had a few boys crushing on her. She was unemployed at the moment, due to a misunderstanding at her job in the mall, but with her personality and her healthy résumé, finding a job never proved to be difficult for her.

The A train was a block away. She walked freely toward it, not knowing she was being watched. As she was about to cross the street and approach to the subway, the attack came suddenly—like out of thin air.

Pearla swung at that bitch first, her fist meeting flesh, and Rebecca stumbled. Jamie came in next, attacking from behind, and punched her in the back of the head. The girl fell like a drunken misfit—confused and unaware. She struggled to her feet, but she was savagely being thrown left and right, punches raining down on her like a hailstorm.

Pearla, sweating fire and scowling, stared in Rebecca's eyes. Before she struck again, she screamed out, "You snitch on us, you fuckin' bitch?"

Rebecca caught an uppercut to the bottom of her chin, and blood spewed. She dropped face down to the concrete in serious pain.

The three girls attacked viciously, ripping apart her yellow sundress and beating her maliciously in the street. There was screaming and yelling.

Rebecca tried to get up, but she faltered, and Roark swiftly kicked her ribs in. She howled from the pain.

"Snitching bitch!" they all yelled.

It went on for less than a minute, but Pearla and her girls continued to be animals and unapologetic for their violent behavior.

They left Rebecca cowering on the dirty street, bloody, her dress ripped apart. Pearla had been fighting and knocking bitches out since she was twelve years old. The darker skin girls would always tease and pick on her while growing up, so she learned to scrap at an early age. Rebecca was lightweight to her; hardly a challenge.

They all retreated.

They could already hear the sirens blaring. Pearla decided to go a separate way from the others. It wasn't smart to walk around in a group after they'd brutally assaulted a young girl.

Pearla moved briskly, walking up the avenue nonchalantly. The NYPD cop car went speeding by her. She smirked. They didn't have a clue she was involved.

The day went by with her chilling from one place to the next—over Jamie's place where they watched music videos and smoked weed, then she and Roark hung out on Pitkin Avenue, window shopping and scheming what store they could take from next.

All day, no matter what she was doing or who she was with, she thought about Cash. Since the block party, she couldn't stop thinking about him, wondering if he would be the one to call first. She didn't want to look desperate and call him first. She hoped to maybe run into him while hanging out with her friends in Brooklyn, but it was to no avail. Anyway, Cash wasn't one to walk around leisurely. He was always driving or doing something mischievous, probably fucking some bitch or stealing a car.

Why do I like him so much? she asked herself. There were so many things wrong with him. He was a womanizer, but there was something intriguing about him, something about his quaint personality that stuck on her.

"You thinkin' about him, aren't you?" Roark asked.

"What you talking about?"

Roark sucked her teeth. "Pearla, I ain't stupid. I see that look on your face. You feeling him like that, huh?"

Pearla tried to play it off, but she couldn't. She wasn't about to play herself like some cheap floozy. She wasn't going to sell herself cheap, giving up the pussy so easily, becoming a one-night stand in his book and never hearing from him again. She was too smart for that.

Once again, Roark warned, "If you fuck wit' him, just be careful, Pearla. You know his reputation."

"I know. You don't have to keep telling me about him," Pearla replied, sounding a bit perturbed that Roark was talking to her like she was some off-brand bitch from the country.

The two drove around Brooklyn in her Benz, trying to make moves. Since the Roosevelt Field mall incident, their shoplifting organization took a backseat. It was time to lay low for a minute and figure something else out. Pearla was always good at figuring things out.

Her cell phone rang as they were cruising down Fulton Street. Her heart started to beat rapidly, as she was thinking and hoping it was Cash calling. Her expectation washed out quickly when she saw it was only Chica. She was happy to see her friend calling, but she had been frantically thinking about Cash.

"Hello," she answered.

"Bitch, it's about time you answer your fuckin' phone. What you been doing all day that you ain't got time to call your favorite bitch?" Chica hollered bubbly.

"Hey, Chica," Pearla replied.

"Don't *hey* me, bitch. You cheating on me?" Chica joked.

"Just been busy."

"Uh-huh. Busy beating some bitch's ass in the streets, from what I've heard."

"How did you hear about that already?" Pearla asked.

"Bitch, I hears everything that goes on in Brooklyn. You don't know? I'm queen bee bitch out here."

"Hey, Chica!" Roark hollered from the passenger seat.

"Who that? Roark?" Chica asked. "Tell that Indian-lookin' bitch she ain't right too. She doesn't know how to call somebody either. Tell her don't fuck wit' me, 'cuz I'll scalp her tribal-lookin' ass."

Roark heard the comment and could only laugh. Chica didn't hold her tongue for anyone. She was a transvestite and gay man with more attitude than Rupaul and Lafayette from *True Blood* put together.

"Anyway, where you at, bitch? We need to talk," Chica said.

"On Fulton," Pearla said.

"Well, take your ass off of Fulton and come this way, bitch, quickly, like you were riding on some good dick."

"I'll be that way in fifteen minutes."

"Bitch, don't keep me waiting."

"I won't." Pearla hung up.

"She a trip," Roark said, laughing at Chica's crazy antics.

"She is," Pearla agreed.

Chica was a get-money bitch like Pearla, and Pearla had nothing but respect for the six-one, drag queen. Chica taught Pearla everything she needed to know on how to become a skillful shoplifter and a player on the streets. When Pearla was fifteen, Chica took her under her wing and molded her into the hustler and businesswoman she had become. In fact, Chica was like a big sister to Pearla.

Pearla hurried Chica's way, moving through the Brooklyn traffic.

"How did she know about Rebecca?" Roark asked.

Pearla shrugged. "I have no idea. That bitch be knowing everybody's business."

"I know, right?"

Twenty minutes later, Pearla was pulling up to Chica's place in Canarsie, a working- and middle-class residential and commercial neighborhood in the southeastern part of Brooklyn.

They got out the car and walked toward the like-new apartments on the corner of Avenue D. It was stairs only to Chica's alcove studio on the top floor. Pearla knocked on the door.

Chica's door came flying open like a gust of wind had hit it, and the first thing Pearla heard from her friend was, "Bitch, I said fifteen minutes, not twenty. You know my time is valuable, Pearla."

"Blame it on traffic," was Pearla's excuse.

Chica sucked her teeth. "You see, bitch, don't get smart."

"Whatever." Pearla replied coolly. She and Roark walked into the apartment.

Chica closed the door behind them. She quickly snapped her fingers repeatedly, saying, "Um, y'all bitches forgetting something—y'all shoes, take them off like you give a fuck about my place. You know I don't like germs up in here. Understand?"

"Damn! You meticulous wit' a capital *M*," Roark stated.

"That's right, 'cuz a clean bitch is a lovely bitch."

Chica greeted them in a sexy satin, animal-print chemise. She wore a blond wig, and her makeup was flawless—lips glossy and long eye lashes applied better than any professional.

She greeted everyone with *bitch* like a regular hello.

"Bitch, you got a cigarette?" she asked Pearla. "'Cuz I need my fuckin' nicotine right now. I've been having a stressful fuckin' day."

Pearla reached into her purse and pulled out her pack of Newports. She passed Chica two cigarettes.

"You a lifesaver, girl, 'cuz a bitch didn't feel like walking to the store in this heat." Chica lit up, took a few pulls, and enjoyed the nicotine flowing through her system.

Roark and Pearla stepped deeper into the place. Chica's place was decorated precisely in the art of Feng Shui, a system that concentrates on the flow of good energy.

Chica had a thing for Japanese culture too, with the zen bed, the Japanese flower-tree birds plastered on her walls, the Japanese decorative mask Okame, and the large vintage decorative paper umbrellas.

"So, what is this I hear about you acting like some savage and fuckin' some bitch up on the street?" Chica asked.

"She almost got me and my crew locked up the other day in Roosevelt Field mall," Pearla explained. "She had it coming."

"Bitch, you supposed to be a bitch about class. You can't be fuckin' up bitches out in the streets and chance getting locked up. Pearla, didn't I teach you better than that?" Chica said, moving her index finger as she talked.

"I know, Chica, but that bitch was a snitch."

"And that bitch supposed to get fucked up, but you a diva bitch. There's more than one way to skin a cat, girl, and sometimes you don't have to get your hands dirty."

Pearla nodded.

"And, Roark, I know your Cherokee ass wasn't out there fighting too."

"I had to have my girls' back, Chica."

"Uh-huh, sure. You Rocky Balboa all of a sudden, huh?"

Roark shrugged.

"Listen, bitches, be about that money and don't be about stupid."

"We won't next time," Pearla replied.

"Anyway, I called you, bitch, because I might need a favor from you." Chica walked into the room and sat on her couch and crossed her legs like a lady in front of them.

Pearla sad, "I'm listening."

"I need one of your bitches to get married," she said.

Pearla and Roark looked at her confused.

"What?" Pearla said. "Run that by me again."

"Bitch, you fuckin' heard me. I need a bitch to get married."

"You're confusing me," Pearla said.

"Okay, bitch, I need you to listen like this is a fuckin' hearing test. I know this guy, he's from Nigeria. He got money, and he got a fuckin' problem—he needs his green card. Let's just say, he's a friend of mine."

"He's gay?" Roark chimed.

"Like a rainbow," Chica said, sitting back and puffing on her cigarette. "But he needs to stay in the country. He needs a bitch willing to marry him—nothing serious, just a ceremony, some fuckin' cake after the 'I do' and shit."

Pearla looked at Roark, and immediately Roark spat, "Don't fuckin' look at me!"

"Oh, and he's willing to pay five thousand dollars," Chica added.

"Word?" both girls exclaimed simultaneously.

"The nigga got money. So you changed your mind, Roark?" Chica asked with a grin.

"No."

"I can find somebody, but what's our cut?" Pearla asked.

"Well, you know I play fair . . . sometimes." Chica giggled. "But you find me a good bitch for this fuckin' Nigerian, and let's say, twenty-five percent."

Pearla nodded. It sounded like a fair agreement.

"But, bitch, I need somebody reliable, not some dumb, hood-rat bitch. The bitch gotta show up at City Hall, memorize the questionnaire with the likes and dislikes of their future husband and go to all the appointments at immigration."

"I can find somebody." Pearla was very sure.

"I know. Why you think I called, bitch?"

The trio continued to talk about the marriage hustle, and the more they discussed it, the more Pearla liked what she was hearing. It was a genius plan. Illegal immigrants or immigrants who were in the country by means of a work or school visa didn't want to return back to their country when their visa or time expired in the States. So they were desperate and willing to do or pay anything to stay in the country, and maybe become an American citizen.

At the end of their discussion, Pearla was already plotting to get more in her cut. Twenty-five percent out of five thousand was less than fifteen hundred. The girl would get two thousand, and Chica would get the rest. If she was going to do all the leg work, she felt she deserved a little bit more.

Pearla and Roark left Chica's place feeling good that they had another hustle to jump into. Shoplifting was okay, but it was too risky. On the other hand, this immigration/marriage scheme had the possibility to take off if operated right, and it felt like there were fewer risks involved.

SEVEN

Twenty-four hours passed, and he hadn't called yet. It didn't worry Pearla too much, but she couldn't stop thinking about him. Yearning to hear his voice and see him again, she was ready to call him. When she was away from Chica and Roark, she took out her cell phone and scrolled down to his number. All she had to do was press the dial button, but she was nervous. Why was she nervous? She was never nervous, but thinking about calling Cash made her heart beat fast like drums at a rock concert.

"Fuck it!" she told herself. She hit the dial button, put the phone to her ear, and listened as the ringing started.

Three rings later, he answered, "Hello." His voice was cool and attractive.

"Hey, it's me, Pearla," she said softly into the phone.

"I know, beautiful. How you been?"

"I'm fine."

Pearla heard laughter and loud voices in the background. It sounded like he was busy, maybe around friends. "Did I call you at a bad time?"

"Oh, nah. I was just thinking and talking about you, matter of fact."

"Oh, you were? I hope it was something good."

"Pearla, it's always good when your name comes up."

She smiled, but she couldn't allow herself to become too gullible to his gift of gab. She took a deep breath. "So what you doing?"

"I'm just chillin' wit' my peoples, you know, gettin' our drink and smoke on. And you?"

"I'm just leaving a friend's place."

"You wanna hook up?" he asked effortlessly.

"I don't mind. When?"

"Tonight?"

It was late, two hours from midnight.

"I can't do tonight. Tomorrow night is better for me."

"A'ight, cool. It's a date then," Cash said.

"It's a date."

"You gonna wear somethin' nice for me?"

"Of course. And you, the same?"

"Beautiful, I wouldn't come see you any other way."

"A'ight, bye."

"Bye, beautiful."

Pearla hung up feeling good about herself, but she knew she had to be careful with Cash. She couldn't help but speculate. Was he really trying to go out on a date with her to get to know her better? Or was it a sly attempt to get between her legs and get him some quick pussy? If that was the case, he was going to be shut down and disappointed. She really liked him, but not to the point where she was about to degrade herself and fuck him on the first date.

✳✳✳

Pearla pulled up to Petey Jay's apartment, parked, and killed the ignition to her Benz. It was a beautiful evening, warm with a spectacular sunset over the city. Cash had instructed her to meet him at his friend's apartment, which wasn't a problem. She climbed out of her car and right away got on her cell phone to inform Cash that she was outside.

"Hello."

"Hey, I'm downstairs," she said.

"A'ight, cool. I'll be down in one minute."

Pearla looked around the quiet block. Cash's friend didn't live too far away from her homegirls. She pulled out a cigarette, lit it, took a few drags, and waited patiently for him to step out the building.

She was excited and nervous at the same time. She wanted to look stunning for Cash, so she wore the dress she'd stolen out of Nordstrom a few weeks earlier—a white YSL minidress with six-inch Fendi heels.

Pearla was about ready to finish off her cigarette. She hated to be kept waiting, but she wasn't going to rush off without him. She blew the last of smoke from her mouth and flicked her cigarette into the street.

Moments later, Cash walked out the lobby cheesing like a Cheshire cat. "Damn! You look beautiful, love," he said with his award-winning charm, admiring her outfit from head to toe.

"Thank you," she said, blushing.

Her car caught his attention.

"Yo, this you, ma?" he asked. He moved by her and walked toward the car like it was hypnotically calling out his name.

She smiled. "It is."

Pearla's Mercedes 240 gleamed. It was a big-boy toy for hustlers doing big things. She felt proud to be in such a category.

Cash gently touched the hood of the car. He looked like he wanted to fuck the car.

"I like this. I see you doin' big things, beautiful."

"I try."

Pearla stood close behind him, smiling and feeling great about this evening thus far. She was dressed to hit the city, but he was dressed like a thug in a wife-beater, his muscular physique and multiple tattoos showing, a pair of faded blue jeans that just covered his black sneakers, a long diamond gold chain with diamond-encrusted skull pendant around his neck, and a colored bracelet on his wrist.

He smiled Pearla's way. "Can I drive it? Can I chauffeur you around tonight?"

"I don't mind," she eagerly allowed, handing him the keys.

Cash slid into the driver's side, while Pearla found herself in the passenger seat of her own car. He started it up, and then he revved the engine, making it sound like he was ready to compete in the Indy 500.

"What kind of engine you got under the hood?" he asked.

Pearla had no idea. She just drove the car and didn't have a clue. "I don't know."

"Sounds nice, though. And the interior . . . you got taste when it comes to cars. Believe me, I know."

Pearla grinned. "I like to ride around town in style."

"I see."

Cash didn't have a license, but he was ready to race to wherever and start his date with Pearla. Being behind the wheel of a Mercedes-Benz made him feel great. For a quick second, only a second, he thought about stealing the car and taking it to Perez, but he couldn't do Pearla like that—not yet anyway.

"What you feel like doin'?" he asked.

"I'm hungry."

"I know a place." Cash smiled. Pulling away from the curb, he briefly glanced at her legs and the dress she wore.

He took Rockaway Turnpike and headed for Applebee's, the grill and bar restaurant near the Far Rockaway area. He was doing about sixty on the Turnpike, and the way he drove her vehicle showed he was a natural behind the wheel of any car.

"So how long have you had this?"

"About three months now."

"You should throw some chrome rims on this baby, tint the windows, throw in a nice sound system, and you'd be the talk of the town."

She smiled. "Talk of the town, huh?"

"Hells yeah!"

"I'm the talk of town now."

Cash laughed. "Oh, you are?"

"I am," Pearla replied smugly.

"Yeah, I hear your name do ring out."

"So, it never rang in your ear?"

He chuckled. "I might have heard a few small bells; kinda faint, though. You know what I'm sayin'?"

"Oh, fuck you!" she replied, nudging him lightheartedly.

Pearla had a good feeling. They were making each other laugh. She couldn't wait to get her eat on. Her stomach was growling a little bit because she hadn't eaten all day. She was just hoping it didn't growl so loud Cash heard it.

She walked side by side with Cash, ready to enter Applebee's, but before they could walk in, his cell phone went off.

Cash didn't hesitate to answer it, snatching it off his hip like it was on fire. Pearla didn't mind—It wasn't her business; they'd just met.

Lingering outside the restaurant, he said into the phone, "Hey, what's up?"

Pearla looked at him stoically.

"Oh, word? It be like that . . . I feel you. I know, right . . . yo, that shit be crazy . . . a'ight," he said to the person on the other end. Then he laughed. For a moment, he wasn't paying her any attention.

Pearla waited patiently for him to end his call. She didn't know if he was talking to some bitch or a friend. It almost felt like he'd forgotten about their date, talking on the phone for several minutes like he was alone.

Pearla had to clear her throat around him to snap him back to reality. "How long you gonna be?" she asked him coolly.

"Oh, yo, let me call you back," he said. Then he hung up the phone.

"Business call?"

"Something like that."

Pearla just smiled and shrugged it off.

They walked into the restaurant and quickly got a table. It was a weekday, so the place wasn't crowded at all. They ordered a few appetizers and their drinks.

"I haven't been to Applebee's in a while," Pearla said.

"You and me both."

Before their appetizers could arrive, Cash's phone chimed again. He picked it up off the table, read the text, and smiled. He texted back and then placed his phone back on the table.

Not even a minute went by, and his phone went off again. He read a few text messages from whomever, while Pearla sat opposite of him in the booth, playing it cool.

When the appetizers came, Pearla decided to try and make an impression on him. She picked up one of the crab cakes, dipped it in mustard sauce, leaned over the table and tried to feed it to him.

Cash couldn't help smiling. "Oh, I see you're giving me the VIP treatment up in here."

"You know it."

He opened up and allowed Pearla to place the food into his mouth. Cash chewed it up and smiled.

"Is it good?" she asked.

He nodded.

She tried the crab cakes herself and was ready to devour them all at once.

They talked for a moment, joking around, trying to connect.

Cash's cell phone started to ring again. He didn't hesitate to answer. "Hey, what's good?"

Pearla shook her head and laughed it off. She'd turned off her phone so Cash would have her undivided attention. It was a shame he couldn't do the same thing for her.

She continued to eat the crab cakes while Cash was on his phone, almost ignoring her like she wasn't even there. She looked around the restaurant, taking in all the sports memorabilia that decorated its walls while he chatted.

"A'ight." He laughed. "That sounds like a plan. Hit me back later tonight," she heard him say.

Pearla finished off all the crab cakes by the time he got off his phone. Hearing him say "Hit me back later tonight," she wondered, *Did this muthafucka have the audacity to set up a booty call while I am sitting right across from him on our first date?*

"So, what did I miss?" he joked.

"You tell me. I see you're a very busy man."

"Just business."

"I see."

"You jealous?"

"I'm not a jealous bitch."

"That's good to know . . . because you know I got fans."

"I do too, sweetheart."

He laughed. "We like Beyoncé and Jay, huh?"

"I don't like Beyoncé," Pearla said out flat.

"What? I thought every bitch liked Beyoncé."

"Well, first off, I ain't every bitch, I'm *this* bitch. And I think that bitch is fake."

"What? Let me find out you hating on Beyoncé."

"It ain't hate, Cash. I just don't like that bitch."

"Then what you call it?"

"Why is it when a girl doesn't like someone, everyone gotta call it hate? What's up with that?"

"Because, usually, everyone hates on the pretty bitch—especially when she got talent, got money, can sing and dance her ass off, and she's a married woman."

"So, what that supposed to mean?"

"It means she's living the American dream three times over."

"And I'm living it too."

"Yeah, illegally."

"Look at you, the pot trying to call the kettle black."

"So, you're not a hater. Then what that makes you?"

"Like I said before, I just don't like that bitch, but that don't make me a hater."

"And what reason?"

"I already gave you my reason—she's fraud."

"Beyoncé fraud. You talk about her like you know her."

"Look, I'm not trying to spend this entire date talking about Beyoncé," Pearla said sharply.

"Okay, I feel you. You win," he said, raising his hands in defeat. "You ain't gotta cut my head off."

Being the charmer, Cash said, "You know, you're much prettier than her."

"Thank you."

The waiter walked over to take their order, but before Cash could tell her what he wanted from the menu, his phone chimed again as another text message came through. He picked up his phone and read it. Another smile appeared on his face.

Pearla ordered first while Cash stayed on his phone like he was the president handling foreign affairs. *Here we go again,* she thought.

When she finished ordering, Cash stared up at the waitress and smiled. She smiled back. His eyes lingered on her figure, and then he said, "Do you come wit' the menu?"

Pearla couldn't believe he'd asked that. "Really, Cash?" she said sharply.

"You know I'm just playing, Pearla."

Pearla sighed heavily. *Rude muthafucka!*

The waitress continued to smile, keeping things professional, and took down his order.

When the waitress walked away, he locked eyes with Pearla and smiled. "You know I don't want that bitch. I'm here wit' you, having a good time, and we gonna have a great night, right?"

Pearla didn't answer him right away. She looked at him and thought to herself, *Damn! He's fine.* She fought hard though, trying not to become that stupid bitch around him. She knew better. He had bitches chasing.

Pearla had niggas chasing her too—hustlers, pretty boys, and professionals—but she kept them at arm's length. She hadn't had dick in over two months.

The last lucky nigga to get between her legs was Randy. They grew up together and had always been cool with each other. Randy was a dope boy; a big-money nigga moving weight from New York to the South. He always had love and respect for her.

After years of friendship, it took one night of drinking and talking for things to turn intimate between them. A lasting stare transitioned into a longing kiss, then to pleasing touches, clothes being removed, and then a heated sexual episode with hips thrusting and deep penetration. It was the best sex Pearla had ever had.

Two weeks later, Randy was shot and killed during a drug transaction in North Carolina.

Cash and Pearla walked out of Applebee's feeling content—good food, good conversation. Before they could get to her car, Cash's cell phone went off again, and he answered it.

Pearla sighed. She climbed into the car and sat in the passenger seat. She was being nice. If it was any other muthafucka, she would have *been* lashed out and ended the date. She was giving him way too many passes.

After he ended his five-minute conversation, he looked at her and said, "It's still early. What next?"

EIGHT

Cash drove up to the liquor store near the Applebee's they'd just left, saying to Pearla, "You don't mind if I get my drink on?"

She shrugged. "Nah. It's cool with me."

He jumped out the car, be-bopped toward the liquor store, and disappeared inside, leaving Pearla waiting inside the Benz.

She lit another cigarette. It was getting late, but she wasn't ready to go home yet. She smoked and hoped the date didn't go left. The last thing she wanted to do was check this muthafucka if he tried to disrespect her.

She turned on her phone to see if anyone had called. Nothing. She only had a few messages from Chica, inquiring if she had a girl yet for the hustle. She texted back NOT YET, and put her phone away.

Cash came walking out the liquor store with a plastic bag in his hand. He was smiling, looking excited. Pearla watched him approach with such a confident stride. She admired his swagger and liveliness. His smile was magnetic, causing her to smile also. He moved like he owned the world and was untouchable. It was alluring to her. He definitely had that bad boy charisma drenched all over him.

He slid into the car, still smiling. "Now it's a party." He removed the fifth of Hennessy from the plastic bag. He had no cups, just the bottle. He didn't hesitate to twist open the bottle and take it to the head in front of her. He downed some of the brown juice like it was water.

"You want a sip?" he asked, placing the bottle in front of her.

Pearla fancied herself to be a champagne-and-wine kind of girl, but she wasn't offended by the offer. She took the bottle out of his hand, placed it to her lips, and took a large gulp. Cash laughed.

"What's so funny?"

"You just surprised me, that's all." He thought she was going to reject the Henny and look at him sideways.

"What you was thinking? I was gonna shun you?"

"Nah, not that."

She smiled. He smiled. For a few minutes, they lingered in the parking lot, talking and drinking.

On the ride back to Brooklyn, they took turns passing the bottle back and forth. Pearla didn't seem to mind that he was drinking and driving, though it was her car he was driving.

Cash gazed at her velvety, long legs that were crossed over each other and licked his lips. He wanted some pussy. He wanted her. He was becoming super horny. "You know you're beautiful, Pearla. I love your style."

"Thank you."

"And I love your fuckin' legs. Yo, I know you work out."

Pearla didn't, but it was a nice compliment.

When they came to a stop at a red light, Cash placed his hand against her exposed thigh. "Damn! You're so fuckin' soft."

Pearla didn't overreact. She kept her cool and stared at his hand, which was now gently massaging her thigh. She could feel the strength in his grasp. He moved his hand between her thighs, and she could feel him urging to move it upward, underneath her dress and between her legs to grab a handful of some pussy.

"What you doing?" she asked politely.

"Massaging you."

"Oh, you are massaging me?"

"Yeah, you like that?" he asked, a lecherous grin aimed her way.

"Yeah, I do. But I know what you're doing, and I ain't gonna fuck you, Cash," she flat out told him.

"Who said I was tryin' to fuck tonight?"

She looked at him and smirked. "You gonna play stupid, huh?"

He continued to grin. "Nah, I'm just sayin'—"

"What you just saying, Cash? Talk to me."

"I like you," he said, at a loss of words.

"I like you too, but that don't mean you gonna get some pussy tonight."

Ugh! It was like a blow into the stomach for Cash.

"We can continue to hang out, and if you want, you can spend the night at my place. But we're not gonna fuck."

The look in Pearla's eyes said it all. She was standing strong with her choice, and drinking Hennessy with him wasn't about to loosen her up and make her change her mind.

Cash removed his hand from her thigh and focused on the road.

"So what we gonna do?"

Cash knew what he wanted to do, but the date had gone left. It was obvious he wasn't going to get any ass from her.

"I gotta stop at my friend's place first, where you picked me up from," he said.

"Okay, cool, and then what?" Pearla didn't want to just be wandering around Brooklyn doing nothing.

"We'll figure it out from there."

Cash pulled up on the block where Petey Jay lived. The night was still early, and now the block was flooded with people hanging out, unlike when Pearla picked him up.

Cash killed the ignition to the car. "I need to clean up and change clothes real quick. I'm feelin' kinda sweaty."

Pearla was puzzled by what he said. He looked fine, but she didn't argue with him. "Are we going somewhere special?"

He simply smiled. "Being with you is special enough."

"You don't quit, don't you?"

"Should I?"

Pearla smiled his way. "Not really."

He was definitely a colorful guy with his wild antics. Pearla never knew what craziness would spew from out of his mouth.

He stepped out of her car, and she was ready to wait patiently for him again. He didn't invite her up, and it didn't bother her. In fact, it was good he didn't, because there was no telling how many niggas were in his friend's apartment.

Pearla decided to light a cigarette and chill. As Cash walked toward the lobby, she noticed a woman hastily approaching him wearing a miniskirt and long, bad weave. Seeing her coming his way, Cash stopped. She vigorously walked their way like she was on a mission, scowling and marching closer.

Pearla stared at her, feeling like there was going to be trouble. It was written all over the woman's face and her body language. Her body was amazing in the miniskirt, but her face was below average.

"Cash!" she screamed out. "Why you ain't answering my fuckin' phone calls?"

Cash looked taken aback. "Yo, Stephanie, you need to chill," he said.

"Nah! I sucked your dick and give you five hundred dollars to bail your fuckin' moms out, and you ignoring me."

"Yo, ain't nobody tryin' to ignore you. I just been busy."

Stephanie spun around and glared at Pearla seated quietly in the passenger seat of her Benz. "This the fuckin' bitch you been busy wit'?" she yelled.

Suddenly, Pearla found herself the focus of Stephanie's wrath.

Stephanie stormed toward the car and shouted, "You fuckin' my man, you fuckin' bitch! Get out the fuckin' car, bitch!"

Whoa! Pearla kept cool though, smirking and hoping things didn't go past her hollering and yelling. But the bitch looked ignorant and stupid as fuck.

"Fuckin' ugly bitch!" Stephanie yelled. "Get the fuck out the car, bitch! You skinny fuckin' bitch!"

Pearla didn't say a word. She simply sat in the passenger seat, looking unfazed by the insults thrown her way and stared at Stephanie carrying on and hollering around her car.

Stephanie banged her fist on the hood of Pearla's Benz. "I'm gonna fuck you up, bitch!"

Cash didn't even rush over to defuse the situation. He shouted, "Stephanie, what the fuck you doin'? You embarrassing yourself out here."

"Fuck you, Cash! I'll fuck you up too!"

A crowd started to gather around the dispute.

Pearla didn't have time for it. She sighed heavily. As Stephanie ran up in Cash's face, angrily thrusting her finger into his face and shouting heatedly like a banshee, Pearla coolly stepped out from the passenger seat and went around to the driver's side. She was about to leave, disappointed that it was going down this way. Cash had yet to defend her, and she realized he wasn't going to leave with her.

Pearla didn't even have a chance to open the driver's side door before Stephanie marched her way like a raging bull, shouting, "Where the fuck you goin', bitch?"

Pearla spun around on her pricey, six-inch heels and glared at Stephanie. She wasn't about to be physically abused by Stephanie.

"You fuckin' this skinny bitch?" Stephanie growled through her clenched teeth.

Cash didn't say a word.

Pearla kept her eyes fixated on Stephanie. There was a crowd around them all of a sudden, and everyone was expecting a fight. Pearla found herself the center of attention. It looked like the fight was going to be one-sided, because Stephanie was a big, thick ghetto bitch with a reputation, and Pearla was slim, reserved and ladylike.

"What, bitch? What the fuck you gonna do, bitch?" Stephanie taunted.

Cash looked on, low-key excited that he had two women about to fight over him.

Pearla quietly clenched her fists and scowled back. If the bitch wanted a war, she was going to get one.

Without warning, Stephanie swung at Pearla.

Pearla sidestepped to her right from the attack and retaliated with a right hook that smashed into Stephanie's face, spewing blood and almost breaking her nose.

Stephanie howled and stumbled like she was on wobbly ground. Everyone, including Stephanie, was shocked.

Pearla was on Stephanie like stink on shit, repeatedly striking her in the face, crippling her.

"Ooooh!" someone yelled out.

Stephanie tried to swing back, but she was overwhelmed by Pearla's hand skills. It felt like she was fighting Laila Ali.

"Yo, she fuckin' that bitch up!" another spectator screamed out.

"Bitch, don't fuck with me!" Pearla yelled out.

Bang! A fist to the temple.

Bang! Another fist to her chin.

Pearla dug her long nails into Stephanie's face, yanked out her bad weave, and dragged her thick body to the ground before being pulled off by Cash and Petey Jay.

"Get the fuck off me! Let me fuck that bitch up!" Pearla screamed out. "Fuck that bitch!" Pearla struggled with Cash, moving wildly in his grasp, desperately trying to free herself so she could finish what she started. "Look at you now, bitch!" Pearla was now the one doing the taunting. "Your blood and face on the fuckin' ground. Get the fuck off me!"

Stephanie was hugging the concrete, her clothes torn apart, her weave ripped out, and her nipples on display for all to see.

"Yo, chill, love," Cash said.

Pearla was ready to fight him next. "Get off me, Cash!" she screamed.

Petey Jay and a few others helped Stephanie off the ground. She was a complete mess. She looked like a speeding truck hit her.

Someone laughed. "Yo, that bitch got fucked up."

When Cash finally released Pearla from his grip, she glared at him and shouted, "Fuck you, nigga!" and stormed toward her car. She jumped in, started the ignition, and took off down the street like a bat out of hell.

A block away, Pearla picked up her cell phone and dialed a three-way call to Roark and Jamie. The minute they answered, she exclaimed, "I just had to fuck this bitch up!"

"What?"

"Over this nigga Cash."

NINE

Cash was never one to chase pussy, but the past two days he'd found himself repeatedly calling Pearla, not to apologize, but to check on her. He was sorry how everything had gone down but wouldn't admit it directly to her. He refused to leave messages. He didn't like leaving messages on any bitch's phone. He didn't want any bitch playing his messages to anyone and using it against him, to make him look like he was desperate.

Pearla wasn't answering his phone calls. It kept going straight to voice mail. She was still upset. Stephanie made her come out of character, and she had to fuck a bitch up.

Pearla was expecting a huge apology from him, but she never received one. She was expecting him to chase her relentlessly after what happened, but within forty-eight hours, he'd lost interest and moved on. Oddly enough, it made her like him even more. Pearla felt like Cash was a dick for not defending her and a bitch-ass nigga for not kissing her ass after their disastrous date. Somehow she also felt that she could train him to be the type of man she needed in her life. Bottom line, Cash was a challenge. However, she wasn't about to chase after him like some bird bitch. Though she really liked him, she still had her dignity and wasn't about to start acting like some thirsty chickenhead bitch.

Cash and Stephanie walked through Kings Plaza mall doing some shopping. Stephanie had tried her best to disguise the bruises on her face, but Pearla had definitely put a hurting on her. With a partially closed black eye and busted lips, she looked like she'd fallen off a building and landed face first.

Cash was still with her, not ashamed to trick on her to make it up to her. He bought her cheap shoes from Express, some jewelry, and a few outfits for the summer. In total, he spent $1,200 on her. Yeah, she wasn't the prettiest bitch in the hood, but she knew how to really suck dick, and with her wet pussy, it always felt like he was dipping his dick in a pool. She knew how to fuck, and her body matched Melyssa Ford's. Too bad her face didn't.

They walked through the mall on a weekday afternoon. Stephanie had called out from work the past two days. She didn't want to go into her job looking the way she was, plus she wanted to spend some quality time with Cash. It seemed that she'd forgiven him for his infidelity, though it was never official that he belonged to her in the first place.

Walking toward the mall exit, with a few bags in her hand, Stephanie smiled and then slipped her hand into Cash's. She wanted to hold hands.

Cash was reluctant. Stephanie was relentless. Cash surrendered, thinking about the treat he was going to get later.

"You love me, Cash?"

The question came out of left field. It caught him off guard. No, he didn't love Stephanie. She was just his plaything—his mind-blowing freak. He loved the way she made him feel when they got together in the bedroom, or in the car, or in the park, the rooftop, the elevator, the parking lot. Stephanie was that bitch down for whatever, whenever, and wherever, and she loved anal. Cash busted some good nuts with her.

Cash smiled. He didn't want to upset her. He wanted some pussy and a blowjob afterwards, and after what she had gone through, she deserved some nice treatment, hence the small shopping spree. He owed her a lot.

"I got love for you, Stephanie," he replied flatly. "You know that."

"But I love you."

"I know, and you my favorite girl, fo' real, Stephanie. Who else would I spend on like this? No one but my favorite girl, and that's you. You know that, right? And when we get back to your place, I'm gonna fuck you so good and eat that pussy out like a hungry slave. I'm gonna show you how much love I got for you."

Stephanie smiled. She was always gullible to Cash's words and excuses. She was a rough, ghetto bitch, but when it came to loving Cash, she was vulnerable like an open target.

"You know I'm sorry about everything that went down." He continued to butter her up. "It was just one date wit' that bitch."

"I know, Cash. I ain't even thinkin' 'bout that bitch right now, and you shouldn't be either. I need to give you better things to think about."

Cash smiled. "Oh, word?"

She nodded. "Uh-huh."

"That's what's up."

The two exited the mall into the parking garage and walked toward the black Escalade Cash had stolen from Queens the night before. It was a beauty of a vehicle, sitting on 22-inch chrome rims with white leather seats.

Stephanie enjoyed riding in it. She felt like a queen. She wished it was his. She wished her and Cash were a legitimate couple, and he would stop fucking with other bitches. The sex was good, but being around Cash was fun and exciting. He was funny and handsome. Stephanie felt that Cash completed her. She did everything she could to please him, from giving him great sex, to sucking his dick like a porn star, and giving him money and a place to lay his head. She wanted the same respect in return like any other woman would.

They climbed into the truck with the shopping bags in the backseat, but before he could start the ignition, Stephanie leaned closer to him and kissed him sensually on the lips.

"Thank you, baby," she said softly.

"You're welcome." He smiled.

He felt her hand touching his crotch. She caressed him gently through the fabric. He liked the way she touched him. It was making him hard.

"What you need me to do to you to officially thank you?" she asked with a teasing smile.

"Damn! I can think of a few things."

"I know you can. And I can think of a few things too, but how about right now, I'll show you one way." She stuck out her long tongue in a provocative way and then slowly licked her lips.

It was turning him on.

He felt his jeans being unzipped. Stephanie wiggled her hand inside and gently pulled out his growing erection. His big dick was in her silky hand, and she began stroking him nicely, coaxing him to full hardness.

"Mmmm," he groaned quietly. "You know all this only belongs to you, right?"

"I know, baby."

"So appreciate it."

"I will."

She wrapped her hand around the smooth flesh, feeling the veins, the head, and the weight of it within her grasp. She squeezed his dick and began fingering his balls, too, rolling them around in her hand.

Cash squirmed around a little. "Oh, shit."

She started jerking him off faster, harder, stroking him to the edge of climax, but then stopping, continuing to tease him. He was antsy. He was ready to feel her lips around his dick. He was ready to feel her strong suction around him. It felt like he had a gallon of come inside him that he was ready to churn out either into her mouth, or her wet, tight pussy.

Stephanie buried her face in his lap, opening her mouth and placing the head of his dick into her mouth and sucking gently,at first, savoring the feel of his hardness, enjoying the taste of his pre-come. Her head slowly bobbed up and down, her full, juicy lips enveloped around dark flesh.

"Ugh! Ugh! Ooooh!" he cooed.

She slipped her fingers past his balls and rubbed the tender flesh of his asshole. Her freak was coming out in the parking lot. Her pussy was getting so wet from sucking Cash's dick. She was ready to pull off her jeans and play with herself. She swallowed his dick whole, taking him deep in her throat.

"Damn, ma! I like that shit," Cash said, spreading his legs with his big dick being taken alive.

She spat on the dick, and chewed it up. She took his balls into her mouth and rolling them around, licking, sucking, and pulling on them.

Cash's knees were shaky, and he whimpered like a baby. He loved every second of it.

She deep-throated him, using her tongue to paint pleasure up and down his hard shaft. He tried to hold back his release, but Stephanie turned it up a notch, fingering, licking, sucking, and stroking.

"Oh shit! Oh shit! Damn, baby! That feels so fuckin' good!" he cried out. "You gonna make me come!"

Hearing Cash coo and groan turned her on even more. Her lips felt like a vacuum around his dick. She felt him pulsating in her mouth, the veins bulging in his dick, and his nut brewing.

Cash tried to hold back, but he couldn't. The way Stephanie sucked dick, she could pull a golf ball through a garden hose.

"I'm gonna fuckin' come!" Cash erupted vigorously, releasing his hot seed into her mouth and down her throat. He looked spent.

Stephanie lifted her face out of his lap and wiped her mouth. "To be continued," she said.

"No doubt."

"You liked that?"

"I fuckin' loved it."

"I do that because I love you, Cash."

After the splendid nut, the two got themselves right. Cash fixed his pants, and Stephanie sat back in the passenger seat. Cash drove out of the parking garage and headed to her place.

"You stayin' the night wit' me, Cash? You know there's more where that came from.""No doubt, ma. But I gotta take care of some business tonight."

"You sure it's just business?"

"Stephanie, it's just business, a'ight! Stop being so fuckin' jealous."

"Then stop makin' me so jealous. I want you and only you, Cash."

He smiled. He had the bitch going fanatic over him. He continuously played with her heart and emotions. He wasn't in love with her and would never be in love with her. She was just a convenience in his life for the moment. Stephanie smiled like the world was made of gold. She loved spending every minute of her life with him.

"Yo, turn left right here," Petey Jay said from the passenger seat.

Darrell made the turn. Manny and Cash were in the backseat, passing a blunt back and forth. They were riding around Queens, moving through a ritzy area called Jamaica Estates. They were in a stolen Dodge, cruising the streets looking for a particular car to steal—a Honda Accord or Civic in mint condition, if not, then a Toyota Camry. It was a still night. An hour after midnight.

Everyone was quiet, smoking and keeping an eye out for police.

They drove deeper into the posh neighborhood. It was a good distance away from their Brooklyn home. The residents were asleep. The houses were dark, luxury cars lined the driveways and the streets. It was the perfect opportunity—get in and get out. See Perez, get paid, and enjoy the remainder of their night with some bitches.

Cash took a pull from the burning blunt and handed it forward to Darrell. Darrell took the weed with his right hand while steering with his left. He looked like a pro at getting high and driving. He took a strong pull and drove smoothly.

The weed was taking its effect on Cash. It was some potent shit straight out of Colorado with a high strain. He was ready to steal this car and hit the strip club afterwards and get his groove on. Smoking always made him horny or hungry. He was both tonight. Riding around in the backseat, he grabbed his crotch and thought about some pussy.

Out of nowhere, Petey Jay said, "So what's up wit' you and Pearla?"

"We just chillin'," Cash responded.

"Yeah, I seen y'all two gettin' all comfortable wit' each other at the block party," Manny said.

"I know, right. You fucked her yet?" Petey Jay asked.

Cash laughed. He never lied on his dick. "Nah, we ain't fuck yet."

"What! It's almost been a week and you ain't fuck that bitch yet?" Darrell chimed.

"I got a lot goin' on."

"Well, I'm gonna need that two hundred soon. You know I like makin' that money," Petey Jay said, a smile plastered on his face.

Cash ignored his friend, thinking about Pearla for a quick second and then erasing her from his thoughts. "It ain't over till the fat lady sings."

"Well, let that bitch sing then," Petey Jay quipped.

His friends laughed.

Five minutes later, the crew rolled up on a 2013 Honda Civic. It was white, looked like it came fresh off the car lot, and it was calling Cash's name, saying to him, "Come get me."

"There we go," Cash said, his eyes on the vehicle.

Darrell stopped next to the vehicle. Cash and Manny jumped out, ready to put in work. Darrell and Petey Jay remained nearby in the idling car, ready for their niggas to go to work.

Cash looked inside the car, and the factory issued alarm, which is located under the dashboard was on—just as he figured it would be. He had the slim jim in his hand and quickly broke into the car. The alarm sounded, and he dipped inside and quickly disabled the siren.

Manny was watching out. He was keeping his cool, waiting to get it over with. There was no telling who that alarm had woken up. "C'mon, Cash, hurry the fuck up," he said.

"Yo, give me a few seconds," Cash replied. He was dismantling the dashboard and hot-wiring the Civic, which was taking him longer than usual.

Petey Jay and Darrell remained in the idling car, swiveling their heads left to right, keeping a keen eye out for approaching vehicles or unwanted company in the area. Underneath the driver's seat was a loaded .45. It had never been fired. It was for protection, just in case things got heated. They were car thieves, not drug dealers or enforcers, but in their line of work, things could go from good to bad in a split second.

The Civic's engine roared to life all of a sudden, and Cash hollered, "There we go!"

"Damn! 'Bout fuckin' time," Manny exclaimed. "You slippin', Cash."

"Nigga, I never slip."

Manny ran around the Civic and jumped into the passenger seat. Darrell sped away, and Cash was right behind him. He had one hand on the steering wheel and the other playing with the radio. The radio had been left on some oldie, but goodie station and Cash needed to listen to his rap tunes.

"Yo, don't get us locked up tonight," Manny said.

"Nigga, you in great hands," Cash replied. "You know I need to listen to my station."

Hot 97 started to blare inside the car. Cash nodded to a Wale and Rick Ross song and said, "There we go, son. This my joint right here."

"Just drive, nigga."

Cash simply smiled at him.

The crew pulled up to Perez's chop shop on Liberty Avenue. It was nestled furtively in an industrial area with mechanic and body shops flooding every block.

Darrell parked near the shop, while Cash rode up to the garage and called Perez, letting him know they were outside and waiting. They didn't want to linger in the area with a stolen car. It was dark, but it was a risky area, especially with the headlights shining against the gate.

Within seconds, the rolling garage gate started to lift up, and Cash drove the Civic inside. He and Manny stepped out of the car.

Perez walked toward them with a deadpan gaze. This was his place, his home. He was six feet, two inches tall and weighed 180 pounds. He was a slim man with strawberry blond hair that was neatly parted on the side. It was hard to tell his age and his background—Spanish, Italian, Cuban. He spoke multiple languages, had tan skin and satanic tattoos running up and down his arms, and he smoked cigars regularly. He had a knack for business and had been running chop shops for over ten years. It was rumored around the hood that he had strong mob and cartel connections.

"See? We got it for you, Perez. Easy as one, two, three," Cash spoke, nodding to the 2013 Honda Civic.

"You boys always do good work for me," Perez said.

Cash smiled.

Perez stared at the Civic. His facial expression indicated that he approved of it. There were no damages to the vehicle, and the parts alone would be gold. The chop shop stayed busy 24/7. A half-dozen men were dismantling stolen cars. It wasn't a huge warehouse with rows of expensive sports cars and teams of mechanics sending sparks flying as they worked like in the movies. It was quite messy and standard.

Perez turned to Cash and said, "I'm gonna need three more of these in four days, plus a Chevy and a Dodge. You think you can handle that?"

"Perez, we got this under control," Cash said. "This is what we do."

Perez nodded. He handed Cash an envelope filled with cash. There was $2,500 inside.

Cash took the money and was ready to go out and steal more cars. He wanted to impress the man. He admired and respected Perez. The man knew his shit when it came to running a chop shop and making tons of money off stolen cars. His workers could dismantle a car into its components in as little as one or two hours. Dismantling the car could be extremely profitable, since the price of an entire car's worth of replacement parts is usually much higher than the resale value of the car. The profit margin increases for older model years, since legitimately salvaged parts become more difficult to find as the cars become harder to find.

Perez and his mechanics would remove personal items and license plates from the car and destroy them. Next, they would unbolt the front end of the car from the frame in one piece, which included the fender and the hood. They then would cut out the windshield and unbolt the doors and seat. Using an acetylene torch, they would cut the roof supports at the front, and then cut through the floor under the steering wheel. The dash section was especially valuable for the airbags.

If they didn't dismantle a car, then they would sell it to a foreign country. In underdeveloped countries, there were often fewer rules and less enforcement of laws pertaining to plates and title paperwork, so the car would be less likely to be noticed.

Perez also got creative when it came to dealing with the VINs. He would completely replace the VIN on a stolen car so that the car could be sold intact. He would purchase cars at salvage auctions that had been destroyed in accidents or fires. He wanted the vehicles mostly for their VINs. Once they had the car and its VIN, they would steal a car of the same year, make, and model. Then they would be able to switch the VIN plates on the two cars and claim that they'd repaired a totaled car.

Perez was like the master chef in a five-star restaurant. If he needed more cars within several days, Cash was ready to deliver. He needed the money.

Cash and Manny walked out of the chop shop with $2,500 to split between four people. They climbed inside the vehicle Petey Jay and Darrell were waiting in.

"Everything good?" Petey Jay asked.

"Yeah, everything's copasetic," Cash replied.

Before they drove away, Cash removed their payment from the envelope, quickly counted it, and then started to divide it between his crew. In total, they received $625 apiece. Cash looked at the bills in his hand, and truth, it wasn't enough for him. Earlier, he'd spent $1,200 on Stephanie. He needed to recoup what he spent. He needed a little more and had the thought about stealing cars by himself to receive the full payout.

The fellows were happy with their split. It was a good night.

"Yo, we goin' to the strip club?" Manny asked.

"No doubt," Darrell answered. "I'm ready to be around some pussy."

Cash didn't respond. He was quiet, thinking.

"What you thinkin' about?" Manny asked.

"Nah, it ain't nothin'," Cash replied.

"What you need to be thinkin' about is some pussy tonight. You know Cream is jumping tonight, like every night. And I know you thirsty to get your dick wet," Darrell said.

"Let's go then," Cash said halfheartedly.

The boys headed toward the strip club. Cash strangely thought about Pearla. He wondered why she was coming into his mind, but he quickly erased it from his head and thought about having some fun at Cream.

TEN

Maribel was twenty-one years old and average-looking with dark skin, short hair, and a nice figure. She had an associate degree in business and communications from Brooklyn College, and she wanted to try and get her bachelor's degree next. The problem was, she couldn't afford the tuition. School was expensive. Her rent needed to be paid, she was on the verge of being evicted from her apartment, her lights were about to be cut off, and her jobs at Burger King and the clothing store sucked.

But there was a light at the end of her dark tunnel.

"So you gonna pay me to do what?" she asked Pearla with disbelief.

"To marry this Nigerian man and help him get his green card," Pearla explained to her nice and slow.

Pearla had chosen her easily. She was from the projects, never had anything growing up, parents on hard drugs, no kids, and she wanted a come-up. Maribel was perfect for the hustle. It just took some coaxing for her to join the program.

"So you're willing to pay me to marry some man I never met before?"

"You get fifty percent, and it's easy money, Maribel."

Maribel looked somewhat reluctant. "I don't know, Pearla. It sounds crazy."

"It's not. We have everything set up to work out smoothly."

"Do I gotta suck his dick and have sex with him?"

"Listen, chances are, you won't even have to live in the same apartment with him. All we need you to do is go down to City Hall and get married. It's cash money in your pocket. What you need to do is memorize the questionnaire we'll give you with his likes and dislikes, remember his birthday, birthplace, and whatnot, and he'll remember your likes and dislikes, and go to all appointments at immigration."

Maribel sat across from Pearla in her run-down apartment where the heat barely worked in the winter and air conditioner was always on the fritz in the summer. She looked like she was struggling, clad in her Salvation Army wardrobe, and always exhausted from working two to three dead-end jobs just to make ends meet.

"Is he cute at least?"

"It's just business, Maribel. You don't even have to stay married to him. Within two years, file for a divorce. But get your money. He's willing to pay for a bride. The man is desperate, and he's caked up, so being married to him can come with perks and benefits. Think about it—What's two years of your life? You're twenty-one now. By the time you're twenty-three, twenty-four, your life will be much easier than it is now."

Maribel looked deep in thought. It was still something she didn't want to rush into, but the bills piling up on her rickety coffee table reminded her that she needed to come up with some type of financial solution quickly.

"If you don't jump on this now, I guarantee someone else will quickly."

Pearla trusted Maribel. She had known her for a long while. She was an introvert, but she put the other girls she talked to through a grilling interview before anyone was hired. She had to trust each one completely, because they could go to jail.

Pearla wasn't about to give up on Maribel. She needed to make this money. It looked like an easy hustle to get into, setting up American women with desperate foreigners eager to get their green card and stay in the country. Everyone wanted a piece of the American dream, thinking the streets in America were paved with gold.

"I get fifty percent, huh?" Maribel said.

"Yes, that's two thousand for now, but there can be more money where that came from. The trick is that we keep milking this guy."

Maribel looked around her surroundings. She hated to live hand to mouth. She was ready to go back to school. She was ready to make a change in her life. Being poor, and struggling to keep her head above water was a fucked-up feeling. With a strong sigh, she looked at Pearla and said, "I'll do it."

Pearla smiled. "You're making the right decision, Maribel, believe me. Your poverty days will soon be far behind you."

Maribel hoped her friend was right. She needed something far-reaching to happen.

Pearla sat with Maribel for an hour, and they worked out all the details to make the marriage happen. It was her first match, but Pearla was thinking that there were going to be plenty more. Chica had turned that light on inside of her head, and she was going to run with it.

After talking to Maribel, Pearla walked out the project apartment feeling happy about herself. She strutted toward her car with her cell phone in her hand and with a lot of moves to make. She called her friends and wanted to meet up with them, maybe have dinner at some nice restaurant on her, since she was feeling generous.

But behind her happiness and her sudden generous mood, there was also some frustration that Cash had stopped calling. She'd ignored his call a few days earlier because she was still upset and she needed some time. She wanted him to apologize, but he didn't. When he'd called her phone, he'd left no voice messages—nothing sincere or remorseful from him since the day of the incident. She wanted to call him, but it would be playing herself. She constantly kept thinking about him and wondered if he was thinking about her too.

Their date was fun, and different. He made her laugh. She felt comfortable around him. But did he have a girlfriend, and did he lie to her? Pearla wasn't about to become second to any bitch, especially one that wasn't even pretty like her. She wanted to be Cash's priority, not his alternative. She was willing to bide her time and wait for her next opportunity, if it ever came.

Pearla climbed into her Benz, started the ignition, and sped off, her expensive heels pressing down on the accelerator. She was about her money, and she didn't have time to dwell on love—love should dwell on her.

Pearla stepped out of her mother's home looking like she was ready to walk down the red carpet at a prestigious event. Everything was on point with her—makeup, hair, nails, and feet. With her clutch gripped in her manicured hand, she walked through the messy living room and said to herself, "I need to get the fuck out this house."

Living in the projects, the Brooklyn ghetto, she felt like a diamond covered in shit. *Soon*, she always said to herself. Soon she would be in her own palace and living the way she was born to live.

She stepped outside onto the porch, and there he was waiting for her, propped up against his silver Audi A7, looking like a don posing for a photo shoot. He was wearing a V-neck T-shirt that fit snugly around his muscular physique, tattoos showing on his arms, designer boot-cut jeans, his tan Timberlands looking like they were fresh out the box, and his bald head gleaming. He was swimming in bling—platinum chain with the diamond-encrusted dog pendant hanging around his neck and the diamond pinky ring with matching bracelet.

Seeing Pearla walk out the lobby in her outfit, Hassan smiled, showing his bright, white teeth. Hassan was a drug dealer, moving kilos of cocaine to states like Connecticut, Rhode Island, and Albany in upstate New York. He was half-Jamaican half-Chinese.

For the past two weeks, he and Pearla had been kicking it. Hassan was infatuated with Pearla, but the feeling wasn't mutual.

They'd met on the street. Hassan was driving by and noticed Pearla getting into her Benz. He quickly threw his Audi in reverse and pulled up beside her passenger window and caught her attention. He was a silver-tongued gentleman, always smiling and polite. He spoke proper—no Ebonics, no pickup lines. He simply said, his voice deep and clear, "Excuse me, beautiful, can I have a minute of your time?"

He had Pearla's attention the minute he backed up to her in his nice-looking car. He continued to compliment her, making her smile and feel like she was the prettiest woman on earth. They exchanged numbers, and he drove off. It felt good to be noticed and wanted, especially from a man of his style and status. He wasn't Cash, but, damn it, he came close.

Pearla knew she was definitely going to call him and see what he was about. They started to hang out, getting to know each other. He was a beautiful man with a warm personality. It was hard to believe he was a notorious drug dealer with a violent reputation.

Walking closer to Hassan leaning on his car, she heard him say, "You are so beautiful."

She smiled. "Thank you."

"I mean it. You are breathtaking, Pearla."

"You trying to get some pussy tonight."

Hassan chuckled at her brash reply. "I'm just speaking the truth. But if it's helping, then hey, who wouldn't want to taste some of that honey?"

"And my honey is good."

Hassan escorted Pearla to the passenger side of his Audi and politely opened her door, allowing her to climb into the vehicle, for everyone hugging the block on a sunny, spring evening to see. She was being treated like Cinderella on her way to the royal ball. For her, it definitely felt good to shine around the haters.

Hassan climbed into his car, and they rode off. He was whisking Pearla away to a blissful evening. First, it would be dinner at his cousin's extravagant restaurant in Long Island—Blue Outlet, a posh and expensive place frequented by some of New York's elite. Hassan could afford it. After dinner, they would go for drinks and then a movie.

Three hours into her evening with Hassan, Pearla was feeling right, like she was on cloud nine. Everything was going smoothly. Touring Long Island with Hassan was fun. Cruising around in his Audi A7 made her feel like a queen.

She sat back against the plush leather seats, crossed her legs, and smiled his way. It was obvious she was flirting with him. She wasn't fiending for dick, but she ate up the attention he was giving her. Hassan had that Adonis look about him, a pretty boy thug. Besides, she had to do something to take her mind off Cash. It was hard not to think about him. He'd left something behind on her—a magnetic attraction—though he had pissed her off.

They rode around Long Island, the sun a memory until the next day's dawn. It was a warm evening, so they drove with the windows down, music playing, and the wind blowing through her hair, the traffic flowing like champagne on New Year's Eve.

"You okay, beautiful?"

"I'm fine," Pearla replied with a calm, easygoing tone.

She threw another smile his way, and he threw one back.

Hassan glanced down at her legs. "I hope you're having a good time with me."

"I'm having a wonderful time, Hassan. I haven't been out on a date this fun in a long while."

"You and me both. I know when we first met a few weeks ago, I'd been really busy. This game has me moving around like a chicken with its head cut off."

"Believe me, I understand. I get my hustle on too."

"You look like a shorty that gets that money. When I saw you getting into your Benz, looking so pretty, I had to stop and get your attention."

"Well, I'm glad you did."

Hassan nodded and grinned.

They were on their way to the movies at Sunrise Cinemas. It had been ages since Pearla had gone to the movies. Her lifestyle kept her busy like rush-hour traffic.

Driving down Sunrise Highway, Hassan smoothly placed his hand against her thigh. Pearla didn't push it away. His touch was sensual, and she knew he probably was looking for some pussy tonight, but her mind wasn't on sex. She saw him as another bridge to cross, a connect for some business opportunity; knowing him could benefit her in the future. If she fucked him, then it would be on her terms and when she wanted it.

"You have some really soft skin."

"Thank you."

As long as he kept his touch respectful, then she wouldn't have a problem with him. Pearla didn't want her pussy fingered and she didn't want to be fondled. She wanted their night out to remain casual.

Hassan pulled into the parking lot of Sunrise Multiplex Cinemas. He killed the ignition to the Audi and said, "We're here."

The parking lot was packed with cars. The theater had a crowd that night. The castle white building was showing over twelve movies, but Pearla was interested in seeing one film. She was into romantic comedies. When she had time to watch movies, she preferred to see a film that would make her laugh and smile. She had so much drama in her own life that she didn't want to view it on the big screen too.

Hassan stepped out of the car and hurried around to the passenger side to open Pearla's door.

Pearla got out with her smile. "Thank you."

The two walked arm in arm toward the theater. There was a small line at the ticket window. It moved though, and they didn't have to wait too long. They looked like they were overdressed for the movies, and they received fleeting looks from other casually dressed couples in the place.

The gripe Pearla had was going through the metal detectors. "Who puts metal detectors in a fuckin' movie theater?"

She didn't know if she was about to watch a movie or get on an airplane. She had to walk through it while placing her belongings in a plastic tub and then have a security guard wave a wand around her like she was on Rikers Island.

After it was all done, they walked into the lobby, which was flooded with people. The concession stand had another long line, and the video games were all occupied. If it weren't for Hassan, Pearla would have gone home, but he was paying for it all, and she didn't want to be rude. It was another fifteen minutes before their film started.

Hassan suggested they get some popcorn and some drinks. He stood on the long concession line, while Pearla just stood around being observant.

Pearla thought about her new hustle with Chica. Maribel was down. Now she needed a half-dozen girls or more to really benefit from the marriage scam. She was smart enough to know, if executed correctly, they could make some real money from these men who were desperate to stay in the country, and it could balloon into something bigger.

She'd immediately started working with Maribel and Fallou, her husband-to-be. He was black like tar, tall and lean with nappy black hair, and teeth white as snow. He was a nice guy. Fallou wanted to become a doctor and was intelligent and ambitious enough to make it happen.

Pearla read Fallou like a book. He didn't come to America broke. He came to the States to pay for an education.

Pearla needed to make the introduction. She needed to make it feel like it was a real marriage, especially when immigration came sniffing around asking questions. There was no room for errors. A mistake could have Fallou deported and Pearla and everyone else investigated and looking at jail time. With the wheels turning on that scheme, Pearla needed some time for herself.

"From Brooklyn to Long Island, I see you everywhere just like me," she heard him say from behind.

Hearing his voice, Pearla spun around and couldn't believe her eyes. Cash was at the movie theater too, and, of course, he wasn't alone. He was with a shapely brown-skinned woman with a long weave and hazel contacts. She was under his arm, looking like a simple bitch, her big tits squeezed into her tight shirt.

"What you doing way out here?" she asked.

"I'm everywhere. You ain't know?"

"I see."

Seeing Cash again a few weeks after their first date was an overwhelming feeling. It came so unexpected.

"Oh, I'm being rude," Cash said. "Pearla, this is Mia; Mia, Pearla."

Pearla looked Mia up and down, sizing the bitch up. Cash definitely liked them thick and stupid. Mia looked like the typical gold-digging bitch ready to spread her legs tonight because some nigga took her to a dinner and a movie.

"Nice to meet you," she said dryly.

The two ladies greeted each other rather tamely. It was obvious that they both liked the same thing and weren't interested in becoming friends.

Cash stared at Pearla, in awe at how good she looked tonight.

With Mia nestled underneath Cash's arms, the two of them looking like a lovely couple, Pearla felt like an oddball suddenly. She was sinking fast in quicksand without any support to pull her out. *Where is Hassan?*

"So, you here alone?" Cash asked.

She was about to say no, but then she didn't have to answer his question. On cue, Hassan came walking up to everyone holding a large bag of buttered popcorn and two large drinks in his hands. He saw Pearla engaged in conversation and decided to make himself known. When he saw Cash, the two locked eyes like two rival pit bulls in the ring.

"You here wit' this nigga?" Cash growled, contempt in his voice.

"You got a problem, nigga?" Hassan retorted.

"I thought you had better taste than trash, Pearla."

Hassan told him, "You better watch your mouth, Cash."

Unbeknownst to Pearla, Cash and Hassan had been rivals since grade school. Back in the days, the girls either went for Cash or Hassan—two pretty boys who were also thugs, every hood rat's dream. As the years moved on, Hassan became a boss in the drug game, moving heavy weight and making money like a kingpin and locking down his name on the streets, while Cash became a low-level car thief.

Cash instantly became jealous that Hassan was with Pearla. The only thing he could think about was his rival fucking Pearla. He was consumed with thinking Hassan was going to succeed where he'd failed.

Hassan said to Pearla, "You ready to go inside, baby? The movie is about to start."

Pearla smiled. "Well, it was nice meeting you, Mika—"

"Mia," Cash's date corrected her, rolling her eyes and craning her neck.

"Oh, okay."

Pearla spun around and walked next to her date.

Cash watched them intently. Seeing Pearla again, especially with Hassan, appeared to spark new interest inside of him.

Pearla was enjoying the movie with Hassan. They were munching on popcorn and laughing, his arm around her in the dark. But from time to time, she thought about Cash. It was a funny thing running into him in Long Island. She wondered if it was fate. Was it meant to be between him and her? What were the chances of them going to the same theater in Long Island, miles away from Brooklyn?

She sighed.

"Everything okay?" Hassan whispered into her ear.

"Yeah, I'm fine."

ELEVEN

Cash parked the Chrysler 300 on the block and stepped out in his long khaki shorts, wife-beater, and fresh white Nikes. It was a sun-drenched day, and he felt good. His date with Mia last night ended with a long blowjob in the front seat of the stolen Chrysler and coming in her mouth. She didn't hesitate to swallow his come. As he was getting his dick sucked, Pearla was heavily on his mind. He wanted to see her again.

He walked toward the liquor store and saw his pops dancing for two young girls. Like always, he was entertaining, making the girls smile and laugh. It felt like a hundred degrees outside, but Ray-Ray didn't care. His dancing and joking around for some spare change was how he made his living. He was clad in a white T-shirt that was too big for his small frame and faded blue jeans that were so filthy they looked black. The red and white sneakers he had on looked a hundred years old.

The girls handed Ray-Ray a few dollars, and he was grateful. "Thank you, my queens," he said, politely opening the door to the liquor store like he was paid to be a doorman, and the girls walked inside.

"Careful, Pop. You might find you a girlfriend if you keep being so charming," Cash said to his father. "You know you too old for them young things; they might give you a heart attack."

Ray-Ray was all smiles when he saw his son. "Boy, I taught you how to pimp."

The two shared a good laugh.

"What brings you my way?" Ray-Ray asked.

"You know I gotta come check on my favorite person in the world."

"So now I'm your favorite person in the world. You sure it wasn't some girl last night?"

"She was okay."

"Okay, boy, I still see you smiling from last night. She must have had some of that good, good shit."

Cash could only smile. Being around his father always brought him in a good mood. He reached into his pocket and put a hundred-dollar bill in his father's hand. "That's fo' you, Pop."

Ray-Ray displayed his toothless smile. "You always know how to take care of your old man."

Cash liked looking out for his father. All his life Ray-Ray had it hard, and if he could make it easier for him, he did whatever he could. Cash knew the money would go to booze or drugs, since drinking, getting high, and making people laugh made Ray-Ray happy.

Cash spent the next hour and a half with his father. Then he said, "Pop, I'm gonna check you later. Gotta make moves."

"Make moves and be safe out there, son."

"Always am, Pop."

He walked back to the stolen Chrysler and drove away. The minute he started driving, he picked up his cell phone and decided to dial Pearla's number. Since last night, she had been on his mind, and he wasn't about to give up on some new pussy.

Her phone rang several times. Then her angelic voice came through. "Hello?"

"Hey, Pearla."

Pearla was speechless for a minute. "Hey, Cash. What's the reason for this sudden call?" she asked unenthusiastically.

"I've been thinkin' 'bout you."

"Oh, you have, huh?"

"Yeah, I didn't like the way our last date ended, and I was wondering, can you give a nigga a second chance? You know, start over and do it right."

"I actually did have a good time, Cash, until that bitch came on the scene and got stupid."

"Well, you ain't got to worry about her anymore. I'm done wit' that bitch."

"So I'm supposed to take her sloppy seconds?"

Cash chuckled at her sudden comment. "Oh, it's like that, love? You think I'm sloppy?"

"When I fuck with a nigga, I fuck with him, Cash. I don't like sharing. I'm too good of a bitch to share my nigga with the next bitch," she said seriously.

"I feel you, ma. I know where you comin' from."

"Do you?"

She was teasing him, fucking with his head—mind games 101. If he thought he was going to call her and ask her out again and she was supposed to jump like the ground was hot, he had another thing coming. Though she really liked Cash and wanted to be with him, she had to let him know it wasn't going to work like that—that she wasn't the average bitch to play with.

"Yeah. When I saw you last night, I was like, 'Damn! I fucked up on that.' I shoulda came correct wit' you," he said.

Yeah, you did. "I'm over it," she said dryly.

"But I do like you, Pearla. You been heavy on my mind since the block party," he lied.

Pearla was listening to him trying to explain his way into her panties. She knew the deal. He saw her out with Hassan looking like a superstar, and now he wanted to call and butter her up. He probably thought they'd fucked and wanted to have a whose-dick-is-bigger contest.

But hearing Cash try to work his way back into her life was pleasing. She felt wanted. She already had it in her head that she was going to say yes and give him a second chance.

"So what you doin' today, love?" Cash asked her.

Pearla had plenty to do today, but she said, "Nothing much."

"So let's hook up and get into something."

Pearla knew what he wanted to get into. It was definitely her. She entertained the idea. She was quiet over the phone. "What do you want to get into?"

"Let's go out to eat and chill."

"That sounds cool."

"So what time you want me to come get you?" he asked.

"Oh, so you're driving now?"

"You know what I drive, ma."

"Something stolen, right?"

"It's the only way I can get around."

Pearla felt Cash sometimes could be small-minded and unambitious. Riding around in stolen cars and selling them to a chop shop for pennies was stupid in her eyes. He probably could do more, but it wasn't her business to get into at the moment.

"I'll drive, Cash."

"You sure?"

"Yes, I'm sure. I'll pick you up in an hour."

"A'ight, I'll be ready."

Cash and Pearla walked into the Olive Garden, off the Conduit Parkway in Gateway shopping center. The restaurant wasn't crowded, and the two were already laughing and smiling, almost looking like the perfect couple.

Pearla, once again, tried to impress Cash by wearing a pink strapless dress, showing off her long legs in wedge heels. She looked like a Barbie doll. The outfit definitely caught his eyes. He couldn't stop looking at her.

Cash wore his Nike Air, blue jeans, a plain white T, and a black-on-black Yankee cap sitting ace-deuce on his head, the brim stopping just short of his sunglasses.

The two walked into the restaurant and were quickly seated. They snacked on appetizers and talked. It felt like they had the place to themselves. She couldn't stop laughing. Cash's humorous personality made her feel like she had front row seats at Def Comedy Jam.

"I know you missed me," he joked.

"You missed me more, because you called first."

"Hey, usually I'm the one receiving the calls."

"Because you cocky, that's why."

"But this is between you and me."

"Our little secret," she replied for a laugh.

After their afternoon dinner at Olive Garden, Cash and Pearla walked a few feet to the small park in the area. With the sun shining brightly down on them, the two decided to take advantage of the weather and lingered outside. They had a view of the cars flying by on the Belt Parkway, beyond which was a mountain of rolling grassy hills that came to an end at the sea. They were in their own little world.

Cash and Pearla took a seat on the bench. For the moment, it was about each other, and they both gave the other their undivided attention. This time there were no cell phone interruptions.

"What's your story, Cash?" she asked suddenly.

"My story?" he repeated, a raised eyebrow thrown her way.

"I know the man I'm always hearing about from the streets. But who are you really?"

The question caught Cash off guard. It boggled him. No one had ever asked him that, not even Stephanie.

Cash averted his attention away from her for a moment, staring off at some distant place, his mind trapped in some nostalgic memory.

Pearla was listening. She wanted to know if Cash could ever have a serious conversation without sex and cars being the topic.

Out of nowhere, Cash mentioned his father Ray-Ray. "My father is a drunk and heroin addict," he said, his voice sad. He rarely spoke about his father to anyone. "You know, my pops, he's a poor and sick man. He never had much while I was growing up, but his view on life is remarkable. He's always laughing and smiling, entertaining folks, even though his own life is fucked up. I guess that's where I get my sense of humor from."

Hearing Cash talk about his father was a good thing in Pearla's eyes. Once he started talking, as usual, he couldn't stop. He went on to tell Pearla how close he was with his father, closer than he and his mother would ever be.

"My moms, she a fuckin' trip. The woman is in her forties and she out there trickin' wit' these young niggas. You know how embarrassing that shit is to me? Sometimes I just wanna spazz out on these niggas that get wit' my moms, yo."

Pearla said, "My mother acts younger than me most times. She curses, dresses like she's a stripper, and fucks everything moving. Me and my mother, we're like night and day."

"Sometimes, I wish we could pick our parents."

Pearla laughed. "Ain't that the truth?"

The two continued to share some heartrending tales about their past, a lot of which was about their parents. It was surprising to hear that they had so much in common.

They talked until the sun began to set behind the horizon. They'd lost track of time.

"It's gettin' late," Cash said.

"It is."

Cash and Pearla locked eyes, their bond stirring up.

"You are beautiful," he said to her.

With evening sweeping over the city, they walked to Pearla's Benz. Pearla drove this time, while Cash relaxed in the passenger seat. Not being able to take his eyes off Pearla, there was one question that plagued his mind. Did she fuck Hassan? In a way, he was too afraid to ask.

Pearla navigated her Benz to her mama's place and invited Cash in.

The house was empty and quiet. Poochie was working the night shift this week. The place was a much different place when her mother wasn't home.

With his hand still in hers, Pearla guided him into her bedroom.

Cash looked around and smiled. He was impressed with the decor. He thought Pearla's infatuation with Mickey Mouse was cute.

Cash gazed into Pearla's lovely eyes and felt drawn to her. Their long stares indicated they both wanted the same thing. He moved closer, placed his arms around her slim waist, and moved his lips toward her. Their lips and tongues became entwined, and their breaths became one.

They tongued each other down slowly, as his hands gently fondled her backside. He slid his touch underneath her dress and removed her panties slowly. They both stripped and kissed at the same time, ready to explore each other's body.

Nestled in each other's arms, Cash ran his tongue across her scented skin and continued to fondle her gently. Her body was nice; smooth, long legs, perky tits. Her small, tight ass and shaved pussy made him hard. He was big, nine inches at least, and his width opened up Pearla's hand.

After positioning herself on her back against her duvet, Cash climbed on top of her with eagerness to claim his prize. His bet with Petey Jay had long expired, but he still felt like he was winning.

"You have a condom on you, Cash?" she said softly in his ear.

He nodded and quickly grabbed his pants from off the floor and pulled out a large-size condom. He rolled the latex back on his thick penis and reclaimed his sexual position between her spread thighs.

He didn't miss a single curve on Pearla, pressing into her as he made her spread her legs some more, and he caressed the soft flesh of her inner thighs. She jerked from him piercing her, feeling his dick parting her soft, pink lips. He kissed her tits and gently teased her nipples to full hardness.

"Ooooh! Ooooh!" she cooed. "Oh, God! It feels so good."

Cash steadied himself until he was deep inside of her, and thus began that brief period of time where nothing but ecstasy existed.

"Fuck me! Ooooh, don't stop! Please don't stop!"

Cash was a pro at sexing. He had this technique down and knew how to move his penis inside of a woman. His strokes were long and deep, but almost sensual and teasing. Her pussy grabbed him tightly with every stroke he thrust inside of her. He pushed her legs back and continued to mount her. Her pleasure zone felt like it was the place he belonged.

Purposeful, steady, strong, and hard, he slid his dick in Pearla over and over and over again. With her legs wrapped tight around him, her nails in his back, and her hot breath in his ear, they were joined together as one.

Her pussy was hypnotizing. She was tight and wet like no other, and she absorbed all of him. Her throbbing punani almost made him want to cry out and come instantly. "Ugh! Ugh!" he moaned.

Trembling and shivering, Pearla chanted, "Fuck me, fuck me, fuck me!" to the heavens.

For an hour straight, they'd fucked hard and sensual, implementing position after position, his hard dick in and out of her like a churning factory machine. He flipped her over and put her on her knees. With her ass in the air, Cash went primal inside her gushing pussy. Minutes later, as if on cue, they both came with a combination of grunts and moans.

Cash pulled a naked Pearla into his arms and held her like she was his lady. Nestled together in the comfort of her bedroom, they started to have some pillow talk.

Pearla gazed into Cash's eyes and said to him, "Promise that you will never hurt me."

He gazed back and, with a deadpan expression, replied, "I promise."

TWELVE

Several weeks had passed since their sexual rendezvous, and so far, all was good. Pearla made it known around the neighborhood that she was in love with Cash. There was minor backlash coming from Stephanie, who was jealous of Cash's new relationship with Pearla.

With her marriage scheme between American women and Nigerian men in full effect and having three girls down for the cause, Pearla was on a roll. She resumed her shoplifting system with more girls and more profit, and felt like a queen bee bitch.

It also didn't take long for Cash to come to her with a new business proposal. The hustler Pearla was, she listened and was willing to try anything new. If it made sense, then it made dollars. Perez had told Cash about a new hustle he thought Pearla might be interested in. All she had to do was report her car stolen, and they would do the rest.

The plan was, Cash would drive the car to Perez's shop on Liberty, and there, they would remove all the leather seats, sound system, tires, and rims and keep them safe in his shop. Then Perez would flat-bed the stripped car and leave it on the city streets. Next, Pearla would report the car stolen to the police and then call her insurance company. Subsequently, when the car was found it would be brought to Perez's shop, and her insurance company would send an adjuster. Once the check was distributed to her for new seats, the stereo, tires, and everything else, Perez would put back the original equipment, and they'll all get a cut of the insurance claim. It was a no-brainer hustle.

Pearla was hyped and ready to execute it. She wanted to know how much the claim could be worth, and they estimated at least twelve to seventeen thousand dollars. She agreed to give Perez half the take, and she and Cash were going to split the remaining half.

Cash pulled up on the block in a Dodge Charger. It was black-on-black with black rims and tinted windows. The minute he stepped out of the car, all eyes were on him. It was a sunny day, and he was looking good and feeling good.

His relationship with Pearla felt solid, but his eyes still wandered, and he gawked at every pretty female that passed by him. He was staying with Pearla at her place. With her moms working nights, it made it easier for him to spend the night and sex it up with his boo, talk, and lay his head.

While he fucked Pearla every night, he still thirsted for new pussy. On occasion, he would receive blowjobs from pretty females in the front seat of stolen cars or in the back of some club. He felt getting his dick sucked wasn't cheating on his newfound boo.

Looking pristine in his designer jeans, chain swinging, fresh Nikes, his waves spinning in his hair, he stepped toward his peoples and talked it up for a minute. He was ready to cop some kush and a few drinks and go somewhere to roll up and chill for the day.

Nosh, the local dealer in the hood, subtly slipped a dime bag into Cash's hand as he passed him a folded ten-dollar bill. Nosh had some of the best weed in the city, and Cash only liked dealing with him. The loud Nosh supplied got him high as a kite and horny. When he smoked weed from Nosh, he and Pearla fucked for hours, and it was some of the best sex he'd ever had.

"A nigga need to get high right now, Nosh. Nigga is stressed and shit.".

"You know I always got you, my nigga," Nosh replied.

"Shit, I need to substitute the grand theft auto business for the weed business," Cash joked.

"As long as you don't step on a nigga's toes."

They shared a quick laugh.

Cash was ready to get back into his car and leave. He had what he'd come for. As he walked toward the Charger, a young teen came running around the corner in haste.

"Yo, Cash! Yo, Cash!" the young man frantically called out to him.

Cash spun around. It was Lil' Con. He was fourteen years old and always looked up to Cash and his crew. The look on Lil' Con's face said to Cash something was urgent or wrong.

"Yo, what's good, Con?" Cash asked coolly.

"Yo, they jumpin' on ya fuckin' pops at the liquor store!"

"What?" Cash said, not believing what he'd just heard.

"Ray-Ray, they fuckin' him up!"

Cash didn't need to hear any more. He took off running in his pops' direction. Lil' Con was following right behind him. He rushed toward the liquor store, which was four blocks away, in a full sprint and got there in a heartbeat.

He turned the corner and saw three goons attacking his father, who was on the ground, curled up in the fetal position, and howling out as his attackers kicked and stomped on him. No one attempted to help Ray-Ray or break up the commotion.

Running full steam, Cash instantly went into berserk mode, kicking one of the goons in his back so hard, he went flying forward and crashed against the concrete.

"Get the fuck off my pops!" he yelled.

The goon he kicked quickly regrouped. Cash was ready for war. He and the goon both threw their hands up, ready to box, exchanging hard stares and foul words.

"Nigga, I'm gonna fuck you up!" the slim goon with cornrows shouted.

Quickly, they went to blows like men, swinging and hitting each other. Cash quickly got the better of him, pulling on his T-shirt and hitting him with a staggering right hand to his face then a left to his right temple. Blood spewed from the man's nose.

Cash continued to fuck him up like he'd stolen something.

It didn't take long for the goon's friends to jump in. One came at Cash from behind, slamming his fist into the back of Cash's head, causing him to stumble. The third came at Cash swinging a bottle.

Cash maneuvered out of harm's way and backpedaled away from him. His hands still up, he glared at all four attackers ready to jump on him. He wasn't going out like no sucker.

He growled through his clenched teeth, "Y'all niggas jumping an old man—that's some bitch shit, fo' real! Fuck wit' me, niggas!"

Cash wasn't about to wait around to become a victim. He went charging at them like a lunatic. Blow by blow, he took them all on. An intense brawl ensued. They attacked Cash, hit him everywhere, and tried to bring him down, but he was determined not to fall and be conquered.

Lil' Con wasn't about to just look on as they jumped Cash. He quickly picked up an empty beer bottle from the curb, charged toward the commotion, and smashed the bottle across the head of one of the men.

"Aaaaah!" he cried out from the attack, blood covering his face.

Lil' Con shouted, "Get the fuck off Cash!"

Suddenly one of the Marcy goons opened fire.

Bak! Bak! Bak! Bak! Bak!

Panic ensued, and everyone quickly scattered for safety.

Cash wasn't so lucky. A bullet grazed his leg, and he dropped to the ground, "Ah fuck! I'm shot!" he cried out in pain.

Shots continued ringing out. *Bak! Bak! Bak! Bak!*

Cash saw his pops on the ground, and his eyes widened like a bug.

The shower cascaded down on Pearla's naked flesh like a tropical waterfall. It had been a hot day, and she needed a long, cooling shower. Lingering in the shower for nearly twenty minutes, she didn't hear her cell phone going off nonstop in the other room.

Thinking about Cash, she played with her clit gently, wishing he was in the shower with her. She yearned for his touch soon. She wanted to nestle in his arms and go to sleep. She had so many high hopes for them. She couldn't see herself being with any other man but him.

She stepped out the shower and quickly toweled off. She could hear her mother moving around in the apartment. Music was playing, which meant her mother either had company over or he was soon to arrive.

Pearla didn't want to be anywhere around Poochie. She had two options: lock herself in her bedroom and wait for Cash; or leave for the night. She knotted the towel around her and hurried into her bedroom.

The minute she walked into her bedroom, her cell phone started to ring again. Pearla picked it up from off the bed and looked to see who was calling. It was Jamie.

"Hey," Pearla answered, pep in her voice.

"Damn, girl! I've been tryin' to call you for over an hour."

"I was in the shower, cooling off and thinking."

"Pearla, Cash's been shot. He's dead."

"What?" Pearla screamed out.

"He got into a shootout in Brownsville—him and his father were shot."

Pearla couldn't believe what she was hearing. It couldn't be true. She didn't want to believe it. Pearla was hysterical. The tears poured out from her eyes, she screamed out, and then collapsed on her knees, dropping the cell phone from her hands. She was feeling like she was about to have a panic attack.

Poochie came rushing into her daughter's bedroom with a heavy frown. "What the fuck is wrong wit' you, Pearla? Did you muthafuckin' lose ya gotdamn mind, bitch? Yellin' in here like someone was trying fuckin' murder you!"

"They shot him, Mama," she cried out.

"Shot who?"

"Cash. My boyfriend. They killed him."

Poochie continued to look at her daughter like she had lost her mind. "It's what fuckin' happens when ya a fuckin' criminal."

Pearla shot a murderous stare at her mother.

"I don't muthafuckin' feel sorry for the nigga. He had it fuckin' coming, being a fuckin' criminal." Poochie pivoted toward the doorway and walked out the room. "He was cute, though. I'll give you that."

Pearla was in a stage of meltdown. Her tears continued to fall. The pain she felt consumed her like a winter cold. Her cell phone rang again. She was hesitant to answer it, her mind ravaged by misery and bad news. She ignored it.

Seconds later, it rang again. This time it was Roark calling. She figured her friend was calling to tell her the bad news.

She picked up, quickly saying into the phone, "I already heard."

"Pearla, I'll go wit' you to the hospital to go visit him."

Pearla was baffled. "What?"

"I know you heard that Cash was shot."

"I know. Why did they kill him?"

"What are you talkin' about, Pearla? He's still alive."

"What?"

"I heard he was only shot in the leg. Who told you he was dead?"

"Jamie."

Roark sighed. "You know she always get shit twisted. Don't be listening to her."

Pearla didn't know what to believe anymore, but Roark brought her some hope and relief. As Roark continued talking and explaining, Pearla's tears stopped, and she rose to her feet.

More calls came in to Pearla's cell phone confirming the same news—Cash was still alive. He'd suffered a gunshot wound to his right leg.

Pearla hurried to get dressed and see him at Kings County Hospital, where he was being treated. It was the only time she regretted having her car stolen to get the insurance money. She had to take a cab to the hospital.

✳✳✳

She hurried out of the cab and rushed toward the emergency room. She bypassed security and went into the triage, her eyes zigzagging everywhere, searching for her man.

"Ma'am, can I help you?" the triage nurse asked her.

"I'm looking for my boyfriend. His name is Cash. He was recently brought here because of a gunshot wound," she said in one breath.

"Okay, you need to calm down."

The triage nurse was very understanding and instead of having security escort Pearla out, she helped her with locating Cash.

The doctor was stitching up Cash's wound as he sat upright on the bed. It was a small graze; nothing serious. Luckily the bullet didn't hit an artery.

Seeing Pearla enter the room, Cash smiled and said with delight, "There go my baby."

Pearla went over to him and hugged him tight, almost breaking out into tears as she held him in her arms.

"Oh my God!" she said. "What happened?"

Cash replied, "Some clown-ass niggas tried to stall on my pops, and I had to jump in."

"What! Why?"

"Don't know the why, but I took care of it."

"Is your father okay?"

"He's in surgery now. They shot him in the ass."

Pearla couldn't make any sense of it. Cash was nonchalant about being shot, but she couldn't help but think that he could have lost his life.

The doctor quickly treated Cash's injury, and he was cleared to go home that same night. With a cane to walk with, Cash signed himself out of the hospital and went home with Pearla. His pops had to stay a few nights, but his injuries weren't serious either.

More than anything, Cash's pride was hurt. He wanted to let it go, but thinking about the way they disrespected him and his father made him irate. He vowed revenge.

THIRTEEN

Cash didn't have to lift a finger for anything. In the comforts of Pearla's bedroom, he relaxed and was treated like royalty. She waited on him hand and foot, while still running a business. When he felt dirty, she bathed him with a side hand-job. When they were alone, they talked. Being around her twenty-four/seven, he was learning a lot.

During the day, countless young women came in and out of her apartment, each involved in one get-money scheme or another—stolen merchandise, illegal weddings, credit card fraud. One way or another, Pearla was getting it in, and all the girls looked up to her like she was a big sister. Cash began to fully respect her. She was a boss.

A week after the shooting, Cash grew restless. He constantly thought about the thugs that did his father dirty. His father was harmless. They beat him down and then shot him. *Why would they beat up an old man and then shoot him?* he thought over and over again.

The more he thought about it, the angrier he became. He refused to let it go. Everyone involved needed to die, and by his hands. He had never been a violent man, but when forced, the monster came out of him. He was ready to get a gun and administer his own street justice.

When the girls were gone and they were alone, Pearla shut her bedroom door and looked at Cash. He was quiet, his gaze turned toward the open window.

She walked to the foot of her bed and took a seat. "What's wrong, baby? What are you thinking about?"

He turned and locked eyes with her. "I can't get these niggas out of my head, Pearla, how they fucked up my pops and shot me. They disrespected me and my family."

"What are you gonna do about it?"

"I'm gonna do somethin' about it. I ain't about to let this shit go. You feel me?"

Pearla nodded. "I feel you, baby." She moved closer to him and took his hand into hers. Looking at him with care, she advised, "Cash, if you do this, just don't get caught."

Cash wasn't trying to get caught. His father had always drilled into his head growing up to do dirt by his lonesome. He knew he could count on Manny and Petey Jay to have his back; they were like brothers to him. But if a nigga got jammed up, it was possible he could snitch. He was going to do it alone. Only Pearla was aware of his plan.

"I just need a gun," he said. Cash was aching to get his hands on a pistol and go hunting, transitioning from car thief to vigilante.

"My mother has a gun," Pearla said. "It's her backup service revolver."

For now, it was perfect.

The minute her mother was gone from the apartment, Pearla picked the lock to her mother's bedroom door and sneaked inside. She had to be careful. Poochie hated when anyone went in her room, especially when she wasn't home. Pearla went through Poochie's closet and found the lock box the gun was stashed in. She punched in the code and grabbed the gun. The plan was to give it to Cash and have him put it to use and then place it back before Poochie even knew it was missing.

"Here," Pearla said, handing Cash the revolver.

Cash took it into his hand, nodded, and smiled. It was all he needed.

Pearla kissed him on the lips and uttered the words, "Be careful."

***

The stolen Pontiac came to a stop at a red light on Myrtle and Throop Avenues. Marcy Projects was right down the street. It was after midnight, and the warm spring weather had the entire neighborhood outside.

Dressed in all black, with a black hoodie in warm weather, Cash stuck out like a sore thumb. He tried to go covert. His plan—kill these niggas and be out. He took a pull from the Newport between his lips and drove closer to the projects. He had gotten word on the crew that had attacked him and his father. The stupid muthafuckas had bragged to their friends about the incident, talking about it in the streets like they had gotten a new toy. Word traveled fast. The streets talked, and he listened.

Cash made the turn leading him into Marcy Projects. It was an active place, wrought with crime and drugs, and well known as being the home of Jay-Z.

With Cash's street connect, it was easy for him to locate the three low-life thugs. It was known that the three men he was looking for constantly lingered in the stairway of a certain building getting high. He parked in the shadows and sprung from the car with the revolver in his hand.

Cash moved stealthily into the seven-story project building on Park Avenue. The area was sparse with people and traffic. He had the heads-up from a source from earlier, so he hid and waited, knowing which apartment one of the perpetrators lived in.

Half-hour later, Cash had his sights on all three men. They disappeared into the third floor stairway as predicted, planning to get high.

Cash took the elevator to the floor below the one they were on. When he got to the second floor, he could hear them laughing and talking. Their voices echoed through the concrete walls, and it sounded like they were close. The thugs sat nestled in the middle of the stairs, one rolling up the haze, while the other two shared stories about bitches.

His latex gloves griped the gun as Cash slowly crept up the stairway. So far, he was out of sight and undetected. There was a short corner leading to the next floor. His heart started to beat rapidly. He was extremely nervous. This was his first time—murder wasn't his forte. But he talked himself into it, thinking about his father being disrespected and lying in the hospital. Neither of them had any health insurance, but it was the principle that mattered the most. The more he thought about his pops, the angrier he became, until his seething hatred reached the point of no return.

"Yo, Sharp, you ain't finish rollin' up that blunt yet?" Cash heard one of them say.

"Nigga, wait the fuck up," Sharp told him. "You know this shit takes time. Rollin' up is an art form."

"Nigga, I'm ready to get high and then see this bitch tonight."

"Nigga, your no-pussy-gettin' ass ain't got no bitch to see. Stop lyin' on your dick."

"Nigga, I'm 'bout to see your bitch tonight, 'cuz she be lovin' the dick."

"Fuck you, nigga!"

It was time. They were distracted; focused on each other and the blunt. Cash took a deep breath and instantly sprung from the short corner with his arm outstretched and the revolver at the end of it pointed at one of the three seated in the stairway. He had the element of surprise, catching them off guard. Their eyes widened with panic.

"Oh shit!" one screamed out.

They scrambled to flee, fumbling over each other.

Cash fired.

Pop!

Instantly, one caught a bullet into his back. He collapsed, sliding down the stairs.

Pop! Pop!

The second man dropped, catching two slugs in his side. He dropped before he could reach the top of the stairs.

The third was trying desperately to get through out of harm's way. He was in full-blown panic. Cash sprinted up the stairs, leaping over the bodies and fired two more shots.

Pop! Pop!

He caught the third just in time before he could escape, both shots ripping through his skull. He was dead before he hit the floor. Cash stood over and emptied the clip into squirming bodies until all movement ceased.

It was carnage in the stairway—three dead.

Cash didn't stick around. He went barreling down the steps, hurriedly went for the exit, and retreated from the building. He jumped into his car and sped away.

Several blocks away from the bloodshed, he had to pull to the side and thrust open his door. He threw up into the street. It was a rush. Within the blink of an eye, he took three lives. Cash couldn't believe he'd done it, but he had. He could now add *murderer* to his rap sheet.

First thing he had to do was ditch the car and burn it. Pearla would be his alibi in case detectives came his way with questions. When he reached her apartment, he was sweaty and hyped.

Pearla took her man into her arms, and by the look in his eyes, she knew he'd gone through with the deed.

"I did it, baby. I bodied these niggas."

Pearla stripped him of his clothing, placed them into a plastic bag, and immediately threw them into the incinerator. Next, she ran her man a nice bath and allowed him to relax and cool his head. "Don't think about it, baby," she said. "Free your head from it. It never happened."

Cash nodded. She was right. He had to erase everything from his head, clear his conscience. It was easier to do when she was around helping him.

Pearla peeled away her clothes and joined her man in the soothing bath, where she straddled him. They made passionate love that night, and it felt like they both were about to give birth to something bigger.

FOURTEEN

Two days after the murders, it seemed everything was back to normal. It was early morning, and the bright morning sun was percolating through the bedroom window. Everything was quiet. Pearla lay nestled in Cash's arms, sound asleep against his chest. They both were butt-naked and still recuperating from the previous night's intense sexing. For weeks, they'd been fucking like rabbits, sucking and fondling each other in special places, exploring every inch of their sexuality.

Then, suddenly, Pearla's door burst open like it had been hit with hurricane wind, and Poochie came charging into the bedroom like a raging bull. "You fuckin' bitch!" she screamed. "How dare you fuck wit' my shit!"

She snatched Pearla off Cash and gave her a rude awakening. Dragging Pearla out of bed, Poochie slapped the shit out of her daughter. She shouted, "You touched my fuckin' gun!"

She didn't give Pearla any time to explain. Poochie was on her daughter, slapping and hitting her insanely.

Cash jumped out of bed butt-naked, dick swinging, and tried to defend his girlfriend. He attempted to pull Poochie off Pearla, but Poochie wasn't having it. She was a healthy-size woman, and she outweighed him by a few pounds.

With the forceful movement of her right arm into his chest, she sent him wobbling backwards. "Get the fuck off me, nigga!" she hollered.

She continued going berserk on Pearla.

Cash fought Poochie, and she fought back with a vengeance. She was strong and nice with her hands, giving him a run for his money. They toppled over things in the bedroom.

Poochie sent Pearla flying over the bed. It was WWF in the bedroom. Blow for blow, Poochie became Mike Tyson on her own daughter.

"Poochie, stop!" Pearla screamed out.

Poochie went crazier. Nothing Pearla or Cash said could stop her from going ham. She felt her daughter disrespected her on so many levels, going into her bedroom and taking her spare service revolver.

She was getting ready to go to work when she somehow figured that her gun was fired. There were no bullets. She flipped. There was only one culprit responsible, and she had to be punished.

Poochie stopped short of retrieving her pistol and shooting them both. Her blood was boiling, her eyes red with madness. She seriously wanted to hurt them bad.

Cash had a bruised cheek, and Pearla's hair was in disarray, her belongings tossed around.

"Get the fuck out my house before I fuckin' shoot the both of y'all!" she growled at them.

Poochie started to grab a handful of Pearla's clothes and hurried to the door and tossed everything out.

An argument ensued, but Poochie wasn't hearing it. She grabbed more of Pearla's things and tossed them out into the street. When Pearla tried to stop her mother, she was met with a closed fist against her right eye. Pearla dropped back, wincing from the pain.

Cash frowned. He and Poochie locked eyes heatedly.

"Oh, you ready to leap again, muthafucka?" she said to Cash. "Go ahead, muthafucka. Try me. Fuckin' try me!"

Cash was ready to go.

Poochie left the room suddenly, and then seconds later, she came storming back into her daughter's bedroom, this time brandishing a loaded 9mm.

Cash stood still.

Poochie pointed the gun at him and snarled, "You think you better than this fuckin' pistol, nigga? Huh, muthafucka? You ready to fuckin' leap now, nigga?"

He scowled, his fists clenched. There was nothing he could do now. "No disrespect, you got it," he said, defeated.

"I thought so, muthafucka! Now get ya big dick out of my fuckin' house. I'm tired of y'all fuckin' bitches."

Poochie hurriedly threw them out, tossing out all of Pearla's clothes, shoes, jewels, and more onto the porch, leaving her out on the street. Poochie was so loud and volatile, the neighbors emerged from their homes to witness the eviction.

With all that was going on, her clothes and belongings scattered everywhere on the porch, Pearla had one thing on her mind—her life savings. It was hidden in a plastic bag in the bathroom toilet. It was the only logical place she could hide anything from her mother in the apartment. In the plastic bag contained twenty thousand dollars. She had to get her hands on it. Without that, her life would definitely be ruined. She'd worked hard to attain that money.

Looking dejected and lost, the couple dressed quickly. Cash and Pearla looked horrid wearing clothes they had to throw together in a heartbeat. Pearla was in tears. Her mother stood in the doorway, smirking. Cash was ready to murder that bitch. She thought she would be able to get her money back later, but for now, she had to throw everything she owned into several black garbage bags that Cash purchased from the corner bodega. It was embarrassing. Everyone on the block was watching. Pearla wanted to disappear.

"I'll be back for the rest of my things," Pearla said dismally.

"Oh, bitch, that's fuckin' everything you have," Poochie hollered.

"No, it's not."

Poochie pivoted on her bare feet and went back into the house, slamming the door behind her.

Pearla was determined to get her money from out of the toilet.

The front door opened again, and Poochie was grinning from ear to ear.

Pearla was in utter shock at what her mother had in her possession—her twenty thousand dollars dangling in her right hand, and her pistol in her left. Pearla's heart sank into her stomach. *How did she know?*

Poochie screamed hysterically, "You come to my fuckin' door again, for this money or anything else, and I'll shoot first and call the morgue second."

Pearla was devastated. She had to leave completely broke and disheartened. No car, no home, and now no cash. The two lovers were completely broke and desperate.

✳✳✳

It was embarrassing, wandering the streets of Brooklyn with trash bags and desolation on their faces. How did it come to this? Pearla felt angry, disheartened and raging all in one. Poochie had twenty thousand of her hard-earned cash, and she wanted it back, but her mother was crazy enough to shoot them both if they attempted to retrieve it. So it felt hopeless.

It was a hot day, and the two lingered by the bus stop on the Avenue. They tried to come up with a plan. Being in a desperate situation, they were willing to try anything. But the first thing they needed to do was find a place to stay.

"I can call up my nigga, Petey Jay. I'm sure he won't have a problem wit' us crashing there for a minute."

Pearla felt reluctant at first, but she didn't have a choice. She'd been down this road before, and she planned on bouncing back on her feet immediately. She still had her hustles going forward, her ambition, and then there was the insurance check that was supposed to come soon. She figured that money would be enough to get them back on their feet.

Agreeing to go with Cash to Petey Jay's place, they jumped on public transportation to go to the heart of the hood.

While riding the bus, seated next to Cash and looking like she didn't have a pot to piss in, Pearla's eyes started to water up. She looked a mess, and she felt even messier.

She placed her head against his shoulder, and Cash placed his arm around her for comfort. He wanted to utter the words, "It's going to be okay," but he kept silent, holding Pearla close to him, thinking of his own moves to make.

FIFTEEN

Two weeks into their slump, Cash and Pearla were living like bums, struggling and scraping, a day here, a night there. Pearla hated every minute of it, and was determined to rise up from her setback. They'd first stayed at Petey Jay's place for a few days, then Darrell's, then Manny's, and a night or two at Roark's, who had to sneak them into her parents' already cramped place.

Now, they were shacking up at Jamie's place. Since her mother was always working all the time and never home, Jamie's place was the most peaceful and relaxing. She didn't mind having Pearla and Cash over. She adored the company, and Pearla was her best friend in need.

Pearla felt ambivalent about the situation, feeling grateful yet humiliated. Bitches looked up to her, but now she had to depend on her friends to give her a place to sleep. Swallowing her pride, she reminded herself that it was only temporary. The one good thing that came from staying at Jamie's was that she had some time to think, since Jamie was an only child and practically lived alone, with her mother constantly working odd hours.

Cash was in and out, so basically it would be just them two, talking, plotting, and getting the wheels turning on every scheme they had brewing. Some nights, it felt like a sleepover with stories and laughter— two young girls sitting in their pajamas drinking Cîroc, smoking weed, and reminiscing about the good old times. And then there were some nights when Pearla felt like a prisoner of war—Jamie's place, her rules.

Cash and Pearla slept on the couch, while Jamie had her bedroom. On their second night there, Pearla was fast asleep. Cash had just come in right after midnight from another night of thieving cars. Pearla had been really stressed and out of it lately and didn't feel like fucking, especially in random homes and random beds. However, after two weeks with no pussy, Cash's hormones were raging.

While Cash took his position on the couch next to Pearla, Jamie, going into the kitchen for a late-night snack, so happened to walk into the living room skimpily dressed in her panties and bra. Cash's eyes were wide open as he took notice of her shapely figure.

Jamie threw a flirtatious smile his way, and that's all it took to get Cash excited. She walked by slowly, parading her figure in front of him, sashaying down the hallway, her phat ass looking tempting. Before she disappeared into her bedroom, she turned around and gave him the perfect invite into her room.

Cash took a deep breath. He was super hard and yearning to fuck. Pearla was asleep, and she was a heavy sleeper. He quietly slid off the couch and made his way down the hallway toward Jamie's bedroom wearing just his boxers. Her door was ajar. He slowly pushed it open, and there she was, lying across her bed like she was posing for some exotic magazine.

She smiled at him. Cash smiled back. His dick had gotten so hard, it started to show through his boxers. He'd wanted her since seeing her at the block party.

"Shut the door," she said softly.

He did. He then stepped into her well-decorated bedroom. It was easy to tell she was well-off, from the bed, to the dresser, to the clothes, and the amenities. But he didn't come in her room to admire the décor, he came for some pussy.

He climbed onto her bed with a look that said he wanted her so badly. He scooped her up in his arms and kissed her passionately. She was soft and so warm. He could feel his dick growing by just being against her.

They began to lick and suck each other in all sorts of sensual places. Cash took the time to give pleasure to her nipples. He sucked on them with delight and then fingered her pussy and toyed with her clit.

Jamie bit her lower lip, stifling a moan, uttering guttural sounds. Cash was rock-hard and her pussy was soaking wet.

She wanted Cash to fuck her mouth with his big dick. She wanted to taste him. "I wanna suck your dick," she said.

She pushed Cash off of her, and he landed on his back, his legs spread, his nine and half-inch dick standing erect like a flagpole.

Jamie didn't waste any time. She opened her mouth and wrapped her full lips around his dick like a blanket, making him coo. She loved sucking dick while her pussy was wet and throbbing. Jamie sucked him like a vacuum, pulling him in with her sensuous lips. Her mouth was like hot velvet, consuming every inch of him, deep-throating him in sensual delight. He was leaking pre-come and horny for more. Jamie was giving him the sloppiest, wettest blowjob he'd ever gotten.

He grunted and moaned, "Oh shit! Damn! Ooooh, that feels so fuckin' good! Shit!"

The sloppy, wet blowjob almost caused Cash to get loud. He forgot Pearla was sleeping in the other room. Jamie stopped sucking him off. She placed her index finger to her lips. "Sssshhh." Wanting to feel him inside of her, she spread her legs.

On his knees, Cash positioned himself between her legs and took precise aim. He lined up the head of his dick with her wet slit and rubbed it up and down. The heat was intense.

Then he shoved himself inside of her in one full stroke, straight raw dog—no condom.

Jamie shuddered from the penetration, wrapping herself and her legs around him as he fucked her. He felt her juices literally run down his dick. She was like a faucet, pouring out sweet honey and purring like a kitten while the dick thrust in and out of her.

The bed shook, and every so often, they had to remind themselves to quiet down and fuck silently.

Her body contorted and twisted with each stroke slammed inside of her. "Fuck me! Ooooh, fuck me!" she whispered.

He began pounding her. Being in some new pussy was a refreshing feeling. He was ready to spill his creamy, white seed inside of her.

Cash worked his dick inside her pussy like he'd created it. He fucked her slowly, deliberately, and hard, hitting the right spots, making her legs quiver. He was deep in her pussy, making it feel like his dick was rooted inside her stomach. The wet, frothy juices on his dick told him she was loving every second of it.

The pounding became more intense. He was driving Jamie crazy, giving her a string of orgasms. The more she came, the harder he fucked her. She wanted to scream out, but she too had to restrain her loud, primal cries of ecstasy, knowing her best friend was sleeping in the living room.

When Cash came inside of her, it felt like he had opened the floodgates. His semen poured out like water from a broken dam.

After it was all over, he went into the bathroom, quickly washed up, and reunited with Pearla on the couch like nothing happened.

The next night, they repeated the same thing, fucking each other's brains out.

And the following night after that, the same thing, sucking and fucking each other while Pearla lay sleeping on the living room couch without a clue that her best friend and her boyfriend had started an affair right under her nose.

✳✳✳

Pearla had to sit outside her mother's home daily and wait for the mailman to come. She was relying on her insurance check, since she desperately needed the money. If Poochie got to it first, there was no telling what she might do with it. She was certain that Poochie wasn't about to call her and let her know about any mail that came for her. With Pearla moving around so much, she didn't have a forwarding address.

She would intercept the mailman before he showed up at her mother's door and ask for the mail to her mother's address. Knowing Pearla's face, the mailman had no problem giving her the mail.

This went on for days, until *Bingo!* The insurance check from the claim she put in a while back finally came. The scam Perez had implemented had come through. The check was for $14,000.

With the check in hand, Pearla needed to think. She wasn't about to lose this pile of cash too. She was ready to invest it and make more money. If she and Cash were going to make it, they had to cut out the middleman, meaning Perez. Yes, he had come up with the insurance scheme and implemented it, but it was her car and she was taking all of the risk.

Ironically, the day before her check came, Perez had repaired her car, and she was back on the road again.

✳✳✳

When Cash heard of Pearla's plan to rip off Perez, he said, "You wanna do what?"

"Why do we have to give him half?" she asked.

"Because he's Perez, and you don't fuck wit' his money."

Pearla didn't care about his name or reputation. She hardly knew the man. He was no one to her. She was about her money and coming up by any means necessary, and if she had to step on a few people to rise, then so be it.

"I'm not afraid of him, Cash. Perez means nothing to me. It's my fourteen grand, and I'm keeping it. If he was so smart, then he wouldn't be so stupid to fully trust you or me," she proclaimed.

Cash continued to protest her decision, pleading with her to honor their deal, but Pearla wasn't changing her mind. If Perez had a problem with it, then she would threaten to turn him in.

✳✳✳

"That's your bitch, and you supposed to have her under control," Perez shouted heatedly when Cash relayed the news to him. "I want my share of the money."

Cash promised Perez he was going to work things out, but there was no guarantee.

Not only did Pearla fuck Perez out of his money, but Cash also lost his connections. Her decision to cheat Perez out of his half also fucked him out of his partnership and dealings with Perez. When it came to stolen cars, Perez was the go-to man, but now that Pearla had burned that bridge down to the ground, it was no longer an option for him.

✳✳✳

"You know, you fucked us . . . you fucked me," Cash complained to Pearla.

Pearla looked at him with a blank stare. "You're better than Perez, baby. You don't need him. Can't you see he was only using you? Now that you're no longer under his wing, this will give you the opportunity to go out and start your own shit."

Then she added, "The cars he has you stealing are worth peanuts, Cash. You need to stop stealing low-end cars and walking away with seven, eight hundred a pop, because you got a crew to divide it between. It's not worth the risk, baby. You need to be stealing luxury vehicles that are sold and shipped overseas. I did my homework, baby. You can get forty to fifty grand for a Range Rover or Benz."

Cash was listening. It sounded sweet. He definitely wanted to stunt harder and become the man, but he didn't have a clue where to start.

SIXTEEN

One Month Later

Pearla walked around the spacious, empty three-bedroom, two-bathroom apartment in Brooklyn Heights, her high heels click-clacking against the parquet flooring. The living room had a soaring 18-foot ceiling, wood floors, and high-efficiency interior and exterior LED lighting. She was exploring the apartment alone, falling in love with the residence as she moved through every square inch of the place.

The tree-lined streets of the neighborhood and the mix of architectural styles, including beautiful historic Greek Revival and Gothic Revival homes as well as Italianate brownstones, made it the perfect location for her. The schools were top-notch, the restaurants were exceptional, and the shopping appealed to the most discerning of tastes. And it was away from the hood.

The realtor, a middle-aged Caucasian woman with long, bushy red hair and clad in a dark pinstriped pantsuit, was about to show her the kitchen.

Pearla followed the realtor into the kitchen as she said, "The kitchen is decorated with Electrolux kitchen appliances, and honed Calacatta Tucci Marble countertops, solid American walnut kitchen cabinets, and a locally sourced eight-bottle under-counter wine storage."

Pearla wanted to move in right away. "How much?" she asked.

"It's thirty-five hundred a month."

"I'll take it," replied Pearla with assurance in her voice.

"Of course, we're going to need run a background check, along with a credit check, proof of employment and whatnot."

Pearla didn't have time for all of that. She wanted to move in right away. It felt like the woman was trying to scare her off, so she had to let the bitch know she could afford the place.

She reached into her purse and pulled out ten stacks. "Here," she said to the pompous bitch. "I said I'll take it, and there's no need for all of that. Now, is there going to be a fuckin' problem? Because I can take my money somewhere else."

The woman was stunned and wide-eyed at the bulk of cash she held in her hand. She responded in a more meek tone, "Um, I guess I can make it work. There shouldn't be a problem at all."

"I thought so."

As the realtor was making phone calls and drawing up the paperwork, Pearla walked toward the windows, admiring the picturesque view of the neighborhood. She was excited about the apartment but knew that it would only be temporary. Pearla had bigger plans. She wanted ownership. She heard someone say own your masters, meaning she wasn't going to be a slave to any landlord. Thirty-five hundred a month was a mortgage payment, and Pearla was about the hustle, not getting hustled. She and Cash would purchase their own home and invest in their future, the American dream.

It'd been a really busy month with no time for sleep or play, but grinding and making power moves that got a few people upset in her world. Just then, her cell phone rang. She reached into her purse and saw it was Chica calling. She released a deep sigh, reluctant to answer the call, but she did anyway.

The first thing she heard from Chica was, "You cunt-ass, muthafuckin' bitch! Who the fuck do you think you are!"

"Is there a problem, Chica?" Pearla asked.

"Yes, there is a muthafuckin' problem, bitch!" Chica said heatedly. "*You* are my fuckin' problem! How fuckin' dare you go behind my back and take from me what I fuckin' brought you into?"

Pearla had completely cut Chica out of the marriage hustle they'd supposedly started together, and she had her reasons. She was the one recruiting the girls and coaxing them to give up their single life for a profit. Chica had the blueprint, but Pearla was the builder, the actual architect of the scheme. Business was booming because of her, not Chica. Pearla figured out that if she found gorgeous, broke girls, the men would pay top dollar to marry them, with the hope of it turning into a real marriage.

In fact, she was borderline running an escort service. The busted project-chicks she was used to dealing with were a thing of the past. She now had a small stable of beautiful, young women eager to make top dollar. She was now charging $15,000 a marriage. She would keep ten and give the girls five. On top of that, she charged $2,000 an hour if you wanted some time with one of her girls. Pearla was the brains, so why should Chica be given a cut?

It didn't take long for her to phase out her former partner. When Chica found out, she was furious.

"Bitch, when I fuckin' see you again—"

"*If* you see me again," Pearla interrupted with her smug tone.

"You fucked with the wrong muthafuckin' bitch, Pearla. I swear this ain't over. I brought you into this game. I fuckin' made you, and I'll fuckin' destroy you, bitch!"

Pearla didn't have time for her idle threats. She simply said into her cell phone, "Bitch, see me when you see me. In the meantime, I'm getting rich."

She hung up with Chica cursing and ranting on the phone.

The realtor walked over with a confused look and asked, "Is everything okay?"

"Fabulous, darling," Pearla replied with a grin.

Cash got out the gypsy cab in Brighton Beach, a shore side neighborhood in southern Brooklyn, known as Little Russia. The area was known for its high population of Russian-speaking immigrants and as a summer destination for city residents due to its Atlantic beaches and its proximity to Coney Island amusement park.

It was a scorching day. Old men played backgammon in Second Street Park. The beaches were crowded, and the area was swamped with tourists and residents. Cash climbed out of the cab sweating like a slave in the cotton field. The cab didn't have air conditioning, and it was a long ride from his hood to Brighton Beach.

He had a meeting with a Russian named Adrian. Adrian was an up-and-coming mobster with ties to former KGB members. Cash was trying to make new connections, while separating himself from Perez and everyone else. Pearla had convinced him to go out on his own and make it happen, and he thought he was ready.

He got word about Adrian from a friend of a friend. The two had never met, but they'd both heard about each other's reputation, though vaguely. Cash was instructed to meet with Adrian at the Bratva Bar in Brighton Beach at 2 p.m., and he was a half-hour early.

Cash arrived at the Russian-owned Bratva Bar, which was located underneath the subway tracks. It was a quaint-looking place, nestled among other Russian businesses on the city block. He took a deep breath and walked inside. The place was dim and not crowded with customers. It was still early. The handful of patrons inside the place was enjoying their flavored tobacco from a communal hookah placed on each table.

Cash, being the only African-American inside the place, had everyone's attention. He looked around, searching for Adrian, even though he had no idea what the man looked like. It could have been anyone.

"You lost?" an employer asked.

"I'm lookin' for Adrian," he said loudly.

Another man removed himself from the hookah table, stared at Cash and said, "Come."

Cash followed the tall, long-limbed Russian into a back room. Before entering, the man said into the room, "We have company."

The room Cash was escorted into had three bearded men seated around a round table, drinking vodka and eating smoked fish. They were speaking Russian. They had all the ingredients for shady, dangerous mob muthafuckas.

Cash swallowed hard. He was nervous, but he refused to show it. He stood tall and remained calm.

A voice from the corner said, "You must be Cash."

Cash quickly turned his attention to the voice. It came from a younger man in the room. He was six feet tall with dark, slick black hair, a lean body, and a narrow face. He had intense eyes and was heavily tattooed.

"Yeah, I'm Cash," he replied coolly.

"Have seat." The man motioned to the chair near his desk. "Let's talk."

Cash walked over. The bearded Russians at the round table fleetingly looked his way and then went on with their business. Cash took a seat opposite Adrian. Being there with the Russians was a chess move for him. Pearla had convinced him that checkers was no longer his forte.

"I hear you good car thief," Adrian said in his thick, Russian accent.

"I'm one of the best."

"Good. Because I have job for you." Adrian took a seat behind his desk. He removed some pictures from his desk and tossed glossy pictures of high-end cars—Maseratis, Maybachs, Range Rovers—in front of Cash. "I'm willing to pay top dollar for these cars," he said. "Can you deliver?"

Cash stared at the pricey cars and thought he might be in a little over his head. But his ego started to do the talking. The money he could make from the Russians would be phenomenal. He picked up the photo with the Range Rover, looked at it briefly, then dropped it back on the desk. He looked Adrian squarely in the eyes and said with confidence, "Yeah, I can deliver. This is what I do—steal cars."

Adrian smiled. "Good to hear. You and me, we can do good business together."

"I'm lookin' forward to it," Cash replied, grinning.

"Have drink?" Adrian suggested.

"Fuck it! Why not?"

Adrian poured Cash a glass of Russian vodka, and then himself. Both men stood up, raised their glasses toward each other, and toasted.

"To business," Adrian said.

"To business," Cash repeated.

They both downed their drinks.

Adrian said, "Another?"

Cash smiled.

His meeting with the Russians went smoothly. Everything seemed good. Now the only problem was, he had to figure out where to get the cars.

✳✳✳

The one person Cash thought could and would help him out with his newfound hustle with the Russians was the woman who was in love with him. She'd persuaded him to push forward on his own, but now that he was asking for her help, it felt like she was shunning him.

"You want me to fuckin' hold your hand for the rest of your life, Cash?" she said to him. "Who got the big dick, you or me?"

"What?"

"You're a grown man, Cash. Figure it out your damn self. I can't always help you out."

"But these Russians are serious."

"So you need to become more serious."

Pearla spun around on her six-hundred-dollar heels and marched out of the room. She had her hands full with various moneymaking businesses and her girls, and she needed a man who could make his own decisions and hold his own.

Cash stood there, frowning. It was hard to hear, but he knew she was right. He walked to the window and gazed outside, contemplating his next chess move. "Fuck it!" he uttered, "Where there's a will, there's a way."

He was determined to find the way. Besides, he was a master car thief. What could possibly go wrong?

SEVENTEEN

It was 3 a.m. when Pearla's phone chimed loudly in the dark, quiet bedroom like an alarm going off. Pearla was sleeping hard. She turned her back to the ringing phone, ignoring it. Whoever was calling would get the hint real soon. It had been a long day, and she'd only had three hours of sleep so far. She cursed the ratchet object for coming alive during a time when everything needed to be dead silent.

Her phone rang again. She turned in her sleep, only to find that Cash wasn't in bed with her. It wasn't unusual for him not to be home around this hour. He was a car thief, so the early morning hours were the perfect time to carry out his craft.

Pearla lifted herself from the bed, sitting erect and staring at the time. She cursed for being awake. She needed her beauty sleep and rest. Tomorrow was going to be another long day for her, starting at eight in the morning. She heaved a sigh and glanced at her cell phone, which had finally stopped ringing.

Half an hour later, just as she was about to fall asleep again, her cell phone buzzed loudly in the room. Annoyed, she snatched up her phone and answered the call.

She got the shock of her life when she heard, "You have a collect call from Cash."

Pearla couldn't believe it. Cash had gotten himself locked up.

***

Pearla hurried toward Cash's arraignment at the criminal courthouse in downtown Brooklyn, her mind spinning with so many things. What charges did he have against him? How did he get caught? How did he fuck up something that he was a professional at? She yearned to see her boo again. She wanted him back home, in bed with her, making sweet passionate love to her. He couldn't do that locked away in some jail cell, so she was determined to get her man out.

At 9 a.m., she was at the criminal courthouse in downtown Brooklyn. The line was long. Everyone was waiting to enter the building, go through the metal detectors, and either see a loved one or go through their own trials and tribulations with the justice system. She couldn't believe it had come to this.

Getting through security was a long, drawn-out process. Over three dozen folks were moving through three active security stations, where everything came out the pockets and into the plastic tub and through the scanning machine.

An hour later, she was in one of the many trial rooms where the morning arraignments were taking place. She sat in the middle of the long pew among so many other people and waited patiently for Cash's docket number to be called. It was really busy—so many criminals, so many cases.

One by one, docket numbers were called, and each defendant went in front of a judge with or without a lawyer.

Another hour went by, still no Cash. Two hours. Then three. As Pearla sat, uncomfortably, for a brief fleeting moment she thought if she'd made the right decision choosing Cash over Hassan?

Right before lunch, the bailiff announced in the court, "Docket Number 5430544, Cash Combs."

Pearla perked up and trained her eyes on the entrance through which they ushered the inmates. She yearned to see her boyfriend. She just wanted to run over to him and hug him and assure her man that everything was going to be okay.

Cash came walking into the trial area, his hands shackled with iron bracelets. He was still in his street attire. For a brief second, Cash and Pearla smiled at each other. His appearance was in disarray. He looked tired and withdrawn. It had been a long twenty-four hours for him.

It was his first appearance in court. He was to face the judge and be advised of the charges against him. He had a court-appointed attorney for now, but Pearla was hoping to hire him a real lawyer.

The attorney representing the State read out the charges against Cash. "The defendant is being charged under Section 154A, for grand theft auto, a felony," he announced.

Cash stood in front of the judge stoically, his court-appointed lawyer doing all the talking for him. Today, he only had to put in a plea of guilty or not guilty. Even though he was guilty as sin, he didn't want to be railroaded by the judicial system. If found guilty, he was looking at maybe a fine and a sentence ranging from one to five years. He was advised to plead guilty, and maybe his court-appointed lawyer could knock the charge down to joyriding, which carried a lesser punishment.

Pearla looked on teary eyed. Either way, it didn't look good for her man. There was a chance he might have to do some time.

"How do you plead?" the judge asked Cash.

Cash glanced back at Pearla. The look on his face said she wasn't about to like his decision. He happened to smile and then turned back around to face the judge.

"I plead guilty, Your Honor," Cash replied.

After being made aware of his rights, he was taken back into custody.

Pearla didn't wait a second longer in the courtroom. Once Cash was out of her sight, she removed herself from the scene quickly. Her eyes were watery. She didn't know what to do at the moment. Now she needed to talk to the lawyer. It was his sentencing she was truly worried about.

Pearla got off the Rikers Island bus with the other females and waited in the long screening line with everyone else, mostly females, black and Hispanic, and a sprinkle of white people. It'd been two weeks since she'd last seen Cash. She couldn't wait to see and talk to her man again. She was devastated with his arrest. Life still went on, but her pussy ached for his touch.

In the morning, she went from one correctional building to the next, moving through multiple metal detectors, being scanned a handful of times by overzealous corrections officers and made to feel like she was an inmate herself.

But it was worth it to see Cash, who was being detained in the GMDC building. He was fortunate not to get a lengthy sentence. His lawyer was able to get him the minimum because this was his first offense, and the judge had sentenced him to six months. He was to do his time on Rikers Island. It wasn't a long time, but it was a long enough absence from the love of her life.

Pearla walked into the visiting area behind a handful of other young ladies anticipating to see a boyfriend, a brother, or their father. The room was packed; almost every small chair and table was occupied. It looked like confusion in one room, but everything was controlled by the corrections officers strategically placed around the room, watching everything and everyone.

Pearla was directed where to sit—near the back, against a brick wall, where she nestled uncomfortably with the other inmates and visitors. She took a seat facing the entrance and waited for her boo to come through the door.

Ten minutes later, five inmates were ushered into the room in single file. Cash was the first one on line. Pearla couldn't help smiling, seeing her man for the first time in two weeks. Rikers Island didn't change him; he still looked like a pretty boy. She was hoping that he wasn't having a hard time in jail because of his looks.

Clad in an orange prison jumpsuit with D.O.C. printed on the back in black letters, Cash looked around the room. The C.O. pointed to where Pearla was seated, and a huge smile splashed across his face. He didn't hesitate to walk over, longing to wrap his baby into his arms and passionately greet her.

Seeing Cash coming her way, a teary-eyed Pearla stood up and greeted him with open arms. "Oh my God! Baby, I missed you so much," she said, her voice cracking.

She and Cash hugged each other like they didn't want to let each other go. The guards had to sternly remind them there was no long display of public affection during visits. The two quickly took their seats opposite of each other, holding hands across the table.

"You look really good, baby."

"And you look good yourself. How are they treating you in here?"

"It definitely ain't home, but I'm good. You know I'm gonna be good anywhere I'm at. I'm Cash, baby—legal tender anywhere I go. I'm temporarily down, but you know, baby, when I get out, it's on. This ain't gonna hold me back."

"I hear you, baby. I love that talk in you. Damn! If you wasn't locked down, you could definitely get this pussy."

"Keep it warm and tight for me for six months, baby, and when I get out, it's on."

Pearla chuckled, gazing into his eyes. He seemed like his normal self and started talking like they were out on a date. He was still lively and humorous.

"What happened?" Pearla asked, referring to the night of his arrest.

"I fucked up."

"How?"

"I just got sloppy that night—rushed things. Didn't plan it out properly. I was hot-wiring this Range Rover, went at it alone when I shouldn't have. Police rolled up on me, literally caught me red-handed."

"At least you got six months."

"But that's still a long time without you."

She smiled. "It is."

"You think you can manage?"

"I have no choice."

"I know you don't," he joked.

"You lucky I love you."

"And I love you too."

The two shared an intimate laugh and continued holding hands across the table.

Cash turned a little serious. He looked at his woman and said, "I need you to do me a favor."

"What is it, baby? You know I got you."

"That's why I'm with you." He grinned.

"So talk to me."

"It's my pops. I need you to look out for him while I'm in here."

"Consider it done," she said without hesitation.

"Another thing. . ."

"What?"

"And if you got it in you, my moms too."

Pearla had met Momma Jones once, and it was a very rude and

unpleasant meeting. Within five minutes of Pearla meeting the woman, it was about to turn out ugly, until Cash separated them.

Cash read Pearla's look. "I know," he said. "She's a hard woman—"

"She's a bitch."

"And your mother ain't," he countered.

"Point taken."

"I'm just saying, no matter what they are, who they are, they still family, right?"

Pearla sighed. "Yeah, you're right."

Cash knew he had nothing to worry about. Pearla would keep her promise. He didn't know what he would do without her in his life. At first, it'd started out as a bet, but then it transitioned into real love for him. Pearla was like no other woman he'd been with. When he was around her, he felt good, he was always smiling. Though he cheated on her with her best friend and got blowjobs from different woman, he felt like he had to make it right by her.

With their visit winding down, Cash gripped her hands in his and looked deeply into her eyes. She gazed back.

"Baby, you know I love you, right?" he started.

"I love you too," she said.

He decided to not beat around the bush and came out with it. "What I'm sayin'—marry me."

"What?"

"I said marry me," he repeated. "I want you to marry me."

"Cash, are you sure?"

"I never been so sure in my life," he said with conviction.

The smile on Pearla's face already revealed her answer. "Yes!" she said excitedly.

The two leaned toward each other across the table and kissed fervently. It took a guard to remind them again about the rules for them to stop.

Pearla was happy. What other bitch could get a player like Cash to marry them? She felt only she could pull it off and change him into a one-woman man.

"The visit's over," the correction officer told them in a gruff tone, towering over the couple with an unsmiling expression.

Cash looked up at the overzealous guard and wanted to smack him for being disrespectful to him and his girl. But he could only hold in his contempt and think about his future. He only had six months to serve and didn't want to chance it by doing something stupid.

They stood up. Pearla hugged and kissed her man lovingly, not wanting to depart from him, but their time had expired.

As she separated herself from Cash and walked toward the exit, she was flooded with so many emotions. Her eyes became watery. Her heart felt like it was about to rip from her chest. She felt alone without him, but she had to stay strong and continue living and continue hustling.

***

Cash and several other inmates were being ushered out of the visiting room and back into lockup. He was in the middle of the line, quiet, thinking about Pearla, missing her deeply, and knowing she loved him so much that she would do anything for him.

There was some regret about his affair with Jamie. The more he thought about it, the more he wished it didn't happen. But it was hard to resist that pussy and her body. He was a weak man that night. And a few other nights. He was hoping it never got out to Pearla, knowing she would be devastated if she ever found out about it.

While waiting on line, he all of a sudden heard one inmate say to him, "Yo, that's ya bitch?"

"What?" Cash replied with a scowl.

"I'm sayin', that's ya bitch in the visiting room, the petite bitch wit' the pretty fuckin' eyes?" the inmate continued.

"What about her?"

"I'm sayin', she used to fuck wit' my nigga Hassan. What ya pretty ass doin' wit' that bitch? Yeah, I heard she suck a nice dick and got that good pus—"

Cash didn't allow him to finish. In a heartbeat, he swung madly, punching the man in the face repeatedly, dropping him to his knees with a bloody lip and swollen eye. He yelled, "Nigga, don't you ever fuckin' disrespect her or me like that!"

Guards hurried over and quickly defused the melee.

Why the inmate said what he said, Cash had no idea, but the damage had already been done. His violent outburst caused him some time in the bing and maybe some extended time on his sentence. But no matter the consequences he faced, no one was going to disrespect him or Pearla while he was around.

EIGHTEEN

'm getting married," Pearla hollered excitedly to Roark and Jamie.

"What?" they both replied simultaneously, not believing their ears.

"To Cash?" Jamie asked, looking in doubt.

"Yes, to Cash. Who else?" Pearla held up her diamond engagement ring, an 18k solid white gold and diamond she went out and purchased herself to boast to her friends about.

"Pearla, you're still a young woman," Roark said.

"And?"

"He's in jail," Jamie chimed.

"He's doing only six months. It's not like he's doing life."

Roark said, "But you had to buy your own ring."

"It's my choice. Y'all acting like y'all not happy for me. What's up? Cash loves me, and I love him."

Roark and Jamie looked at each other like they knew a big secret that Pearla didn't know. They thought she was playing herself, getting engaged to a nigga while he was in jail and she had to buy her own ring. Who does that?

Pearla was obsessed with marrying Cash despite the naysayers. In her eyes, it was probably jealousy, because she'd snagged a fine man like Cash and they hadn't.

"I want y'all to be my bridesmaids."

"Bridesmaids?"

"Yes."

"When is the wedding?"

"We don't have a date, but it will be soon. So, will y'all be my bridesmaids?" she asked again, smiling.

Reluctantly, they accepted.

Pearla was thrilled.

Momma Jones strutted across the street in her tight miniskirt, worn-out heels, and a halter top so tight and revealing her tits looked like they were trying to jump out of her shirt. It was just after midnight, and she was turning tricks in Crown Heights, Brooklyn, walking in the middle of the street and flagging down cars.

She had heard about her son's arrest, but it didn't bother her. In fact, she had smirked when she heard he'd been arrested for stealing cars and was serving time on Rikers Island. She'd said to herself then, "Nigga thinks he's better than me and gets locked up. Serves him right."

She stood on the corner longing to make some money tonight and get high. She was willing to do anything for the right price. Her body was a trick's canvas. They could paint any sexual desire they wanted on her—anal, have her swallow come, suck on balls, fuck on the hood of a car, or even group sex. If they were paying, she did it.

She walked into the street and tried to flag down a red minivan. As it slowed down, Momma Jones hurried toward the driver's side, and the window slid down.

"Hey, sweetie, you lookin' for a date?" she asked with a wide smile.

"Yeah. How much?" the driver asked. He was an older black man with a graying beard and a meek demeanor about him.

"What you lookin' for?"

"A blowjob."

"That's twenty."

He smiled. "Get in."

Momma Jones didn't hesitate. She strutted around toward the passenger side and climbed inside. She was ready to go.

"Where to?" the driver asked.

"I know a place. It's quiet and private, and there I can suck your dick and make you come until you lose weight," she lightheartedly said.

"That sounds like the perfect plan," he replied, chuckling.

"Let's go."

The man didn't budge. He simply looked at Momma Jones and feigned a smile. The way he looked at her, Momma Jones immediately knew something was wrong. And then there it was, her worst nightmare—the badge. He was vice, and this was going to be her second arrest this month.

"Yeah, it don't look too good for you," the cop said, shooting a smug look her way.

She sighed heavily and looked deflated. "Fuck me!"

"Not in a million years."

✳✳✳

The person Momma Jones least expected to bail her out was Pearla, especially after the way she'd treated her when Cash had brought her around. The bail was high. Momma Jones was lucky she had bail, with this being her second arrest for prostitution in one month. The judge was lenient, but he gave her a stern warning. The next time she was arrested for prostitution, she was going to have to do some time.

But what she really needed was a detox program. Drugs were eating away her life.

Momma Jones and Pearla walked away from the courthouse being distant toward each other. Momma Jones looked a hot mess. She glared at Pearla. "Don't expect any fuckin' favors from me. I didn't ask you to come bail me out."

Pearla chuckled. *Is she serious? I can't believe this bitch is serious.*

"I didn't do it for you. I did it for Cash. He asked me to. Don't you see, your son really loves you, and look at you, you're a disgrace to him."

"Bitch, who are you to judge me? Like you God Almighty. Bitch, I know what you are."

"What am I?"

"You a leech—that's what you are. You see a good thing, and you latch yourself to it, draining it dry."

Pearla had to laugh at that one. It was funny to her. "I'm a leech?"

"Yes, and my son is a good thing, a pretty boy making money, and you see a good thing and wanna take from him."

"Wow."

Cash's mother was delusional. She lived in her own world and had a distorted version of the truth. Pearla swallowed her contempt for the woman, though she was rude and disrespectful, and helped her out anyway, as a favor for her man.

✳✳✳

Now Cash's father, Ray-Ray, he was delight to be around. He was such a sweetheart; a really nice guy. Pearla constantly looked after him and kept him posted about his son. Like Cash, she would have long and meaningful talks with him. He made her laugh, like Cash did. He complimented her and called her beautiful, like Cash always did.

Pearla wondered, *For a man to be so smart and wise, why is his own life so fucked up?*

"You're going to be my daughter-in-law. I always wanted a daughter, and a beautiful daughter too," he said to Pearla. "Welcome to the family."

Pearla beamed. Why couldn't his mother be more like his father?

A month after Cash's incarceration, Pearla was out in the streets, keeping her word and holding him down in jail. She was proving herself to be that ride-or-die bitch for her man.

NINETEEN

With fall approaching, it meant Cash's release was soon coming. Pearla couldn't wait. He was scheduled to be released sometime the end of October. By then, she would have everything set up for him. Despite his absence, the summer had been good to Pearla. Money, money, money, it was all she was making—becoming a boss bitch. She drowned herself with Chanel, Gucci, Fendi and many other hot designers, along with the other finer things in life. She'd upgraded her Benz and was driving around town like an A-list celebrity.

Chica was going around the hood talking shit about Pearla, but Pearla wasn't worried. She thought Chica, like Perez, was all bark with no bite. She had relocated to an even better neighborhood, and no one knew her address. She didn't shit where she ate. She became introverted, choosing to keeping her circle tight. She remained close friends with Jamie and Roark, and only they knew her location and her business.

Pearla and Roark rode into Brownsville styling in Pearla's gleaming silver S-Class Benz with chrome rims and a slight tint on the windows. In fact, Pearla's vanity plates read *She-Boss*.

She came to a stop on Ray-Ray's block. She was there to give him a few dollars. He definitely needed it. As usual, Ray-Ray was lingering in front of the liquor store, smiling and cracking jokes, opening the door to the store for patrons and entertaining.

Pearla stepped out of her car looking like a diva with her black lace Manolo Blahnik heels, stylish halter top, and designer jeans so expensive they looked like they were dripping in diamonds. Roark too, looked really good.

When Ray-Ray saw his favorite girl approaching, he smiled so big, his ears felt like they would implode. He looked a little drunk.

As the two girls walked his way, Ray-Ray clapped his hands together excitedly. "Hey now. How good it is to see my son's two favorite girlfriends!"

What? Pearla thought. *His son's two favorite girlfriends?*

At first, Pearla was going to write it off as a drunk talking and foolishness coming from an old man, but when she looked over at Roark, she saw guilt on her friend's face. Pearla planned on getting to the bottom of things.

Pearla had a talk with Ray-Ray and gave him some money, but they didn't stay long. What he had said was lingering in her mind, and Roark was too quiet all of a sudden and looked too guilty about something. She knew if her friend could teleport, she would be gone in a heartbeat.

They walked back to her Benz and got in. Pearla turned up. "What the fuck was Ray-Ray talking about back there?"

Roark looked nervous and scared for a moment. She was definitely hiding something. Ray-Ray had inadvertently spilled the truth about something going on.

"Bitch, don't fuckin' play stupid with me. Let me know something. You're my friend, Roark. Talk, bitch, because I swear, if you don't, it's going be hell up in this car. Are you fuckin' Cash?"

Roark sadly looked into her friend's eyes and came out with it. "I used to."

Pearla was in shock. She couldn't believe it.

"Let me explain," Roark said.

"Bitch, what is there to explain?"

"It happened way before you two even got together. It wasn't even a relationship with him, just sex. Way before you and me became friends."

Pearla was seething. She knew her man was a male whore, but damn! He'd fucked Roark too? Her stomach churned with sickness, knowing her man had dipped his dick into a friend of hers.

"But we haven't done anything in so long, Pearla. I swear to you, I don't fuck with him anymore."

No matter what came out of Roark's mouth, how she dressed it up, or rueful she looked, it didn't change a thing. She had fucked Cash. It didn't matter if it happened last year or yesterday. The thought was still sickening.

"But I know he loves you, Pearla. What we had was a long time ago, and I don't want him anymore. I swear to you, I've been over him."

Pearla heard her talking, but she wasn't listening. The only thing she could remember was Roark being against her dating Cash and giving her warnings about him. *She could be lying,* Pearla thought. Every bitch wanted Cash. For all she knew, it could be a ruse to try and get him back.

"Pearla, I know he's yours, and believe me, I would never go there again. I respect you too much, and you're my best friend. I don't want him anymore. It was a long time ago."

Her blood boiling to a breaking point, Pearla glared at Roark and threw a hard punch to her left jaw that sent her head flying back. "Bitch, shut the fuck up!" she screamed.

Pearla hit her again in the same place, even harder. "Get the fuck out my car, bitch!"

Roark knew not to protest. She clenched her left jaw and slowly made her exit from the car, tears streaming from her eyes. "I'm sorry, Pearla."

"Fuck your *sorry*, bitch!"

Pearla didn't want to hear her apologies. Even though it'd happened before she met Cash, it still was painful. Why did she have to be so in love with this man? She was very aware of his past and was afraid to ask him how many women he'd actually been with.

Her tears fell, and her mind started to spin. She needed to go. She brought the engine to life and sped away, leaving Roark standing on the sidewalk crying with a bruised cheekbone and hurt feelings.

✳✳✳

Pearla had been to Rikers Island over a dozen times to see Cash since he'd gotten himself locked up. She'd looked forward to every visit, but this time she was ambivalent. She needed to hear it from him. She sat in the visiting room trying to hold back her tears. She knew seeing her man again after finding out about him and Roark was going to bring about a flood of emotions. Her heart beat rapidly like an African symphony. She tried to keep her composure, but it was so hard.

Every visit before this one, she came dressed nicely, looking like eye candy for her big daddy, but today she was there in regular jeans, sneakers, and a T-shirt, her long hair pulled back into a ponytail, and she barely wore any makeup. This wasn't a social visit; this was going to be more like an interrogation.

Cash was ushered into the room clad in his ugly, orange prison jumpsuit. When he saw Pearla, he smiled widely, but she didn't return the smile. Walking toward her, he right away knew something was wrong.

Pearla remained seated, no hugs or kisses like usual, just aloofness.

Cash sat opposite her. "What's goin' on, Pearla? Everything okay?" he asked, a hint of worry in his voice.

"No, everything is not okay," she returned firmly.

"Why the look?"

"Did you fuck my friend?"

Cash had that *Oh shit!* look on his face. "Let me explain," he started.

She started crying, unable to hold back the tears. "What is there to explain, Cash? You are such a fuckin' whore!"

"Yeah, I fucked her, baby. I'm sorry. She didn't mean anything to me. It just happened. I know she was your best friend, but I cut the bitch off when I got really serious with you," he said.

His statement brought Pearla into sudden confusion. "What?" She realized he wasn't talking about the past but the present. "Who are you talking about?"

"Jamie. How did you find out? Did she tell you?"

Pearla felt so betrayed and crushed on so many levels. The tears pouring out from her eyes could have left a small puddle around her feet.

Cash tried to console her, but she pushed him away and violently smacked him so hard, the sound of her hand crashing against his face echoed throughout the room.

"Fuck you!" she screamed. "I fuckin' hate you! How could you do me like this? I fuckin' loved you, nigga! You fucked that bitch?" She pushed herself away from the table and abruptly stood up.

By now, guards were hurrying their way.

She spat on Cash. "Stay the fuck away from me!" she screamed and stormed toward the exit.

Cash sat there looking like he had lost his best friend. There was nothing he could say or do.

TWENTY

Pearla cried all day. She locked herself away in her bedroom wishing there was some easy way to take the pain away. She felt hurt and betrayed, especially by both of her friends. Roark had fucked Cash in the past, and Jamie fucked him while they were together. Damn! It felt like a conspiracy against her. She didn't want to talk to or see anybody. She needed some time alone. Being in love was a bitch, and Pearla was deeply in love. It was hard not to think about Cash. Even though she was still pissed at him and hurt, she was ready to forgive him for his infidelity before she forgave her own friends.

She realized that being locked away in her bedroom and listening to Mary J. Blige albums wasn't going to cut it. Life still went on, and hustling never died out. But before she could move forward, she had to handle her business. She felt Jamie punked her, smiling in her face while stabbing her in the back. At least Roark's affair with Cash had happened a long time ago, but there was no excuse for Jamie. She was Pearla's friend, and friends don't fuck each other's man. There was no way she was about to let it go and not confront that snake bitch.

Pearla left her apartment on a mission. She jumped into her S-Class and headed to the old neighborhood in search of Jamie. She wanted to physically hurt that bitch, put her in the hospital. Jamie had the audacity to fuck her man while she put her on and had that bitch getting money out there. She drove her car hurriedly into the East New York hood and went looking for Jamie at locations she was known to frequent.

An hour went by, and there was still no sign of Jamie. She patrolled the area like a squad car, slowly riding down the blocks and looking out her window. All eyes were on the S-Class with the *She-Boss* license plate. She tried calling Jamie's phone, but she wasn't picking up. It was like Jamie was deliberately sending her calls to voice mail, probably knowing it was on.

Pearla made a right onto Pitkin Avenue, and bam, there she was, coming out of the corner bodega across the street from the housing project with another girl. She stopped the car suddenly at the curb and jumped out of her Benz like she was police.

Jamie stood there looking at Pearla coming her way. The way Pearla was approaching her, she knew it was something serious.

Pearla got up in Jamie's face. "You fucked Cash, you slut bitch?"

"Bitch, what?"

"Bitch, you fuckin' heard me!" Pearla shouted. "Cash told me every gotdamn thing about you and him. You were my friend, Jamie. I looked out for you, had you getting money out here and everything,"

"Bitch, I don't fuckin' need you. I got money, bitch!" Jamie scowled, ready to go to war with her best friend. "And besides, bitch, Cash don't want you anyway. He's using you. I love him more than you ever will. He ain't about to marry you."

Pearla had heard enough. She lashed out at Jamie like Mayweather, striking her with a two-piece combination, causing her to stagger. Jamie, however, refused to go down so easily.

They duked it out with a crowd gathering around the fight. There was hair-pulling and blows raining down, but as the fighting intensified between them, Pearla and Jamie kept feeling themselves being pulled away from each other.

Some fool was trying to break it up, saying, "Yo, y'all friends. Y'all shouldn't be fighting, especially over some nigga."

"Get off me!" Pearla screamed. "Get the fuck off me! I'm gonna fuck that bitch up!"

"Fuck you, bitch!"

They quickly broke away and ran smack into each other—hair was in disarray, with jewelry and weave flying everywhere, along with clothing being torn and private areas being somewhat exposed. Jamie was tough, but Pearla was even tougher.

Once again, the two were separated from each other.

"I'ma kill you, bitch!" Jamie yelled.

Pearla wasn't worried at all. Her former friend hadn't seen the last of her. She grabbed her things off the sidewalk and walked to her car, shouting, "That's my nigga you fuckin' with!"

"Bitch, how do my pussy taste?"

"Bitch, I got the ring."

"That you bought yourself, you stupid bitch!"

"You fraud, bitch! I'ma see you, Jamie. Shit ain't over; that's my word."

Pearla was ready to charge at her again. She didn't want it to be over, but she was being forced back by some young nigga she barely knew. She was so upset, she was ready to fight him.

Pearla got into her car still fuming. She wanted to rip Jamie's head off. It was only the beginning.

For the next couple of weeks, Jamie ran with her new crew trying to taunt Pearla. Word had gotten back to Pearla that Jamie had visited Cash a few times in Rikers, but the straw that broke the camel's back was when Jamie got Cash's name tattooed on her forearm with a heart. It drove Pearla insane.

Pearla had never thought of herself as a killer, but blind rage and jealousy was catapulting her into a whole new level. She couldn't see her man being with anybody else.

She sat in the middle of the night, watching the building. Pearla was watching Jamie's every move, studying her routine. It was quiet, the area sparse with foot and vehicular traffic.

Pearla waited over two hours, the large kitchen knife beside her as she contemplated doing the unthinkable. Every minute that passed, every hour, her thoughts became more contorted. Thinking about Cash sticking his dick into Jamie was driving her nuts. She was seething with so many emotions, from jealousy to rage to insecurity. Jamie had a better body than her, tits and ass for days. She knew Cash loved her friend's body. *What if Cash does leave me to be with her?*

It was two in the morning when a pair of headlights drove up. The Infiniti came to a stop in front of Jamie's building. The passenger door opened up, and Jamie stepped out in her high heels and short skirt, looking like she was coming home from a date. Pearla watched her closely.

Jamie, smiling and laughing, kissed the driver good-bye. She shut the door and strutted toward her building. She appeared a bit tipsy, stumbling a little bit to the lobby.

As the truck drove off, Pearla opened her door and got out, the kitchen knife gripped tightly in her hand. The area was dark, quiet, and still. With nobody around, it was the perfect opportunity to kill someone.

Pearla came out of the shadows and hurried into the building and arrived inside just in time to see Jamie stepping into the elevator. She rushed toward it before the doors closed. The minute she joined Jamie inside the elevator, before the doors could close, she plunged the knife into her flesh, catching her off guard.

Jamie jolted from the sharp blow into her stomach, feeling the kitchen knife wedged deep inside her gut. She looked at Pearla wide-eyed.

Pearla pulled out the knife and plunged it into Jamie repeatedly. She could feel her slowly dying. The body dropped before her feet just as the elevator came to a stop on the fourth floor.

There was no one around. Pearla still had her chance to make it look like a robbery turned assault. Before she fled the scene, she ripped off Jamie's jewels and snatched her purse.

Leaving her friend's body dead inside the elevator, Pearla raced out of the building, taking the stairway and hurrying to her car. Being smart, she'd worn latex gloves during the crime and wore a baseball cap and dark baggy clothing, making it look like she was a black male. She believed she had gotten away with murder. Once home, she was going to burn everything and dispose of the knife in the Atlantic Ocean. No evidence, no jail.

TWENTY-ONE

Cash lay quietly on his cot, looking up at the ceiling. He had heard the news that Jamie was murdered. He couldn't believe it. One of his little homies from around the way had relayed the news back to him while they were in the dayroom watching television. When Cash had heard, he simply got up and left the room, going to his cell to be alone. He didn't cry, because Jamie was just a piece of ass to him, but he knew who'd done it. He felt responsible for getting her killed. He'd fucked up and told on himself.

He shook his head and knew to never bring it up around Pearla. She had dirt on him, and he had dirt on her—they both were killers now. But loyalty was what he went by, and he was no snitch. He figured his girl to be crazy, but he still loved her. She killed someone because she was in love with him. He drove her to it. Now, all he could do was reflect on the incident.

Ponce Funeral Home on Atlantic Avenue was crowded like a rap concert. It seemed like everyone from the neighborhood came out to attend Jamie's home-going service. She was a popular girl and well liked, and everyone was devastated by her brutal murder. The news had hit everyone like a really bad dream. She was stabbed four times and robbed.

People were saying a crackhead or heroin addict murdered her. Everyone was angry and wanted justice. Detectives were investigating every angle.

Pearla pulled up to the funeral home alone. Dressed in all black, she got out of her Benz wearing dark sunglasses, ready to put on a performance. She was sad and disheartened, though she was the one who'd killed Jamie.

***

Detectives Jones and Miller, black cops in their mid-forties and veterans on the police force, had come knocking on her door with questions. Word had gotten out to them about her recent beef with Jamie, and they knew about the fight and the threats.

Pearla kept her cool. She talked to them with tears in her eyes, showing she was shocked and distraught about Jamie's death. They asked her the usual questions—Where was she on the night of the murder? She told them home, and she had her cousin willing to support her alibi.

They asked about her fight with Jamie. Pearla was honest and said it was over Jamie fucking her boyfriend. They continued questioning her, but she didn't crack. She answered all the detectives' questions like a professional liar. They didn't have any proof that she'd done it, so they went on their way with no new leads at all.

***

Pearla walked into the funeral home, and everyone she knew was there. She greeted a few friends, talked, and showed her sorrow. She didn't see Roark at the funeral. Pearla wondered why she wasn't there, but she didn't dwell on it. She walked into the room where Jamie's body was displayed in an open casket and broke down crying.

She then had the boldness to comfort Jamie's mother and sister seated in the front pew. "I'm so sorry," she said, tearing up again.

Jamie's mother held Pearla in her arms and cried too. She said to Pearla, "No matter if y'all were beefing or not, my daughter loved you like a sister, and y'all will always be close. I knew y'all beef wouldn't last long."

"I know. I'm gonna miss her so much."

"We all will."

Pearla showed out. Her tears were real, and so was her heartache. She had a hard time looking at Jamie lying in the cherry wood casket, dressed immaculately in a white dress. It was the perfect outfit for her funeral. She was as stylish in death as she was in life. The casket was inundated with flowers and pictures of a very beautiful woman, from adolescent to present. The family went all out for Jamie's funeral.

Pearla lingered around the family for a moment, and then she couldn't take it any longer. She gave her condolences and departed before the pastor got behind the podium to deliver the eulogy.

She jumped into her Benz and sped away. Too much was on her mind. Cash was coming home in a few weeks, and she felt undecided about it. He'd caused her to kill her best friend. She sped down Atlantic Avenue doing fifty and running through a red light like she was looking to get pulled over.

The tears welled up in her red, puffy eyes. She was really crying. She needed a momentary escape, somewhere far, to get her mind right.

A half-hour later, she pulled up to a lounge on Bedford Avenue and got out. The place was busy, packed with people mingling, drinking, and having a good time. She entered the place and caught a few looks. Pearla went straight for the bar and ordered some Pinot noir and sat at the counter, lost in thought.

After five minutes at the lounge, she heard someone standing closely behind her say, "You need some company, beautiful?"

Pearla was ready to tell him, "Fuck off!" but when she turned and saw it was Hassan, she was speechless. He was smiling her way, looking finer than ever in a black shirt that hugged his muscular physique and True Religion jeans.

"Hassan!"

"I'm glad to know you still remembered my name," he said coolly.

It was a shock to see him again, especially since she'd stopped there on impulse. Once again, Pearla couldn't help but think—Did she make a poor choice cutting off Hassan for Cash? He had more money and more class to him than Cash, but her heart wouldn't let Cash go.

"Can I buy you a drink?" he asked.

"You can."

He moved closer to her, brushing against her skin exposed by the black sleeveless dress she wore. He smelled so good. He called over the bartender and said to him, "Whatever she's drinking, it's on me."

The bartender nodded, and Pearla ordered another glass of Pinot noir.

Hassan pulled out a wad of hundred-dollar bills, placed a fifty on the bar top, and sat close to her. "So can I ask you a question?"

"You can."

"Why him over me?"

She smiled. "Are you jealous?"

"Honestly, I am."

"I heard you and Cash been competing against each other since grade school."

"The nigga doesn't have anything on me. I'm a Bentley, he's a Ford."

Pearla laughed. "It's always a who-has-the-bigger-dick contest."

"I really liked you, Pearla," Hassan said, the flame in his eyes burning heavily for her.

"You did?"

"I still do. I heard your boy is doing a few months on Rikers."

"The streets talk, huh?"

"Like Wendy Williams."

She chuckled and took a sip from her drink. The wine was smooth, but Hassan was even smoother. She gazed into his beautiful, dark eyes and was lost in his humorous and intellectual personality. She had a kingpin vying for her attention, and he was able to shower her with diamonds and gold. Still, she couldn't leave Cash—she loved him—but could she get even.

Hassan was sweet-talking in her ear, yearning to take her home with him. He made it clear to her, saying, "I wanna be with you tonight."

Pearla took a deep breath and drank more wine, entertaining the proposition.

Hassan placed his hand against her thigh while seated on the bar stool.

Pearla hadn't had dick in months, and her kitty cat needed playing with. With so much on her mind, she needed to exhale and release. She'd killed her best friend, smacked Roark around, her man cheated on her with her best friend, and she was sexually frustrated. Couldn't she have her fun, if only for one night?

She looked Hassan in his eyes. "I can't."

He was surprised by her response.

"I love him too much," she confessed.

"You do, huh?"

She nodded.

"Even though that nigga cheated on you with your best friend?"

Word had definitely gotten out. Cash had embarrassed her. She was becoming the talk of the town with his affair with Jamie, and now people were thinking she had lost her mind over that nigga.

"Maybe in a next life." Hassan politely excused himself.

"Maybe."

Pearla downed the rest of her drink and left the lounge. It had been a trying day. She got into the car and cried. Thinking about Cash coming home in a few weeks made her break down emotionally. She hadn't seen him since he admitted his infidelity with Jamie. The first thing she wanted to do when he got out was smack him as hard as she could and beat his ass. Then she wanted to fuck the shit out of him so he wouldn't even dream about cheating on her again.

TWENTY-TWO

"Free at last, free at last, thank God Almighty, I'm free at last!" Cash hollered lively as he stepped out of Rikers Island a free man.

Everyone looked at him. Cash didn't care who he offended or what people thought about him. He couldn't control himself. He felt like a bolt of energy, charged and ready to get live like a Jeezy concert. He felt good. There was so much to do, and he didn't know where to start. He jumped on the Rikers Island bus and expected Pearla to be across the bridge waiting for him in the parking lot.

The first thing on Cash's mind was pussy. It'd been a long, long six months, and he looked to jerking off to please himself and bust a nut. He couldn't wait to get his hands on the real thing. He was just hoping his girl wasn't still too upset about him and Jamie.

The cool October air made him realize how long he'd been inside. The leaves were changing colors. He'd missed out on the entire summer.

He rode in the back of the bus, thinking about his options. Being locked up was supposed to rehabilitate someone; make them learn their lesson and not do the crime again. Cash was the same criminal. He was ready to get back into action, being extra careful this time. Inside, he'd made some good connects that put him on how to get the cars he needed.

"Miami," Pablo had said to him.

"Miami?" Cash repeated.

"Miami, my friend. It's sweet down there. Business is good. There are a string of luxury cars all around for the easy pickings, not like New York. It's more relaxed down there, the weather is better, and with the right technique, you can come off good."

Pablo became a good friend to Cash. He was from Cuba, born and raised in Miami, and got knocked for cocaine possession in New York. He was looking at five years mandatory, but he still had his connections down in South Beach. He was handsome and suave, but behind the brown eyes and nice smile, it was easy to tell he was a gangster. He took a liking to Cash. Cash made him laugh, and they looked out for each other in jail.

Cash was ready to step up and make something happen for himself. Pearla was coming up, and he needed to come up right beside his baby. It would look bad if he didn't and was falling behind. Would she leave him if he couldn't pull his weight in the relationship?

The bus crossed over the Rikers Island Bridge and came to the first bus stop at the civilian parking lot. Cash stared out the window searching for his girlfriend. He yearned to see her again, grab her petite figure in his arms, kiss her passionately, and have some privacy with her.

He smiled seeing Pearla standing by her new S-Class Benz, looking like she was ready to model for a photo shoot. Clad in tight Balmain moto jeans, Prada wedge heels, and a butter-soft leather jacket, she looked beautiful.

"Oh shit!" he uttered. He was ready to leap off the bus and run toward her like a kid running to the gifts under the Christmas tree on Christmas morning. He was that excited.

The bus came to a stop, and Cash sprung off of it like a gazelle and moved in Pearla's direction. She smiled.

He smiled wider. "There go my baby," he hollered. He grabbed Pearla in his arms, hugged her enthusiastically, then swung her around in the parking lot.

While they kissed fervently, Cash ran his hands all over her body, squeezing her ass and ready to fondle her tits, not caring who was watching. He made it known that he wanted some ASAP.

"I want you so fuckin' bad right now," he whispered into her ear.

She giggled.

Cash had something to prove. He'd been in the shithouse ever since he'd come clean about Jamie.

Before he got into her Benz, he said, "Damn, baby! I see you been doin' big things since I've been locked down, huh? I like this." He moved his hand against the hood of the car and smiled like it was his.

When he climbed inside, he was even more impressed with the interior and dashboard. He couldn't wait to drive it. Cars like these turned him on. If he could, he was ready to fuck Pearla in the backseat and bless the car his own way.

During the drive home, he mentioned Miami to Pearla. He told her about his new friend Pablo and his new connect in South Beach.

"That is kind of far."

"When it comes to gettin' that paper, ain't no such thing as far."

"It's simple, baby. From what Pablo has been telling me, the dealerships down there have high-end cars out on the lots with only a chain keeping the riffraff out. I mean, cars are wide open down there. So I go to the dealership and convince the salesperson I'm legit, I can afford any car on the lot. I take it for a test-drive and, in the process, switch the real key. Later that night, I come back with the keys and drive the car off the lot."

Cash made it sound so simple. He was positive he could pull it off, but Pearla wasn't so sure. There had to be a catch.

He continued talking about the hustle.

Pearla had to trust her man, but she didn't want to see him get locked up again, especially in a different state. All she could say to him was, "Just be careful, baby. Florida is a whole new state. Different ball game."

"I know, babe, and I will."

Pearla raced her S-Class to their Brooklyn home. She had a nice surprise waiting for him once he walked through the doors of her expensive Brooklyn Heights home. Did he deserve it? Probably not. But she was loyal to her man and believed in giving him a second chance.

There was nothing like being home, and Pearla went all out for her man being released. Spread out on the living room couch was high-end clothing and over a dozen shoeboxes. She'd gone on a shopping spree and spent five grand shopping for him, so when he came home, he wouldn't look like a bum.

Cash smiled at the clothing and sneakers. He pulled Pearla into his arms, her back toward him, and couldn't resist filling his hands with her breasts and kissing her lovingly. "You're the best, baby," he said.

"And don't you ever forget."

Cash knew not to fuck with Pearla. He done seen the beast come out of her on a few occasions and knew she was nobody to play with. Her petite frame and prettiness had a lot of bitches and niggas fooled. She was gangster, and a stone-cold killer. Hearing how Jamie was murdered, it was hard to believe a woman like Pearla could pull it off.

Before long, the couple was groping each other, kissing, and ready for some hot and heavy action. Cash was so horny and so hard, his dick hurt, and Pearla was nearly naked.

"Let's go to the bedroom," she suggested, pulling at his shirt and leading him into the bedroom.

Cash felt he needed to make it up to her big time, so he got down on his knees and began kissing his way up Pearla's legs, spreading them. "I wanna taste you," he said.

She couldn't wait. She moaned from the sensation of his lips kissing the tender warm flesh between her legs. She leaned back, and he pulled her forward more, her ass on the edge of the bed.

Maneuvering her panties down her legs, Cash tossed them to the floor. He then wasted no time in diving in, eating her out like she was dessert.

"Ooooh! Ugh! Ooooh!" she cooed, feeling Cash's tongue lapping her pussy, licking, sucking, and feasting on her sexy ass. His tongue was in overdrive, licking his lady from her clit to her asshole and back again.

Pearla squirmed and moaned loudly. She was losing her mind. She grabbed Cash's head and held it to her pussy. She was chanting, moaning, and purring like a kitten. The way her man ate pussy, it should be a damn crime. She was grinding on his face, feeling her pussy being devoured like good cooked food. She couldn't take his wicked tongue, feeling her clit being licked and her pink walls being sucked.

One minute, she was telling him she was going to come, the next minute she was saying stop. Cash's oral action had her twisted and confused.

She bit down on her bottom lip and continued to squirm. "Fuck me!" she cried out.

Cash was ready to fuck Pearla like there was no tomorrow. He had been backed up for six months and needed to feel the real thing and release his semen into her.

"Fuck me," she pleaded. She wanted Cash to put his throbbing dick where his tongue had been moments earlier.

Cash climbed between her legs, his dick super hard, throbbing for some action. He penetrated her. She was tight and hot and wet. With her legs on his shoulders, he fucked her like a high-paid porn star. Cash tore it up from the back, the front, the side, and the middle. Then all of a sudden, he felt her tense up, he saw her eyes shut, and he heard her scream out, "Oh shit! Oh nooo! Oh shit! I'm fuckin' coming!"

Pearla was all over the place, spilling and pouring out her fluids all over the dick. With his dick buried deep inside her, and her muscles milking him, he felt her body tremble and her legs tense up.

Cash felt wave after wave of come shooting out of her pussy. He loved every minute of it. It was good sex—the best sex. Giving her good dick like this, she had to forgive him and forget. Cash didn't want her thinking about the past, so he fucked her so good, he wanted to give her amnesia.

Fifteen minutes later, they were fucking their brains out again.

✳✳✳

Cash's trip to Miami had been set. He had his airline ticket and his connections in South Beach. Pablo was a man of his word, and in return, Cash promised to hit him off with ten percent of the profits.

Prior to his departure for Miami, Cash and Pearla went on a shopping spree. He bought a few Tom Ford suits, some hard-bottom shoes, got a manicure and haircut, and a pair of expensive cuff links. He needed to look legit, not like a thug.

Pearla gave Cash a ride to JFK Airport in Queens. He came with only a carry-on. His flight was to depart in two hours. He looked so debonair in his expensive suit and hard-bottom shoes. He gave off the air of a serious businessman, no longer looking some playboy thug.

"How you feel?" she asked.

"I'm good."

"You'll be okay, baby."

He nodded. He'd never been on a plane before, so he was a little nervous. He took a deep breath and then leaned Pearla's way and gave her a long, passionate kiss good-bye. He stepped out of the car, removed his carry-on from the backseat, and walked into the airport with his ticket in one hand and his luggage in the next to board a nonstop JetBlue flight into Miami.

Several hours later, Cash's flight landed safely in Miami International Airport. Cash couldn't wait to get things started. Walking through the terminal, the first thing he did was get on his cell phone and connect with Pablo's people, who had made some arrangements for him.

The terminal in Miami was just as busy as JFK. Cash followed behind the crowd of arriving passengers toward the exit and into the streets. He was both excited and nervous about being in a different city. He'd spent his whole life in New York. Now he felt like someone different, moving among the crowd dressed in his suit and tie, looking like a businessman taking a business trip.

He stepped out of the terminal into the beautiful weather of Miami, a popular city within the Sunshine State, with its sandy beaches, ideal weather year round, alluring club life, and beautiful women.

He got into a cab and told the cabbie, "South Beach."

Twenty minutes later, he was checking into the Hilton in downtown Miami. Cash's hotel room was breathtaking, with a large overstuffed sofa, lovely accent furnishings, massive flat-screen TV, a marble bath featuring a deep soaker tub, and a panoramic view of the white coral sand beaches and the blue ocean water.

An hour after checking in, there was a knock at the door. Cash answered, and there stood a man—a handsome Cuban wearing khaki shorts, a T-shirt, and white loafers. He was bald, had thick eyebrows, and held a cigar. He looked like he could be related to Pablo.

"Cash, I presume?" he said.

"Yes."

"I'm Marc."

The two quickly got acquainted with each other, and Cash soon found himself involved in a major car theft operation. They sat out on the balcony drinking Bacardi and Coke and going over every minute detail of how the hustle would go down.

Marc explained it best when he said, "It's about supply and demand—give the customers what they want. And high-end luxury cars for a reasonable price is what they want."

First, Marc would walk on the lot of a dealership wearing suit and tie, making the salesperson believe he was going to buy a car. He'd take the car for a test-drive and get friendly with the salesperson. During the test-drive, he would subtly exchange the real key for a fake one and continue buttering up the dealer.

Dealerships in Miami were known for not securely locking up their cars. After closing time, they would come back with the real key during late-night hours and ride off into the dark with a stolen Maserati, Porsche, Lexus, or Range Rover. Then the car would get a new identity through vehicle identification number cloning. It was easy to go to any salvage yard for a VIN.

Marc talked with experience. He'd done it plenty of times, so his face was too recognizable in Miami. They needed new people with a fresh look.

He told Cash, "New car thieves use a key. If it's built by man, then it can be defeated by man."

Cash nodded.

Marc went on to explain to Cash that if they couldn't get the key from the dealer, they had to look into purchasing a transponder key programmer, which was able to make additional keys for a vehicle. They ranged in price from $7000 to $10,000, but it was easy to find a knock-off on the Internet for $150.

Cash was learning a whole lot. Technology was advancing on both sides, and he was ready to take advantage of it on the illicit side.

"We start tomorrow, so rest up and have some fun. This is Miami—beautiful women, beautiful nightlife," Marc said with a smile.

Club 01 on Ocean Drive was Cash's club of choice for the night. It was the place to be with seductive burgundy and a caramel-colored ceiling, huge leather chairs, a beautiful champagne bar with gemstone chandeliers, and an intimate dance floor.

He downed champagne and danced with beautiful and seductive-looking women most of the night. Then he saw her, looking stunning in a black halter dress, legs as long as a skyscraper, and looking voluptuous and ripe to eat. He offered to buy her a drink, and she accepted. Her name was Melanie.

Cash was once again falling victim to infidelity. He wanted to be faithful, but he was a creature of habit. He was butt naked on the balcony, fucking Melanie doggy-style, a condom tight around his dick.

Melanie's dress was on the floor, shoes kicked off in the corner, as she took his big dick with her legs spread wide. "Fuck me!" she cried out, curved over and gripping the railing to the balcony.

It was a beautiful night with the multihued skyline displayed in the background. Cash was deep in the pussy, grabbing her hips. He was enjoying the scenery, her lovely backside, and the kaleidoscope of bright colors in the distance. This was living for him. He could definitely get used to this.

When Cash was done busting a nut, he sent Melanie on her way. He needed his rest. Tomorrow would be a whole new ball game for him, and he was ready to step up to the plate and hit a home run.

***

Cash was busy throughout the day. He'd hired a car service with a driver once he was in Miami to take him around to the lots.

First, he visited Legend Nation on Southwest 8th Street. There, he took a Mercedes CLS for a test-drive. Mission accomplished. Then it was

Miami International Wholesale & Export on Northwest 7th Street, from which he took a Porsche for a test-drive. Then he test-drove a Jaguar from Miami Exotic Cars on Collins Avenue, a Lamborghini from Lamborghini Miami on Biscayne Boulevard, and a pearl-white Bentley from Brickell Luxury Motors on Southwest 8th Street.

After only three days in Miami, Cash had already gone through dozens of car dealerships and test-drove many cars, switching keys to almost a dozen. On his fourth and fifth days down there, his crew stole countless cars from the dealerships he had frequented.

Cash made close to seventy-five thousand dollars for his involvement— tax-free cash money. It was the most money he'd ever seen at one time in his entire life. He couldn't wait to call Pearla and tell her the good news.

TWENTY-THREE

In the past month and a half, Cash had been traveling back and forth from New York to Miami. He had his hustle down to a science. His business in Miami with Marc was going so well, he was able to purchase something nice for himself to drive around in—a midnight blue Porsche Cayman, a two-seat coupe. Cash fell in love with the car, which he drove around Brooklyn flaunting like a pretty new bitch on his arm.

With money to burn and feeling a good thing could never come to an end, Cash was on top of the world. Getting locked up and doing some time on Rikers Island was the best thing that had ever happened to him. Finally, he was able to hold his own and not depend on Pearla to do everything for him. He was right there by her side, making his ends by the thousands of dollars and feeling at home in New York and Miami.

While Cash was making a ton of paper in South Beach, his boys were becoming sour because they were still currently stealing low-end cars, and yet he didn't put them on to his hustle. Petey Jay, Manny, and Darrell felt Cash was being too greedy. He didn't want to share, and they wondered why. His excuse to them was, it was all Pearla's money he was spending, but they didn't believe him.

But there was one man Cash felt he needed to make amends with, and that was Perez. It still didn't sit right with him the way Pearla had reneged on their deal. Perez was a dangerous figure in the underworld. Cash was surprised that retribution for their betrayal hadn't happened yet. He never wanted to be in the crosshairs of a man like Perez.

Cash reached out to him, via a friend. He arrived at the chop shop in his Porsche and felt nervous like a long-tailed cat in a room filled with rocking chairs.

"From the sheep to the shepherd, I see," Perez said, entering the garage, staring intently at Cash.

"Hey, Perez," Cash said meekly.

Perez walked up to Cash and smiled. He looked past Cash and fixed his eyes on the Cayman. "I see you brought me a gift. I like it."

"It's not a gift, Perez. This me."

Perez chuckled. "This is you? I like this car."

Cash nodded.

"I see you came up. I've been hearing things about you out there, Cash, and obviously, the rumors are true."

Cash tossed Perez an envelope.

Perez caught it and looked at it confused. "And what's this?"

"It never sat right wit' me how Pearla dissed you out of your cut, but I never had the money to change it. So I'm here to make it right."

"You're here to make it right? That's what you're telling me?"

Cash nodded.

Perez peeped into the envelope and saw the money.

"It's seven grand, half of what we agreed upon," Cash said, feeling like he was doing a good thing.

Perez chuckled once again. It was a creepy laugh. He positioned himself closer to Cash and placed his arm around him. They both leaned against his Porsche. Cash couldn't help but feel a tinge of nervousness build up inside of him.

"You know, I thought about killing you and that bitch for y'all betrayal, but then, I changed my mind."

Cash took a deep breath.

"You wanna know why I changed my mind, Cash?"

Cash didn't respond right away. He stood still, feeling Perez's arm tighten around him. He then responded, "'Cuz you like us?"

Perez laughed. "You was always a funny dude, Cash. No, not because I liked you, but because I always found you useful. I knew one day you would become more of a benefit to me than a problem, and that day has come. You think you can just walk up into my shop, throw fuckin' peanuts at me after a few months, and everything's supposed to work out okay?"

"What is it that you want?" Cash asked, feeling the lump in his throat.

"Now that's the million-dollar question of the day. What is it that I want? I want in on what you have going on down in Miami. You think I wasn't going to find out?"

"What?"

"I hear good things about South Beach, and you owe me big time, Cash. In fact, you owe your fuckin' life."

"Perez, I'm just a small fish in a huge pond."

"So shrink the fuckin' pond. I want in, and I want you to get me in."

Cash didn't know what to say or do. There was no way he was going to allow Perez to come into something he'd started. It was his operation, his connect. Cash started thinking it was a mistake to show up in the first place.

"I expect to hear from you in a week, Cash, with the answer I expect. And if not, then I'm sorry to say, Cash, but this time, I will see you as a problem. I don't allow problems to linger around for too long."

The two men locked eyes. Cash had no words. He'd put himself in a dangerous predicament, and somehow he had to figure a way out.

He was about to get into his car, but then he heard Perez shout out, "No, leave the car. Let's just say you owe me interest, and blue is my favorite color."

Cash had no choice but to walk out of the shop with his tail between his legs. Perez had punked him—taken his Porsche *and* his dignity. But he wasn't about to allow him into his Miami scheme. He was making too much money. Cash knew he needed to do something before it was too late.

They were living like number one stunners—nice cars, money, jewelry, fancy clothing— and now they'd purchased their dream home in Jamaica Estates. Pearla had hustled all her life to end up living this way. The house came with hardwood flooring, granite countertops, crown moldings, ensuite master bedroom and Viking appliances. However, to put their home over the top, Pearla hired a contractor to add a Trex deck for entertaining and purchased an outdoor fireplace, lounge chairs, and a high-end grill for Cash to barbeque for their family and friends. Next Pearla went all out and hired an interior designer who furnished the home with designer furniture, Persian rugs, and expensive Parisian paintings. When the designer was through their home looked as if it belonged in a magazine. There was one last thing Pearla bought to add a personal touch, which was an outdoor bronze plaque that read: The House that Hustle Built, Circa 2014. When Cash came home and saw it he had a good laugh.

They toasted to their success and then fucked their brains out in each room, blessing the house with their love.

"We did it, baby," Cash said, smiling brightly.

"Yes, we did, and I'm proud of you, Cash. You stepped up like a man should."

Cash beamed. It felt good being praised by his queen.

"When do you head back to Miami?"

"In a few days."

Pearla nodded. One day, she planned on taking the trip with him into the Sunshine State to get some rest and relaxation, but at the moment, she was too busy to step away from anything. Everything needed her attention, and her girls needed her guidance. With the boosting, credit card scams, illegal marriages, a little bit of extortion, and her escort agency blossoming, she felt like Magic Johnson.

The investigation of Jamie's murder had reached a brick wall, and was becoming more of a cold case with every passing day.

As Cash shared an intimate moment with Pearla, Perez was in the back of his mind. He didn't tell Pearla about it, because he wanted to handle it on his own. Two weeks had passed since their meeting, and Cash had chosen to ignore the threat and take his chances.

Fuck it! After coming this far, he wasn't about to share or lose out on his money-making scheme. Getting Perez involved would only complicate and fuck things up.

As the two were about to soak themselves into the Jacuzzi and become intimate, Cash's cell phone rang. He sighed, wondering who could be calling him at night. He wanted to ignore it, but something in his gut made him answer the phone call.

"Who this?" he abruptly answered.

"This is Kings County Hospital," a woman's voice said on the other end. "Can I speak to a Cash Combs?"

Cash had no idea why Kings County Hospital was calling him, but he knew it couldn't be good news.

"Yeah, this is Cash."

"I'm calling on behalf of your father, Mr. Ray-Ray Combs," she said.

Cash clenched his cell phone tightly and braced himself for the bad news. "What about my father?" he asked, his voice cracking with worry.

Pearla listened in on the conversation and perked up, knowing something had happened. The look Cash had on his face made her move closer to him and be by his side.

"He was admitted this morning due to a heart attack, and he listed you as his next of kin," the woman explained.

"Heart attack?"

"Baby, is your father okay?" Pearla asked, concerned about Ray-Ray's well-being.

"Listen, I'm on my way."

Cash hung up and quickly got dressed, and he and Pearla were out the door in a heartbeat.

✳✳✳

Cash and Pearla charged into Kings County Hospital with worry and grief written all over their faces. Cash didn't know if his father was alive or dead. He headed to the emergency room and bombarded every hospital employee with questions about the whereabouts of his father. He was pointed to a back room and hurried to be with his old man.

Cash pushed open the door and saw his father lying on the gurney in a hospital gown, plugged to several machines, looking like a character straight out of *The Matrix*. He almost broke down seeing his father in that condition.

"What the fuck, Pop!" he hollered. Seeing Ray-Ray out of commission immediately brought tears to Cash's eyes. He loved his father, and not hearing the jokes, and not seeing the dancing and entertaining, made it feel like the world had stopped spinning.

Pearla was right with him, looking worried about the man too.

Ray-Ray was asleep, and Cash decided he was going to remain by his bedside until he woke up and saw a familiar, loving face in the room.

The next day, Cash was relieved to hear that his father had only had a minor heart attack, but due to his heavy drug use and drinking, he was in very bad shape. Doctors warned Cash that if his father continued with the drug use and reckless lifestyle he would be dead within a year.

When Ray-Ray woke up, the first thing Cash said to him was, "You tryin' to kill yourself, old man? Die on me and leave me here alone?"

Ray-Ray smiled. "Hey, if you gotta go, go with what you love doing."

Cash became serious. "Listen, doctors said you need to slow down or you'll die. I'm not arguing wit' you about this, Pop. When you get discharged, ya comin' to stay wit' me—I'm not having a debate about this. We got a new place and plenty of room."

Ray-Ray saw the look his son had in his eyes. "It's not like I have a choice, right?"

"You damn sure don't," Cash said.

"Okay, I just hope you have a small bar," Ray-Ray joked.

Cash knew his pops was impossible to get through to, and despite the doctor's warning, he wasn't going to ever quit drinking or using. He felt that if his father was closer to home, then he could be easily monitored.

As Cash talked to his father, his cell phone vibrated against his hip. He looked at the number and didn't recognize it. "Pop, I'll be right back."

Cash hurried out of the room and went into the street to answer the call. After he picked up, he heard Perez say, "Nigga, time's been up. You ignore me, so now you're a full-blown problem."

Click.

Cash stood there silently and motionless. There was no other way around it—He had to do the unthinkable. He'd killed before and was certain he could do it again.

Cash chain-smoked while seated behind the wheel of a dusty, beat-up stolen Ford that would be set on fire later on. He was lurking and watching Perez's chop shop like a hawk, the 9mm with the extended clip sitting in his lap.

His heart beat rapidly, and he was extremely nervous. Killing Perez was certain to come with repercussions because he was a connected man in the underworld.

But Cash's life was in danger. No question, Perez was going to kill him if he didn't act first, and there was no way he was about to share his Miami profits with anyone but Pablo. Cash thought he had been fair giving Perez what was owed to him, plus his Porsche. There was no way he was going to allow the nigga to keep digging into his pockets. He had to eat too.

Cash flicked his cigarette out of the window. He was ready. It was dark, and the street was quiet and still, and nobody was around. Adrenaline was pumping through him like gasoline. Once he did this, it would certainly create a domino effect.

Cash knew there were about five guys inside the place. Would he have to murder them too? Probably so, if they got in his way. He pushed the door open and stepped out of the car, which was parked a half block away. He was hyped. He wore dark clothing, black boots, and he wore gloves to cover his prints.

He began marching toward the shop with the gun in his hand. If he died tonight, then at least he went out trying. He didn't want to think about Pearla or his father. He kept his mind blank. He didn't want to back out of it, knowing if he did, he was a dead man anyway.

He marched closer ready to play the Terminator—Kill anything moving. As he moved closer, all of a sudden flashing blue and red lights came out of nowhere and rained down on the shop like a heavy thunderstorm.

Cash froze up as marked and unmarked police cars raced by him and came to a screeching halt in front of Perez's chop shop. Then a swarm of police officers and detectives raided the place.

"Oh shit!" Cash looked on in shock at the action.

The cops kicked in the door and charged inside like a swarm of bees attacking.

Cash kept his cool and little by little backed away from the area. Slowly, he went back to the Ford and got back inside. "That was close," he said to himself. If he had gone in a few minutes earlier, he would have been fucked. Fate was definitely on his side.

Cash sat slumped behind the wheel and observed the authorities haul off Perez and his crew in handcuffs. Perez could be seen cursing and shouting. He didn't look too pleased with his sudden arrest. Cash smirked. It was a miracle. Tonight, Perez met with an arrest instead of death. Cash felt like he could continue his life in peace without having to worry about any interruptions.

TWENTY-FOUR

Pearla stepped out of her baby-blue Bentley and stared at her mother's place. She was a changed woman—a whole new bad bitch. She had grown a lot since her mother had kicked her out. Pearla didn't harbor any hard feelings toward Poochie. What's done was done. All her mother did was harden her. If it wasn't for Poochie, then she probably wouldn't have been the sharp, calculating edgy bitch she had become.

Poochie had reached out to her a few days earlier, claiming she wanted to make amends and let bygones be bygones. The real truth was, Poochie had lost her job as a corrections officer for having an inappropriate affair with one of the male inmates. Word had gotten out via an inmate snitching, and the department did a thorough investigation on Poochie. She lost her job, her pension, everything. Down and out, she had no choice but to reach out to her daughter looking for forgiveness, especially since she had heard good things about Pearla.

Dressed for the cold wearing designer jeans, a short mink coat, and her Manolo Blahnik boots, Pearla looked like she was ready to star in a movie. She walked up the steps to the front porch and rang the bell. Pearla didn't really want to be at her mother's place, but she came anyway.

A short moment later, she heard Poochie ask, "Who?"

"It's me, Poochie. Pearla."

She heard the door being unlocked and opened up. Poochie came into her view and smiled. Poochie rarely smiled.

Life must be beating down hard on her, Pearla thought.

"Come inside," Poochie said, sounding humble.

Pearla walked inside and the place was a mess—a fucking pigsty. There was a week of dirty dishes in the sink, clothes were everywhere, the trash hadn't been taken out, and remnants of fast food, weed, and liquor were everywhere.

"Damn! Don't you clean?"

"I haven't had the time," Poochie responded civilly for once.

Pearla didn't understand how a woman with no job didn't have the time to clean her own place, but she didn't gripe because she didn't live there anymore.

Poochie was never the one to beat around the bush, so she pushed some clothes aside on the couch and took a seat in front of her daughter.

Pearla chose to stand, since she wasn't staying long.

"I need a favor."

"Of course," Pearla replied, looking at her mother smugly. "How much do you need?"

"Just a few thousand, something to get me back on my feet while I look for a new job."

"A few thousand? I need a number, Poochie."

"Ten thousand should do."

"Ten thousand?" Pearla chuckled at the request. "You want to borrow money from me, but not give me so much as a fuckin' apology for all the shit you put me through?"

Poochie looked like she wanted to put her head in the dirt and hide. Everything was coming back on her. She looked Pearla directly in the eyes and said reflectively, "I'm sorry."

Pearla didn't give a fuck about her mother's apology. It was the past.

Her sole focus was the present and toward the future. She planned on giving Poochie the ten grand, but her mother was going to owe her. She figured her mother could be very useful in an area she was weak at.

Pearla reached into her mink coat pocket, pulled out a wad of money, and tossed her mother five thousand dollars. "That's all I have on me for now. I'll give you the rest later."

With the cash in her hands, Poochie smiled.

"You owe me, Poochie. And I want you to come work for me."

"Doing what?"

"Never mind the questions," Pearla said sternly. "At ten thousand, I run the show."

Poochie couldn't say a word. She could only sit in her messy home and allow her daughter to talk to her a certain way. The shoe was now on the other foot, and she had to swallow anything arrogant that wanted to come out of her mouth.

Pearla pivoted on her boots and made her exit with a heavy smirk on her face. Her mother definitely could be put to good use in her organization, from the prostitution ring to being a strong voice for her with the bitches she ran.

Pearla climbed into her Bentley and drove away, feeling the heavens smiling down on her.

TWENTY-FIVE

To business, Cash," Marc toasted with a smile.

"To business," Cash repeated, his flute glass filled with champagne and raised Marc's way.

They were in the VIP section of Club Klutch on Collins Avenue. It was a City Tower Entertainment club, a scenic 26,000-square-foot nightclub with vibrant colors and a large dance floor along with many VIP nooks.

Cash loved Miami. He had gotten used to the city, the nightlife, the money, and definitely the women. It'd been months since he started boosting cars from the dealerships and then it grew into other areas, different ventures he undertook with Marc. Together, it felt like they could take over Miami. When he stayed in Miami, he lived in five-star hotels and drove around in high-end cars, flaunting a wad of cash. With Marc treating him like a brother, his name started ringing out, and he enjoyed the perks that came with being good friends with Marc.

"Business is good," Cash said.

"It is," Marc replied.

The music was blaring, and the club was packed with revelers. Nights in Miami felt like paradise with exotic-looking women and luxury cars. Cash planted his eyes on every beautiful woman in the club. He easily had his pick of any bitch. Every trip he took there, he enjoyed the company of a beautiful woman in his hotel suite, sometimes indulging in threesomes, and even a foursome. He loved Pearla, but his money and power was fueling his appetite for sex.

The more money Pearla and Cash made, the more they wanted. They were becoming greedy, mixing business with pleasure and venturing out into uncharted territory. Their illicit businesses were growing rapidly. They had a nice home, no kids and were under twenty-five, and they had lots of money, but weren't saving any money for a rainy day. All they did was make money and spend it.

Cash continued talking to Marc.

"Cash, when you get the chance, I want to pull your coat to something," said Marc.

"What is it?" Cash asked.

"Not now, sometime later. Tonight, we party and we have some fun."

"You know I ain't got a problem with that." Cash grinned. He poured more champagne and downed it like it was water. He trusted Marc. Cash felt there wasn't anything that could go wrong.

They had the best stuff on their table: Cristal, Rosé, and Moët.

The DJ continually shouted them out inside the club, making the ladies look their way with their flirtatious smiles and come-fuck-me look shimmering in their eyes. Cash was ready to make his pick for the night. He wanted the best bitch in the club to suck his dick and throw her legs back. He was ready to fuck all night.

He poured another glass into his flute and looked around the club. He looked mature and distinguished in his silk shirt and black slacks, platinum cuff links, and diamond-encrusted pinky ring. In Miami, he felt like a different man every time.

"I'll be in the bathroom. This champagne feels like it's going right through me," Marc said.

Marc walked away, leaving Cash alone, looking around, and prowling for something or someone to get into. Then he saw her, standing five four, with skin the color of bronze and almond-shaped eyes that danced with the light. She was so beautiful.

"Shit!"

Her beauty, captivated by the sexy pout and the shiny lipgloss that accentuated the most perfect smile he'd ever seen, hypnotized Cash. She wore a sexy, tight top that showed off her voluptuous cleavage and a long skirt that went to the floor and hugged her undeniably round bottom and full hips. She was just blessed with the curves in all the right places.

Cash immediately had to meet this woman and get to know her. She happened to look his way, and they quickly exchanged glances. He didn't hesitate to introduce himself to her. She walked to the bar, and Cash followed her.

Before she could order her drink, Cash intervened, saying, "You are the most beautiful woman I've ever seen. Whatever you're drinking, it's on my tab."

She smiled. Then her full, sensual lips parted to respond with, "Oh really?"

"Yes."

"I'm an expensive girl."

"I have very expensive taste," he countered.

She smiled and laughed.

"What is your name?" he asked.

"Alisha."

"Lovely name for a lovely-looking lady."

She smiled again.

He quickly got acquainted with Alisha. She was from Miami, was 22, and a college student. She had no boyfriend, but Cash didn't care if she had one anyway. She had to be his.

Cash's entire head slipped between the tight opening of her nether lips, and the gripping walls of silky smooth muscles, moistened with her juices, instantly surrounded his dick. Alisha had that good, gushy pussy, and after three hours of meeting, he was stroking himself deep inside of her as her arms and legs gripped him tighter.

"Yes," she grunted, "Fuck me!" feeling Cash's dick sink into her.

Her pussy started sucking as the walls inside rubbed him in a way he'd never felt before. They pulsated like they were trying to pull his dick farther in.

Cash cooed and grunted, fucking Alisha missionary, loving every second he was inside of her. With such pleasures coursing along his dick, his eyes rolled into the back of his head. He tried to pull back, but the opening of her pussy gripped his hard shaft so tight, his mushroom dick head was hard to pull out.

"Ooooh shit!" he howled out.

Her walls were milking his dick crazily. Her lips began kissing and sucking on his neck, her teeth nibbling on his neck. Her pussy gripping and trying to pull Cash in deeper was impossible for him to resist.

He glided his hard dick deeper into the warm wet heat of Alisha's sex. When he came, it was so intense, it felt like his explosion ripped through the condom and splashed inside of her. But it didn't.

Cash rolled off Alisha's sweaty body and collapsed on his back. He was in a zone. He huffed and puffed, collecting himself.

It was official. Cash had found his new side-bitch down in Miami. She had some of the best pussy he'd ever had, and there was no way he wasn't about to come back for more. If they could put a price on pussy, her shit would be priceless.

Alisha started to kiss Cash all over, seducing him again, and then she whispered into his ear, "I hear you do big things, Cash."

"Yeah, I do. Why?"

Alisha didn't answer him. She simply smiled and relaxed in his well-defined arms.

Pearla stepped out of the shower and quickly toweled off. It was a cold January night, and Cash was away in sunny Miami. She sighed with envy. Though she grew up in the cold weather, she hated it.

She had to let go of her boosting business and credit card scams. They were becoming too risky, and the risk was no longer worth the reward. She only concentrated on the green card marriages, and that had steadily transitioned into a profitable escort service, called Pink & Neat. It was catching on discreetly via the Internet and word of mouth. She operated it like it was a modeling agency. Pearla had beautiful women lined up for men willing to pay handsomely for her ladies' time—two thousand dollars an hour.

She had girls like Brandy from the Dominican Republican; Paquitta from Kingston, Jamaica; Isabelle and Gabriella, sisters from Italy; Angelina, Cassandra, Kiara, and Danielle, all from the States; and Farrah, a Bajan.

Pearla had a new crew of friends, and she was tricking on them lovely. She loved being the boss, and she wasn't shy when it came to treating her girls fairly and looking out for them, which included shopping sprees all over the city and fine dining in top-notch restaurants like Nobu and Philippe Chow with Pearla always picking up the tab. But her finest moment was when she took her girls on an all-expenses-paid weekend getaway to Turks and Caicos.

Vacationing there, the girls experienced the pristine white sand beaches that bordered the breathtaking turquoise ocean. It provided an extraordinary milieu at their luxury hotel villa, and the restaurants on the island were exquisite.

Pearla learned quickly that if you give your employees incentives then they would feel appreciated, but if you gave them too much then they'd start to feel entitled.

✳✳✳

Pearla almost tripped over a pile of clothes left in the hallway. "Fuck!" She knew there were only two people who could be so damn messy in her home, and she was getting fed up with it.

Not only was Cash's father staying with them, but so was Momma Jones. She was against it, but Cash argued her down, griping that he needed to take care of his parents. With the two of them in her home, it felt like complete chaos.

Ray-Ray was cool, even though every night he would pass out drunk on their floor or their couch. But Momma Jones was constantly a loudmouth and utterly disrespectful toward Pearla, and the two got into loud arguments all the time. Momma Jones was secretly jealous of the gorgeous young woman and wasn't about to play nice to someone she considered a bitch, though she was staying in her home.

Pearla started to walk to her bedroom. The minute she got dressed, she was about to take up the issue of her home being left untidy with Cash's parents. As she walked to her bedroom, Momma Jones's bedroom door opened up, and a completely naked stranger exited the bedroom.

"What the fuck?" Pearla was in complete shock.

"Ay, what up, pretty?" the man said to her, smiling. He had no shame in his game, dick out and swinging, scratching his ass while he made his way toward the bathroom.

Pearla was fuming. It wasn't the first time she had woken up or arrived home to find a strange man in her house, thanks to Cash's whore of a mom.

"Get the fuck out my house!" Pearla shouted.

The man gazed at her like she was retarded. "Ya house?"

"Oh, you think I'm fuckin' playing?" Pearla screamed out.

She rushed to her bedroom, knowing she could show him better than she could tell him. Still wrapped in her towel, she snatched open her bedroom dresser, grabbed a snub-nose revolver, and charged back out of her room to confront the naked stranger.

She kicked open the bathroom door and fired a shot at his ass. The bullet struck the wall behind him as he sat on her toilet trying to take a shit. She'd missed him on purpose.

The man was suddenly terrified. "What the fuck! You crazy, bitch!" he yelled. He fell off the toilet looking traumatized.

Pearla aimed the firearm at him again and sternly warned him to leave. She gave him five minutes. He hurried out of the bathroom, ran into Momma Jones's bedroom, hastily grabbed all his things, and ran out of the house like it was about to collapse.

Now that he was gone, Pearla went to confront Momma Jones. She wasn't as scared with a gun in her face as her last trick was.

"I told you to stop bringing these niggas into my fuckin' house!" Pearla shouted heatedly.

"Bitch, you better get that fuckin' gun out my face."

The two got into a heated argument, but Pearla had someone for her. With Cash away in Miami, she decided to call up Poochie, who was hired so Pearla didn't have to get her hands dirty.

When Poochie got the call from her daughter, she rushed to her home.

There was no time wasted between Poochie and Momma Jones. They were both hard and belligerent ladies from the streets. Poochie got into Momma Jones's face, but Momma Jones wasn't intimidated. Harsh words were exchanged, and a fight quickly ensued between the two ladies. It was like a hurricane clashing with a tornado. They quickly turned her living room into a mess—broken chairs, overturned furniture, and shattered glass all over the floor.

Ray-Ray attempted to break it up, but he was overpowered and tossed around.

It got to the point where Pearla threatened to call 9-1-1. In her neighborhood, they would have showed up in a heartbeat and arrested both women. Momma Jones and Poochie had their bruises and bloody lips, but if Pearla had to play referee then Poochie clearly out-boxed the crackhead. Although it clearly wasn't over between them.

When Pearla called Cash to tell him what happened, he laughed it off.

"You actually put them two ladies in one room together?" he said, teasing.

"It's not fuckin' funny, Cash. Your mother needs to go now before I kill that bitch!"

"A'ight, baby, when I get home, I'll handle it."

"When are you coming home?"

"The day after tomorrow. I still got some more business to handle, and then I'm on the first flight back to New York."

"Hurry up, baby. I miss you."

"I miss you too."

After getting off the phone, Pearla looked deep in thought about something. *Did he go down there just for business, or did he mix some pleasure in it too?* She already had to kill one bitch because of Cash's infidelity. The next time around, she would kill him and the bitch he was with. She hated when niggas fucked with her heart, because she was a loyal bitch. Cash was her heart, so she had no reason to creep out on a nigga. If she didn't do it with Hassan while Cash was locked down, she wasn't about to do it now. She wanted the same respect and loyalty she constantly showed her man.

TWENTY-SIX

Cash landed in JFK Airport Monday afternoon, strolled out of the terminal with his carry-on, and quickly caught an idling cab outside. It was freezing cold in New York. The temperature was a shivering twenty-five degrees with snow predicted later that night. Cash went from sunshine to frostbite. He so badly wanted to jump back on the plane and fly down to Miami, but his queen was calling, and he needed to see what was going on.

Wrapped snugly in his winter coat, ski hat, and Timberlands, he jumped into the backseat of a yellow cab, told the driver, "Jamaica Estates," and then closed his eyes and thought about what Petey Jay had been calling him about since he'd been in Miami. For more than a week now, Petey Jay had been in his ear about selling cocaine. Petey Jay was sure they could make a boat-load of money. The idea caught Cash's attention.

What he had going on down in Miami was good, but learning from the best, his queen Pearla, Cash knew to never have all his eggs in one basket and to put his hands into other money-making areas as well.

As he was being driven to his home, he got on his cell phone and dialed Petey Jay's number. It'd been months since he'd hung out with his former crew. Things done changed. He got rich, they didn't. There was some tension between his crew, but when it came to money, Cash was listening. He wanted to help out his friends, because his conscience was on his back, and Petey Jay had always looked out for him.

"What's good, Cash?" Petey Jay answered.

"I'm back in New York. Let's link up."

"When and where?"

"Tonight. I'll come by your place so we can talk."

"A'ight, my nigga," Petey Jay said coolly. "I'll be waiting."

Cash hung up. The first thing he wanted to do was get some sleep and then handle his business. He was exhausted. Jetlag was killing him, though he was still in the same time zone.

When he arrived home, Momma Jones wasn't there, Ray-Ray was sleeping on the couch, and Pearla was in their bedroom.

Hearing the door shut downstairs, Pearla immediately knew it was Cash arriving home. She hurried down the stairs to be with him. Seeing Cash, she lit up like Con Edison. She ran over and leaped into his arms, yelling out, "I missed you, baby!"

Cash held her in his arms as she straddled him. Sometimes, Pearla could be like a big kid, playing around and sounding girlie on him. They kissed passionately.

Cash felt on her booty and said, "I'm so tired, baby." He carried her upstairs into the bedroom and undressed.

Pearla missed everything about him, from his humorous personality, to his hardcore sex. She was longing for some dick inside of her.

"Oh, I forgot to mention, I gotta run out tonight, handle some business," he said.

"Tonight? But you just got back, baby."

"I know, but this is important. Money never stops. Right, babe?"

She smiled. "Right."

They kissed again. Pearla didn't hesitate to take his dick into her mouth. He got thicker and harder in her mouth, fucking her mouth more, until the head of his penis was pounding her throat.

Cash moaned. It was the best welcome-home greeting. He laid back and allowed Pearla to do her thing. The way she sucked his dick was a pure indication of how much she missed him. Her sex put him to sleep a half-hour after his arrival.

While Cash was in la-la land, Pearla carefully went through his things to find out if her man was doing dirt down in Miami, but she didn't find anything. Either he was being true to her, or he was careful at covering his tracks.

✳✳✳

After five hours of sleep, Cash was over at Petey Jay's place to talk about business. He walked inside his friend's apartment with his Rolex and diamond pinky ring shimmering like sunlight was in the room. It was only the two of them.

"I see you shining, my nigga," Petey Jay said, his eyes fixated on his friend's jewelry.

"You know I'm tryin' to do my thang."

"Shit. My nigga, we all tryin' to eat. You feel me?"

"I feel you."

"Then let's talk," Petey Jay said.

Cash took a seat and popped open a beer while Petey Jay went into talking about the drug business. Petey Jay needed Cash to become his financial backer for the first batch of cocaine he wanted to purchase from some Colombians out of Washington Heights.

"I got this connect, Cash, and they legit."

"How legit? And how well you know these people, Petey Jay?"

"Well enough to know they making a shitload of money, and I wouldn't be talkin' to you about this if I wasn't sure, Cash. But I'm so sure about this deal, I bet my kids' life."

Cash grasped that Petey Jay loved his kids and would never put them on the line if he wasn't super sure about it all.

"You don't even have to get your hands dirty, Cash. All you need to do is supply the paper, and I'm the only one you'll have to deal wit', while me, Darrell, and Manny do everything else."

"How much you talkin' about?"

"About three hundred and seventy thousand."

Cash whistled at the estimate. "That's a lot of money, Petey Jay."

"I know, but think about the return that will come your way when we flip these birds and start making major moves, my nigga. I promise you five hundred thousand which includes interest within ninety days."

Cash sat back against the couch leery about it all. Three hundred and seventy thousand dollars was a lot of money to give out, even when it came to a drug deal. But the opportunity to make a huge profit without risking his own safety was tantalizing.

Cash looked at his friend, took a deep breath, and said, "A'ight, I'm in."

"My nigga," Petey Jay responded excitedly, glad-handing with Cash.

"But, Petey Jay, don't fuck me on this," Cash said in a stern tone. "I'm trusting you wit' a lot of fuckin' money."

"You my nigga, Cash, and believe me, I ain't gonna burn you."

The next day, while Pearla was out on business, Cash almost emptied out all of their money from their concealed safe in the bedroom of their home.

TWENTY-SEVEN

Cash and Pearla were spending money like it was water. Whatever money could buy, they had it. Wherever money could take them, they went, and whoever it could corrupt, they corrupted. Growing up, they'd never had it like that, and since they didn't work hard for it, they didn't have a clue what money management or saving for a rainy day meant. With the escort and green card marriage business, the stolen cars in Miami, and a few minor investments, how could the money stop?

The sudden letter from the IRS was the start of a storm coming the couple's way. Pearla was being audited. She had no idea why. The IRS was going to audit her income for the past three years. She'd never filed taxes. It was a stupid mistake, and she was bugging out.

How could this happen?

She stared at the letter over and over again. They were coming for her. She looked to her moms and even Cash for help or support, but they were stumped too. No one had any answers as to why the IRS had a sudden interest in her.

There was a number she could call, and she called it. A man answered, and Pearla bombarded him with many questions about the letter she'd received in the mail.

"Why the fuck did I get this letter? Why am I being audited? What the fuck is going on?" she said through the phone.

"Ma'am, I'm going to need you to calm down," the IRS employee composedly said to her.

Pearla took a deep breath.

"Now, I need your name and social security number," he said.

Pearla gave her name and social security number. She could hear the man stroking the keys to the keyboard.

"Well, listen, our records show you haven't paid any taxes at all, and that you have assets but no reporting income."

"What? So what does that mean? Why the fuck y'all in my business?"

"Ma'am, you can't be that naïve," he returned rudely.

"Don't patronize me."

"It will behoove you to follow the instructions in the letter and come as scheduled. Ma'am, don't make it worse for yourself."

"Fuck you very much!" Pearla cursed loudly and hung up.

The phone call spooked her. She looked at the letter again and read it aloud, "Your rights during an audit: A right to a professional and courteous treatment by IRS employees."

The man she spoken with was a direct contrast to that.

"A right to privacy and confidentiality about tax matters;

A right to know why the IRS is asking for information, how the IRS will use it, and what will happen if the requested information is not provided;

A right to representation, by oneself or an authorized representative;

A right to appeal disagreements, both within the IRS and before the courts."

Pearla focused on the last one. Hell yeah, she wanted appeal it, because she disagreed with it completely.

Pearla looked stressed for a moment. Cash wrapped his arms around her. "Listen, don't worry about it. You're smart, baby, and there's always a way around something. We're gonna figure it out."

She broke into a smile, pushing the anxiety to the back of her mind.

With all that was going on, Cash decided to take his woman out to dinner at a nice, Manhattan restaurant. They decided to go to Eleven Madison Park, the restaurant bearing the name of its address. It was an elegant place with two balcony-level private dining rooms overlooking the main dining room, and offering a picturesque view of Madison Square Park through floor-to-ceiling windows. They were dressed to the nines and enjoying what life had to offer them.

Cash and Pearla both had the New York strip with Kinkead's scotch whisky sauce and two glasses of Pinot noir. The food was delicious. They sat by the wall-to-ceiling windows and took in a wintry view of the park.

Cash wanted Pearla to forget about her troubles with the IRS, so he figured a beautiful night out in the city would help. He owed it to her. For weeks, they'd been so busy.

For a moment, they talked and laughed.

Then Pearla gazed at Cash like he had a disease. They had been together going on nine months and it felt like a lifetime for her. She sat her glass down in front of her and continued looking at her man. She then held up her left hand and showed him the diamond engagement ring, something he'd seen so many times.

"You see this?" she said, referring to her ring. "This means a lot to me, Cash. Even though I bought it myself, it's a symbol of our love."

"I know, babe," Cash blurted out.

"Do you?"

"I love you, Pearla. I never loved a woman like I love you, babe. What we built together, what we created, this is only the beginning."

"It is."

Pearla took another sip of wine and then suddenly confessed to him about killing Jamie. "She was my friend. But I killed her because I was jealous. I was thinking that she was going to take you away from me.

"I stalked her, and then got her when she was alone and vulnerable, and when I plunged that knife into her stomach, I felt relieved, because she was no longer a threat to me . . . to us and our relationship. I killed her because I love you so much."

Cash looked around to see if anyone was listening, or eavesdropping on their conversation, but no one was. It was like she was looking to get caught by confessing to him so suddenly in a public place.

"You did what you had to do," he coldly replied.

Cash wanted their past to stay the past. Bringing up Jamie's death was risky. He killed, she killed, and their bond was solidified with deadly secrets. He loved her, and with Pearla by his side, he felt they could do anything, achieve anything.

"I don't want to ever feel like that again, Cash. I don't want to share you with anyone. Do you understand me?" Pearla said in a stern tone.

"Yeah, I understand."

"That feeling I felt when I found out about you and Jamie, it almost drove me insane. I don't want to ever lose you, not to another bitch or to these streets."

Cash reached across the table and took her hand into his. "And you won't lose me," he said. "I promise."

"I better not," she replied coolly.

While talking to Pearla, Cash thought about Alisha. She had texted him from Miami asking when she was going to see him again. Cash knew he had to be careful, because the way Pearla was talking, she was indicating implementing some biblical shit.

"I have to fly down to Miami again in a few days. Marc hit me up, more business to take care of."

"Just when you're down there, think of me," she said simply and then smiled.

"I will."

✳✳✳

Cash landed in sunny Miami in the middle of the afternoon and moved through the busy terminal like he was on a mission. Marc had texted him and said he needed to see him. It was an emergency. Marc couldn't go into details, and that worried Cash. So many questions flooded his mind. He was nervous, but it didn't show on his face. He was confident that everything was okay.

The minute he stepped off the plane, he texted Pearla letting her know that he landed safely.

Alisha had also texted him, yearning to see him too.

With his carry-on slung over his shoulder, Cash walked outside and saw Alisha parked outside the terminal in her convertible coupe, smiling ear to ear when she saw Cash exiting the terminal. She hopped out of the car and hurried in his direction, throwing herself into his arms, excited that he was back in Miami. They hugged and kissed.

"I missed you, baby," she said to him.

"I missed you too."

Alisha grabbed his crotch. She didn't care who was watching. "You wanna go play right now?"

He smiled. "Business first."

Cash tossed his bag into the backseat.

"You drive," Alisha suggested.

Cash jumped behind the steering wheel and drove off.

Leaving the airport, he got on his cell phone to call Marc. His call went straight to voice mail. He lit a cigarette and jumped on the Dolphin

Expressway doing seventy, headed to the Hilton Hotel in South Beach. With Marc's call continuing to go to voice mail, he decided to spend his time with Alisha.

Moving toward the city, Alisha smiled and did the predictable, leaning into his lap and undoing his zipper.

"What you doing?" Cash asked, looking shocked when he shouldn't.

"I wanna taste you."

She gripped his dick, sliding her hand up and down it, causing a moan to escape from his lips. Then she threw it into her mouth, down her throat and gulped him down like a good, tasty drink.

With one hand on the steering wheel and the other pushing the back of Alisha's head to deep-throat him, Cash swerved a little on the expressway but quickly regained control of the car. Alisha's head game was fierce, matching his fiancée's.

"Damn, love, you tryin' to make a nigga crash," he joked.

With her glossy lips wrapped around his cock and feeling the speed of the car moving on the expressway, Cash was about to explode inside her mouth when suddenly his cell phone rang. He didn't want to answer it, but the caller ID showed it was Marc calling him back.

His breathing was ragged when he answered, "Marc. What's good?"

"Where are you?" Marc asked.

"I landed an hour ago. I'm driving toward South Beach now."

"I need you to meet me."

"Where?"

"Everything all right?"

"Yeah, ugh, everything good," Cash replied.

Alisha was still sucking his dick, her head bobbing up and down in his lap. He tried to conduct a normal conversation with his friend, but with her full lips sucking him crazily, he almost wanted to pull to the side and deflate.

"Cash, meet me at the bar near the American Airlines Arena in an hour."

"A'ight. Marc, is everything okay?"

"Yeah, everything's cool."

"Then why the emergency text?"

"I'll tell you when I see you, Cash."

"A'ight."

Cash hung up and hurried toward his favorite hotel in Miami. Alisha was determined to finish him off as he drove. She was a freak bitch and wanted to take advantage of the full hour they had before his meeting with Marc.

Within the hour, Cash checked into the luxurious Hilton in the South Beach area, fucked Alisha quickly, unpacked, and hurried out the room, his freak bitch following right behind him.

He jumped into her convertible and hurried toward Port Boulevard.

Marc wanted to meet at the Largo Bar and Grill, across the street from the arena, located in the heart of downtown Miami.

Cash pulled up to the area with Alisha and looked around. The area was teeming with people drinking and mingling, everyone having a good time. The Miami Heat were scheduled to play the Knicks in a few hours, so the area was flooded with people and activity. Every bar and lounge was busy.

"Stay here," he told Alisha.

She nodded. "Don't take long, because we still gotta do round two."

Cash grinned. He got out of the car and walked toward the destination. His eyes searched for Marc. He saw him seated near the railing, overlooking the bay waters, with yachts and boats docked all around.

He went over to Marc, seated alone and looking aloof from everything happening around him. He took a seat at the table with Marc and asked, "What's goin' on? Why we meeting here?"

"I wanted to kick it, you know, catch up before we go out and steal more cars." Marc's voice was a bit louder than Cash thought necessary. He looked around and smirked.

Marc kept talking. "So, how was your flight?"

"Long." Cash was irritated but couldn't quite put his finger on why.

"Yo, how much did you get for that Maserati that you stole from Exotic Cars of Collins a couple weeks back?"

"Maserati? You got me mixed up, son. I don't boost cars."

"Nigga, what you smoking?" Marc tried to relax, but his bottom lip was trembling. "This me you talking to. I just need to know how much you got for it 'cause I'ma cop me one and sell it to this cat in Houston."

Cash was deadpan. "Muthafucka I ain't smokin' shit. I just said I ain't boost no car, therefore I can't sell what I don't have. I came out here to see my girl and have a good time. End of story."

Cash could see that Marc was frustrated by his answers. Then out of the blue, he saw them swarming in around him, local police and federal agents charging his way with their guns drawn and shouting, "Get down! Get down now!"

People in the area quickly moved away from the trouble after seeing chaos ensue. Cash was utterly shocked. Over a dozen Miami PD officers and agents came rushing his way like he was Tony Montana in *Scarface*. Surrounded and outnumbered by law enforcement, he had nowhere to go. It was obvious that Marc had set him up.

He was thrown to the ground and handcuffed in front of the public, feeling like he was in some crazy public exhibition.

"Officer, why am I being arrested? I ain't do shit." Cash tried to remain calm, but he was nervous.

"We don't need your admission, asshole, we got you on surveillance tape!"

Being dragged off the ground with his arms cuffed behind him, he glared at Marc, knowing he was a snitch. "Why?" Cash asked through clenched teeth.

"It's a dog-eat-dog world, Cash, and I'm sorry. I didn't have a choice."

"Fuck you!" Cash growled, wishing he could break the man's neck.

Cash knew his arrest in Miami was going to break Pearla's heart. He felt ashamed. He was ushered to a marked police car with his head down and they shoved him into the backseat.

When Alisha saw who they'd arrested, she leaped from her car and ran over to Cash and the officers. "Baby, what's going on?" she hollered.

"Just keep cool, baby," he said. "Everything's under control."

TWENTY-EIGHT

Hearing about Cash's arrest in Miami made Pearla cry and cry. She couldn't lose him, especially in a state so far away. Seeing it was his second arrest, there was no telling what the consequences would be this time. She had no other choice but to go down to Miami as soon as possible. It was going to be her first time there.

Immediately she began packing her bags and making arrangements. Her man needed her, and she was about to be there in a heartbeat. Once, she thought the heavens were smiling down on her, now it felt like hell was trying to pull her under.

With what was going on around her, she was ready to go. Her home was in shambles. Between a drunken Ray-Ray and her feud with Momma Jones, she was going crazy. She wanted them out of her home. She wanted everyone gone around her. She needed to think, to get her life back on track. Since she'd found out the IRS was auditing her, she felt like she was losing control of things.

For once, her home was quiet, with no Ray-Ray or Momma Jones around to disturb her or get in her way. The reason she kept them around for so long was because she loved Cash. Ray-Ray was a nice guy, but his drunken stupors and Momma Jones funking up her home with her whorish and ghetto ways was becoming too much to deal with.

They were doing drugs in her house. She started to find things and money missing, which meant they were stealing from her.

Cash would look the other way, make excuses for his parents' behavior, but Pearla didn't want to tolerate it anymore. Because of them, she and Cash were sometimes at odds with each other, arguing and fussing. It was embarrassing to her that she had control over so many things, but in her own home there was mass chaos.

Pearla decided to take a soothing bubble bath for an hour or two. She closed her eyes and dreamed of Cash being in the tub with her, but the doorbell ringing interrupted her pleasant thoughts and solitude. Annoyed by the sudden company, she removed herself from the tub and donned a long robe.

She made her way downstairs and looked to see who it was. She remembered his face. It was one of Cash's friends. *Why is he here? What does he want?* She wasn't about to take any chances.

She retrieved her gun and carefully answered the door. Looking him in the eyes, she asked, "You're Petey Jay, right?"

"Yeah. I'm here for Cash. He home?"

"No, he's not."

Petey Jay stared Pearla up and down and smiled.

"Why are you here?" she asked seriously.

"Just business," he responded.

He looked jazzy in some new clothes and a gold Rolex around his wrist. Parked outside her home was an Audi R8. His appearance screamed drug dealer or something.

He reached into his coat pocket and pulled out a wad of money—forty-five thousand dollars to be exact. "I owe Cash this," he said, placing it in Pearla's hands.

"Owe him for what?"

"He invested in me, and it's paying off."

"Investment?" It was the first time she'd heard of Cash investing with a friend. "What did he invest in, and how much?"

"He didn't tell you?"

"Obviously not."

"Well, it's not my business to tell. But tell Cash there's more where that came from." He winked at her and then turned around and left.

Pearla figured Cash was dealing in drugs now and keeping it a secret from her. She was furious. Something told her to check their money in the safe, hoping he didn't do what she thought he did.

She slammed the door and hurried to her bedroom. She went straight for the concealed safe in the closet. When she opened it, it was almost empty. Cash had taken a large amount of money without letting her know. She was devastated. Why would he do it without running it by her first? They weren't supposed to keep secrets from each other.

She sat slumped on the floor, looking despondent. In two days, she was flying to Miami to help him out and be by his side, but at this point all she wanted to do was turn her back on him.

*** ✳ ***

The flight into Miami went smoothly. Pearla did a lot of thinking during the trip. She realized that she and Cash needed to tighten their purse strings, kick out his parents, and that she needed to cut off her mother completely. She had bought Poochie a Yukon Denali. Though Poochie had proven useful to Pearla and her organization, she was also becoming a handful, always needing a hand out, creating unwanted problems, and spending her money like it was free.

They also needed all the money that Cash had invested with Petey Jay. Pearla was determined to work around the clock to keep what they'd built. With the IRS breathing down her neck, and with Cash arrested, that meant spending money on lawyers and bail, meaning money was going to start going out faster.

Pearla was a stranger to Miami, so she needed the assistance of a sociable cab driver to drive her around. She was able to bail Cash out of lockup. His bail was $150,000.

In all, the Miami Attorney General charged twenty people a few days earlier in the takedown of a major international carjacking and stolen car trafficking ring. The media was all over the story, reporting that approximately 160 stolen cars worth more than $8 million were recovered during the operation. The ring targeted high-end vehicles—particularly luxury SUVs, Mercedes-Benz, BMW, Maserati, Porsche, Jaguar, Bentley, and Aston Martin. The defendants used electronic keys fobs, critical to the resale value of the car, to steal the vehicles from various locations in the South Beach and Miami-Dade area. The ring then shipped them to West Africa, where they resold them for large profits.

Cash was caught up in the criminal operation and was looking at multiple charges, from conspiracy in operating a criminal organization to money laundering—six counts of grand larceny, six counts of conspiracy to commit grand larceny, two counts of breaking and entering, and two counts of conspiracy to enter a dwelling with intent to commit larceny or felony. As he thought, Marc had turned snitch/informant and sold him out, among twelve other people. As the officer had stated, they had several surveillance tapes of the cars being driven off the lots, and Cash was in more than one tape. It would have greatly helped the prosecution's case had Marc gotten Cash to admit his involvement.

The list of charges made him want to bury his face in his hands and cry. He was looking at three to seven years in Florida.

When he saw Pearla there to pay his bail, it felt like an angel had walked into the courthouse. He hugged and kissed her, not wanting to let her go.

The first thing Pearla wanted to do was get him a lawyer. Brent Donaldson was one of the best Miami had to offer. He had a ninety percent acquittal rating and came highly recommended. The problem was, lawyers like him are costly, and with the case Cash had lingering over his head, it was going to be expensive to try and pay for his freedom. There was no choice but to hire him, since they couldn't afford for Cash to go away. The retainer alone nearly broke them.

Pearla informed Cash of her plans to cut off the hemorrhaging, and he was with it. People were bringing them down, and it was time to clean house. Together, they came as a team, and it was going to be them against the world.

TWENTY-NINE

It felt cruel, but it needed to be done. Ray-Ray was sad and pitiful when he was told that he had to leave the house. He put Cash on a huge guilt trip about being kicked out from his own son's home. He'd gotten used to eating good food and having shelter from the cold. He didn't want to go back to living on the streets.

Despite Ray-Ray's complaining and bickering, Cash understood that he had to remain strong. He had to remove his father from his home. "You can live in a shelter, Pop," he suggested.

"A shelter? You know what they do to people in there. You know what they will do to an old man like me inside a shelter."

"Shelters are safe, Pop, and you'll still have me."

"I would rather live back on the streets than go stay in a shelter."

It was tough on Cash to make his father go. With his criminal case in Florida pending, he needed to save money and make things right. And Cash didn't truly owe him anything. He was his father and he loved the man, but Ray-Ray didn't raise him at all, nor gave him a dime.

Momma Jones was pure hell. She wasn't about to leave so easily. She was there to stay. She was a street bitch, and she'd gotten accustomed to living the good life. When Pearla demanded she pack her things and get the hell out of her house, it was a problem. They started cursing at each other. Pearla was sick of Momma Jones's shit. She wanted her gone.

"Bitch, make me fuckin' leave!" Momma Jones shouted.

Pearla was tired of her. The bitch was too disrespectful. The straw that broke the camel's back was when Momma Jones picked up a few things and tossed them at her, leading to a brawl between them. Momma Jones went berserk, trying to scratch up Pearla's pretty face, and then spitting and biting, acting like a wild animal.

Pearla hit her with punch after punch. "You dumb bitch!" she screamed, wanting to take Momma Jones' head off.

The fight between them spilled out into the street.

Being a high-class neighborhood, the neighbors immediately called the cops when they heard the disturbance. It wasn't the first time officers had showed up at the couple's home. When uniformed officers arrived at the residence, Pearla and Momma Jones were cursing each other out, throwing nasty threats back and forth. Cash was in between his mother and his fiancée, trying to keep them separated to prevent them from tearing each other apart. Both ladies were bloody and bruised.

"Fuck you, bitch!" Pearla yelled. "I'm sick of your shit!"

"You ain't shit, bitch! Fuckin' bring it, wit' ya little ass!"

Both ladies were instantly arrested.

Cash watched on in horror seeing his fiancée and his mother thrown into the backseat of a squad car. The nightmare continued when the female officer told Cash and Pearla that they couldn't kick out his parents. Apparently they had rights as tenants because they'd been there more than thirty days, and if they wanted them out, then they would have to go to landlord and tenant court. Pearla and Cash were dumbfounded by the news.

Just like that, their dream home had turned into the house of horror.

The next morning, Pearla and Momma Jones were released from jail. Cash was there to pick up Pearla, not his mother.

It had been a long, long night. Pearla looked dazed and sick. Her hair was in disarray, her clothes were torn and dirty, and she didn't know what to do anymore. Their money was low, and she was stuck with his parents. She wasn't going to survive too long under the same roof as Momma Jones.

"What fuckin' rights do they have?" Pearla was fuckin' furious.

Cash helped her into the car. He didn't know what to say. He'd made so many wrong decisions that he didn't know what was right anymore.

"Cash . . . Cash. . ." Momma Jones called out. "You not gonna take me home too?"

Cash ignored his moms and shot her a dirty look. Momma Jones twisted up her lips and got into a cab.

Pearla remained quiet during the ride home, thinking and crying. She leaned her head against the window and stared out the windshield.

"We gonna be all right, baby," Cash said. "They gonna fuckin' leave our place. I'm gonna make sure of that."

It sounded good to hear, but Pearla wasn't too sure. She sighed heavily and didn't reply, choosing to remain silent.

Cash drove up to their home and parked in the driveway. Pearla gazed at her beautiful home and didn't know what to think. It started to feel like a prison. Everything was changing and not for the better.

"C'mon, let's go inside, and I'll run you a nice bath and give you a massage," he said.

She managed a smile.

They exited the car and walked toward the front door hand in hand. The second they were about to walk through the front door, two detectives seemed to appear out of nowhere.

"Are you Pearla Baker?" one asked. He was a tall, white male with short, cropped hair who looked eager to carry out his job.

"Who's asking?" she replied nervously.

"You're under arrest for racketeering and fraud," he said.

Pearla was shocked. Immediately, they started to arrest her. Pushing Cash away, the detective grabbed Pearla's arms behind her back and placed the iron bracelets around her wrists.

"What the fuck is going on?" she hollered.

The second detective started to read out her Miranda rights. "You have the right to remain silent. Anything you say or do may be used against you in a court of law. You have the right—"

"I know my fuckin' rights!"

Cash yelled, "Yo, is this fuckin' necessary?"

"Sir, please do not interfere," the tall detective warned.

Cash had to helplessly watch them usher Pearla to their unmarked car and take her back to jail when she was just released. He stood there stunned, not knowing what to do.

✳✳✳

During her arraignment, Pearla learned about all the details in her case. Cash was there front seat and talking to her lawyer. She was being charged with racketeering for green card marriage and fraud, which carried up to three years in prison and a huge fine toward restitution. Apparently, one of her girls, a bitch named Karen, took it upon herself to try and extort her arranged husband for more money. When he refused, and shit hit the fan, she went to the police and named Pearla as the one who'd set everything up.

Pearla pleaded not guilty and was ready to take her case to trial. It was costly. With money dwindling fast, she didn't know how she and Cash could stay above water.

THIRTY

Several weeks after Pearla's second arrest, the tension in the home was so thick, it could be cut with a knife. Cash and Pearla both had open cases that, if convicted, could have them serving a few years in prison. It was a stressful time for them both.

Momma Jones and Ray-Ray had turned their house into a pigsty. There were dirty dishes piled up in the sink, dirty clothes and junk everywhere, fast-food remnants scattered throughout the house, and company coming and going. Things continued to go missing, and it was always one thing after the next. Each time Pearla or Cash would start beefing, Momma Jones and Ray-Ray would threaten to call the cops, which always backed the couple down.

With the two of them so busy trying to avoid incarceration and to keep their funds in order, they couldn't risk catching another case.

Cash's parents had made it where the young couple didn't want to live in their dream home anymore. It started to feel like they were the guests. There was constant arguing and disrespectful. But what hurt Cash the most was that Ray-Ray had changed. He was no longer the philosophical jokester. He'd become as mean, bitter, and vindictive as Momma Jones .

✳✳✳

Early one evening Cash pulled beside Petey Jay's Audi R8 in the parking lot of the grocery store. Petey Jay wanted to meet with him to talk about more business, looking to borrow another $100K from him. However Cash grew leery of his friend. The two exited their high-end cars and greeted each other with hugs and the glad hands.

"My nigga," Petey Jay hollered, sounding excited to see Cash.

Petey Jay looked fresh like a superstar in a black-and-green Gucci ensemble topped off with a platinum diamond necklace that sparkled in sync with the diamond-filled Rolex on his wrist.

"What's good, Petey?" Cash said dryly. "I see you ballin' and shit."

"You know, nigga, I'm tryin' to do my thing, come up like you and shit. You feel me?"

"Yeah, I feel you," Cash replied halfheartedly, eyeing Petey up and down.

"Yo, I know Pearla gave you that forty-five *K*, right? Am I good for the hundred thousand? I got shit moving soon."

"Nigga, forty-five *K* is peanuts. Where's the rest of it?"

"I got it comin', my nigga. I'm just sayin', shit is crazy out here. We got hit in Harlem. Some niggas ran up in our stash house, disrespected us, and took our shit. But we lookin' for these niggas. Believe me, it ain't goin' down like that," Petey Jay said, fidgeting around while he talked.

Cash knew it was a lie. He frowned and clenched his fists. Petey Jay was probably getting high off his own supply, or some other supply. Cash felt he was tweaking.

"Yo, I heard about that shit that went down in Miami. Crazy, yo."

Cash scowled. "Fuck what went down in Miami. I gave you almost four hundred K, and I ain't seen no real money come back yet, Petey."

"I got you covered, Cash. Yo, why would I be tryin' to play you? I don't even get down like that. C'mon, my nigga, we go way back. If it was like that, I wouldn't even gave you the forty-five."

Cash felt like he was being played, especially with his friend wearing a Rolex and driving new shit. He realized how his friend did it. He'd never had any drug connect, and he'd never planned on turning a profit. Cash strongly felt Petey Jay took advantage of their friendship and lied. He took his nearly 400k, gave him back 45k, only to try and get another 100k, thinking he was some sucker or pussy. It was a fucked-up Ponzi scheme.

Cash growled, "Yo, I want my fuckin' money, Petey."

"I'm gonna get you ya money, nigga!"

"Nah, I mean I want my fuckin' money now. I ain't playin' no fuckin' games wit' you, nigga. Real talk!" Cash shouted heatedly.

"Yo, why you comin' at me like I disrespected you?"

"Because you are, nigga! You think I'm fuckin' stupid?" Cash marched closer to Petey and got in his face, his 9mm tucked in his waistband.

"Yo, Cash, you need to chill."

"Nah, fuck that *chill* shit, nigga!" Cash screamed out. "I want my fuckin' money, Petey!"

Cash wanted to punch his friend in his face, but they were in a public parking lot, and there were too many witnesses around. He had to calm down. There was already too much heat on him and his girl. He didn't need to add any more fuel to a fire that was already raging.

"You know what, I'm gonna see you, Petey, real soon. Best believe that, nigga," Cash said coolly, stepping away from Petey and glaring at the man. He already had it in his mind that he was going to murder Petey Jay, soon.

Cash jumped into his car and drove away, fuming. His friend was a dead man.

Pearla and Poochie got into a heated argument about money. Poochie felt that Pearla wasn't keeping her promises and blessing her with the money she felt she had earned.

"Look, Pearla, I got fuckin' bills that need to get paid," Poochie whined.

"Don't we all?" Pearla screamed. "I got a fuckin' case pending and they threatening that I do hard time, ma. I got the IRS up my ass and now I gotta take care of you too! A grown fuckin' woman?"

"Bitch, I earn mines. I ain't Momma Jones or Ray-Ray. You ain't never or will ever take care of a smart bitch like me."

Pearla rolled her eyes. She was spent.

To add to the list of woes, word on the street was that someone had snitched on her to the IRS, and she speculated that it was Roark.

✳✳✳

With hell going on around them, Pearla and Cash needed a slice of heaven. Trying to escape all the drama surrounding them and the pressures of impending court cases, they decided to go out for another intimate dinner. This time they went to Odeon on West Broadway. The restaurant, with its old-school ambiance, made it a popular daily lunch spot for those below Canal, as well as the perfect place for a romantic dinner or a relaxed evening with friends.

The place was semi-crowded, patrons enjoying the tasty food and the friendly service.

"You're beautiful," Cash told Pearla, smiling and gazing at his queen in her watercolor dress.

"Thank you."

Through the drama and chaos, the two of them continued to make time for each other. The atmosphere around them was settling. Pearla dined on the warm goat cheese salad, and Cash had the unbelievable BLT. They had a warm, stimulating conversation and wished the evening could linger on forever.

"It's gonna get better," Cash told her.

Pearla replied halfheartedly, "I know."

They talked about their criminal court cases. With both of them catching cases, they couldn't really hustle in their respective fields, trying to keep a low profile until the fire was put out and the smoke cleared.

They'd blown a few million dollars in a year or two and needed to recoup what they'd spent. Cash's lawyer in Miami had prolonged the trial for months, and Pearla's lawyer, Jonathan Gray, was attempting to do the same thing. Both attorneys were desperately trying to look for any technicalities to have their cases dismissed.

The couple was now closer than ever as they went through their trials and tribulations.

"Us against the world, baby," Cash said, smiling. "And you know what? We gonna win."

Pearla chuckled. "I know."

They kissed lovingly.

Dinner went on for two hours. Then they went for a walk in Central Park, despite the cold and snow on the ground. After that, they went for drinks at a local bar, and then it was home to make love.

Their romantic and lovely night together came to a shocking end when they arrived home to find police at their home and their place shot up. There were bullet holes in the door and the windows were shot out.

"What the fuck!" Pearla exclaimed. "Why does this keep happening to us?"

Cash shook his head in exasperation. He was blindsided.

Pearla suspected Poochie was the one behind the shooting. Her mother was a vindictive and evil bitch when she wanted to be. However, Cash felt it could be a number of people, not to mention Petey Jay.

"I'll kill 'em all before I let them hurt you," Cash said.

"I know you will, baby. I know you will."

Never did the couple think, after everything they'd done for family and friends, that they would do them so dirty. With so much going on, threats looming from everywhere and family bringing them down, they decided to move out of their house and into an apartment until they could legally force Momma Jones and Ray-Ray out.

Flying back to New York from Miami, Cash smiled widely. He was ecstatic. His lawyer had pulled it off, and now he was a free man. He had just beaten his case in South Beach on a technicality. The surveillance tapes that had led to Cash's arrest weren't collected with a warrant; therefore, the evidence thrown out. It almost brought tears to Cash's eyes. His lawyer was worth every damn penny.

If someone could win the lotto twice, then it happened to Cash and Pearla, because Jonathan Gray had Pearla's case dropped too because of lack of evidence. Karen wasn't a reliable witness, with her extensive criminal history.

The extra blessing came when Housing Court finally evicted Cash's parents from their home.

It was now time to get money again. Too much time had been wasted with litigations and drama. Now they had to work extra hard to regain the momentum they once had.

But there was a problem—both their reputations had been tainted. The hood had started whispering about them. Rumors began to spread. How did they both beat their federal case? How were they able to walk away?

To make matters worse, Petey Jay, who had gotten arrested in a drug sting, was telling everyone listening that Cash was a snitch, and that he had set him up. Petey Jay had gone to buy some recreational weed when five-O kicked open the door to a known stash house. There was more than three hundred pounds of kush, guns, and drug money. He'd fucked up big time.

The couple, once admired and respected, were now hated and shunned by their peers.

Pearla had to constantly defend herself and her reputation. Her bitches from the escort service turned their back on her, no longer remembering the exotic trips and shopping sprees, or when Cash would peel off thousands so they could have a good time.

Cash was now being depicted as shady and untrustworthy. His reputation in Brooklyn had been trashed. Too much had gone down with him and Pearla, from everyone knowing that they cut Perez out of the insurance scheme before his sudden arrest at the chop shop, Jamie's still unsolved murder, Petey Jay's untimely arrest after Cash had threatened him, Roark putting Pearla on blast after feeling slighted by her, and their sudden freedom from two federal cases.

Rage, anger, and feelings of betrayal coursed through so many hearts, it should have been no surprise that someone wanted them dead.

EPILOGUE

The pearl-white Benz came to a stop in front of the Jamaica Estates home. Cash and Pearla lingered for a moment, looking, reflecting on the past a little. The place looked peaceful and quiet. It was hard to believe that drama and hell went on inside for so long. Summer was flourishing in the area, and like the winter season, their problems seemed to fade for another pleasurable season to take place. It was a new beginning, and for them, it felt so good to breathe again.

"This is it," Cash said, smiling at his queen.

They had arrived home after leaving a few weeks earlier. Pearla had rented a bungalow in Montauk, a block away from the beach, and the two just chilled.

Pearla set her eyes at the front entrance. With all they had gone through, she wanted to go inside and take a nice, long hot bath.

"You ready?" Cash asked.

"Yes, I am."

Slowly, they stepped out of the car and approached the house. Before they stepped inside, they vowed to never make the same mistakes again after almost losing everything they'd worked so hard for. This time, they were going for bigger things—first, setting a goal to get one million or more and then retire from the game.

Pearla had hired a tax attorney to straighten out her finances and deal with the IRS on her behalf, and their circle of friends had gotten much, much smaller.

When they walked inside, it was a horror story. Cash's parents didn't leave peacefully and respectfully. They decided to vandalize the house, which they did by knocking many holes in the walls, smashing everything they could get their hands on, breaking mirrors, windows, ripping up carpets, smashing furniture, and stealing everything of value that wasn't nailed down.

"Those muthafuckas," Cash uttered softly.

They walked into the ransacked home and inspected the damage. From room to room, everything was destroyed, including clothes bleached and ripped.

Cash could understand Momma Jones doing something like this, but not his father. Not Ray-Ray, the always genial and gregarious man who couldn't hurt a fly, who liked to make people laugh, and always seemed contented with his life, no matter what he was going through.

Cash looked around, at first looking despondent, maybe angry, but then he heard Pearla say, "You know what? I don't care."

"Huh?"

"I said I don't care."

Cash right away adopted the same attitude. "You know what? I don't care either."

Everything could be replaced. They were planning to rebuild anyway.

During the course of the evening, Cash and Pearla straightened up in certain areas, including the bedroom, and fixed what they could, and then they focused on each other.

After a long, stimulating shower together, the passionate lovemaking began on their bedroom floor, their comforter used as a mattress. A full moon hung heavy in the summer night sky. They ate Chinese food, drank champagne, and looked peaceful in the middle of the broken dishes, taped-up windows, and destroyed furniture.

Their fingertips touched in an act of intimacy. They kissed softly and fondled each other. Their kisses grew more passionate and more compelling then to a fever pitch. It was time for them to enjoy each other.

Cash was on his back, and Pearla straddled him slowly, feeling her pussy penetrated with his hardness. He gripped her hips and pushed upwards into her. She fucked him back, giving him pussy like he'd never dreamt possible.

"Ugh! Aaaah! Aaaah!" they both moaned in unison.

The sweat on Cash's body glistened, and his smooth brown skin rippled with muscles as he fucked her harder and deeper. His ass flexed as he drove his dick in her deeper, making her moan.

The two lovers put on a performance for the unwanted company gazing into their windows. The men outside were witnessing two beautiful black lovers in a passionate moment.

Cash was like a machine, fucking Pearla intensely and with skill, and she was moaning seductively. Their body movements were like a dance. Cash pumped and pumped some more, his steely erection coated in Pearla's juices. He was ready to empty himself physically and emotionally into his woman.

Suddenly, the romantic scene changed drastically when two masked men appeared in their home with automatic weapons. Cash and Pearla were so rooted into each other, they were caught slipping.

The last thing the couple heard before everything got fuzzy was, "This is payback, bitches!"

Then the gunfire followed. *Bak! Bak! Bak! Bak! Bak! Bak!*

There was a long moment of silence.

And then, gasping . . . and again, silence.

Pearla was frozen. All she saw were names swimming around in her head: *Roark, Chica, Perez, Petey Jay, Poochie and Momma Jones.*

Cash wasn't as quiet. "What the fuck! Niggas tried to body us," he yelled, staring at the two bodies that lay at his feet. "Who sent these niggas?"

"Wasn't me."

Luckily for Cash and Pearla, Ray-Ray had fucked up their house with Momma Jones and forgotten that he'd left his stash of heroin in his room. He came back to get it just as the two assailants were breaking in. Thinking quickly, he grabbed Cash's burner off the kitchen table and made his way to their master bedroom just in the nick of time.

Pearla finally got up the courage to snatch the masks off their unrecognizable faces; disappointed that the perpetrators were strangers.

"Now what?" she asked no one in particular.

Both men shrugged.

"What you doing here?" Cash finally asked.

"I'm not." Ray-Ray wasn't trying to get locked up for a double homicide.

Pearla and Cash agreed. They didn't want to be there either.

Ray-Ray grabbed his heroin, but before he left he gave them some words of wisdom. "Whoever wanted y'all dead is still out there. Watch your backs." He took two steps forward and warned, "And get rid of those dead bodies."

With two dead men in their bedroom, some unknown figure gunning for them, and limited funds, Pearla and Cash felt their house of cards crumbling all around them and it was going to take a miracle to rebuild.

As the two lovers wrapped each body in plastic garbage bags for transport they discussed their future.

Cash stopped and looked around at what it had come to. "If we get away with this, how do we survive?"

Pearla didn't miss a beat. "We hustle."

She's So Bad

Bad Girl Blvd

Part 3

Erica Hilton